D1766550

We hope you enjoy this book. Please return or renew it by the due date.

You can renew it at www.norfolk.gov.uk/libraries or by using our free library app.

Otherwise you can phone 0344 800 8020 - please have your library card and PIN ready.

You can sign up for email reminders too.

NORFOLK ITEM

30129 089 006 101

NORFOLK COUNTY COUNCIL
LIBRARY AND INFORMATION SERVICE

Chiselbury

CHAPTER ONE

Teheran, March 16th, 16.15 hours (local time) London, March 18th, 19.50 hours (GMT)

As K pushed his way through the glass doors of the Park Hotel, he realized instinctively why the two stumpy men were waiting by the reception desk. They had come to kill him.

Behind K, the Persian afternoon blazed with its customary eye-aching brilliance; water tinkled in an encrusted fountain.

K's mind instantly absorbed and as quickly rejected both the sight and the sound. Neither had any part of his present danger; they offered no way of escape. His face, sallow from too long in too many hot climates, shone with perspiration like oiled parchment. The walk up the Khiaban Shah from the telegraph office had tired him; he was looking forward to a lager. Even so, years of assuming so many different personalities, so many different pasts, still produced their automatic reflex action of outward unconcern as he faced the strangers. It was the end product of so many risks surmounted; the built-in survival mechanism of the professional spy. Behind the counter of the reception desk, pigeon-holes with room numbers honeycombed the wall. A piece of paper in his own, folded like a pipe spill, showed that someone had tried to contact him. But who? And why?

K looked from one man to the other, assessing his chance with a sudden drop to his knees, throwing the miniature BOAC flag from the desk at one of them as he accounted for the other with his fountain-pen gun. But they read his thoughts as though he had printed them on a hand-out in 48-point Bodoni bold: they had not studied in vain at the Soviet spy school in Kuchino.

One of them shook his head gently, as though sad that one professional should so underestimate another. Only in England was the amateur in these matters still highly regarded. Other countries had long ago abandoned the gentlemen for the players.

'You're coming with us,' he said. He spoke English perfectly, but his voice was flat as a dead balloon. It had no accent, no intonation, no trace of dialect; equally not English.

'Who are you?' asked K, simulating surprise, playing for seconds, hoping that someone would appear to distract their attention.

Neither of them replied, but without appearing to move, they were suddenly closer to him, their hands deep in the pockets of their alpaca jackets.

The man who had spoken first jerked his head almost imperceptibly towards the door. K feinted to the left and dived to the right, but they caught him as though he were a ballet dancer They were half his age and twice as fit and two against one. He might have been in this business before they were born; but they would remain in it after he was dead.

Where was everybody? Why was the hotel so deserted?

Then he remembered. It was Friday, the Moslem holy day, the equivalent of an English Sunday. Most people were at their prayers in the mosque. Those who weren't dozed in their rooms, hoping their compatriots thought they were.

A black Packard pulled out from the shelter of the feathery trees near the fountain as they approached. It was the only car in the yard. Usually, a row of gaudy taxis were parked under these trees. His callers had chosen their time well. But then, the other side always seemed so thoroughly organized, so splendidly competent.

One of the strangers opened the rear door and climbed in. The other prodded K to follow. He did so; he was no hero. The round hard muzzle of the nine-millimetre Lüger automatic pressed against his ninth vertebra had its own inescapable message. As he bent to enter the car, expert hands frisked him, feeling for the gun he didn't have.

Inside, K saw with deepening gloom that the handles had been removed from the doors. It would be impossible to open them quickly. The faintly stirring hope of an escape at a traffic light, a sudden dash for freedom at a crossroads froze within him.

He remembered the German wartime instructions to their agents: *Ein Spion hat keinen Kamaraden* - 'a spy has no friends'. They had hit on the worst aspect of his job, worse than the danger, the discomfort: its loneliness. A man needed friends; all men needed them. K sat down wearily, almost thankfully, on the shabby unpleated leather. He felt old for these adventures; he was a fool to persist.

The man who had been standing behind him suddenly dashed back through the glass doors. He returned with a spill of paper which he handed to K; it was the message from his pigeon-hole, written on a telegram form. K unrolled it. The instructions to the sender were in French, English and Arabic script. In the Persian crest, at the head of the paper, a lion wielded a curved sword in front of a sunrise. Or was it a sunset?

K read: 'Mr Offord. Regarding your telegram to Oil Catalysts Limited, Khartoum. We regret delay in dispatching this owing to technical defects. Supervisor.'

So. This was the last bitterness of all. The message that could have changed the world had not even been sent. What sort of technical defects could have delayed it? A bribe, a breakdown in antique equipment? Or was it simply because to work on Friday was as unthinkable in Teheran as to work over the weekend would be to Civil Servants in Whitehall?

K's mouth felt dry with disappointment and despair. He screwed up the paper into a ball and pushed it into the right-hand pocket of his jacket. At once the man on his right seized his wrist roughly and twisted it. He thought K was reaching for a weapon he had missed.

K opened his hand to show the crumpled form, and then suddenly lurched forward, head on his knees. His companion bent down with him, gripping his shoulder.

'What's the matter?' he asked roughly.

K shook his head as though his agony was too great for speech. He seemed to be gasping for breath, his face contorted as though he were about to vomit. His companions pulled him back against the cushions; had he somehow taken poison?

K closed his eyes, and with a weary gesture, wiped his dry lips with the paper. Then he tossed it out of the open window. There was a faint chance that someone might pick it up. But who - and what could they possibly make of the message?

The man on his left spoke rapidly in Polish. His partner shook his head.

'It's harmless,' he said reassuringly. 'Let's get on.'

None the less, this faded Englishman might be playacting; after all, he was a pro.

'Don't try anything,' he told K harshly.

His English idiom was perfect. Only his enunciation gave him away as not being English. But who would bother about that now? Who could pick up the paper and read thc message it didn't contain?

The Packard began to move towards the rose-covered trellis over the narrow gate into the Khiabari Hafez. The driver paused for a moment to let a yellow Chevrolet taxi, packed with American tourists, enter the courtyard, and then they turned right into the wide, almost empty street.

They headed north, across the Khiaban Shah and then the Khiaban Churchill, with the high brick wall of the Russian Embassy on their right.

Most shops were shuttered and the wayside sweetmeat stalls stood deserted, with canvas sheets tied across the goods on sale to discourage flies and pilferers. Under the trees the beggars waited, blind and mutilated, their hands or stumps of arms outspread for alms. Flies buzzed around their sores; it was the sleepiest time of the day.

Soon they, were out on the Tajrish road, heading towards the blue spine of the Alburz mountains that shimmered in the distance like a mirage. K lay back on the dusty leather seat, the arms of his escort through his own, making him powerless to move.

Who or where or what had been the weak link in his

chain of cover and subterfuge? He tried to trace the flaw, thinking back over the past few days in case he had made the mistake himself, but he felt too tired, too apprehensive, too involved to make much effort.

Although his passport, in the yellow oilskin pouch in the inner pocket of the lightweight tropical jacket he had bought from Airey & Wheeler on his last visit home, declared him to be a university professor, clearly his escort knew his real profession.

Someone had talked, willingly or unwillingly. He hoped he would not be put to the test himself. He dreaded the thought of physical pain; the tweezers tightening on his fingernails, the electric current jarring his testicles. He had heard of their methods so often from others; it was as though he had already suffered by proxy.

Yet, obliquely, K felt a curious surge of feeling, almost of relief, that at last the years of complicated suspense - of pausing before he opened the door of his hotel room for the sound of breathing within; of suspecting any car that parked beneath his window - should be ending.

What he dreaded most during the twenty odd years he had been 'in the field' (how close the mission analogy in so many ways!) had been discovery and capture.

MacGillivray had promised him a spell at home before retirement, possibly a job in the Passport Office or the Public Relations Department of the Ministry of Defence, until he was due for his pension, and the inevitable CBE for unknown, unnamed, unnameable 'political and public services'.

Now the words of the Roman Emperor Septimus

Severus came back like bile in his mouth: *Omnia fui, et nihil expediti* - 'I have been all things and it avails me nothing.'

There would be. few to mourn him, for few remembered him. His wife had died in a Plymouth air raid early in the war; his son, at Cassino. He and his daughter had not corresponded for years, but she would inherit his few possessions: a crate of books and Roman manuscripts in store at Harrods; his three insurance policies - would the companies have sought his custom so eagerly had they suspected the risks involved? - and a couple of thousand pounds on deposit at the Piccadilly branch of Lloyds.

Even when she was.at school K always seemed to be away on his accursed job when he should have been at her sports-days and prize-givings like other fathers. Of course, she had no idea of the real nature of his work, and this made it all the harder for her to understand his absences. Other girls' fathers, she would tell him reproachfully, always managed to be there, even though they were in business, too. But not my sort of business, he would say again and again; not my sort of work.

The car sped on, past the little Renaults, the Vauxhall and Hillman taxis with coloured streamers on their radio aerials. K watched them with fascination, greedily. Was it possible that any of their occupants were, like himself, not what they seemed, but also driving to unknown destinations? But of course. In the last analysis, everyone's destination was unknown, the undiscovered country.

All K hoped was that if this were to be the end, he would feel no pain, and as his old Latin tutor used to say, quoting Cicero, 'The last day does not bring extinction but change of place.'

Well, he would soon see.

The car turned right, off the main road, bumping along an unmade track beyond the wide gardens of the pretentious, pillared villas built by wealthy Teheran businessmen. Cypress trees had been planted carefully and successfully on either side of the track to screen it from their view.

The roughness of the surface increased, until they reached a clearing. They were not its first visitors. Mounds of rotting laths and chunks of white plaster from new houses down the road had already been dumped there. Brightly flowered weeds sprouted from these pyramids of decay amid rusting oil drums, mattresses, abandoned perambulators.

The driver turned the Packard so that it faced the main road, switched off the ignition and put the key in his pocket.

'We get out here,' said the man on K's left. 'All of us.'

They both opened their doors by lowering the windows to reach the outside handles; then they climbed out and stood facing him. K followed more slowly: he had cramp in one leg, and suddenly realized how badly he wanted to make water. He hoped he would not disgrace himself.

The rocky ground felt warm through the soles of his shoes. Beyond the trees, the gentle hills stretched up in a sea of green feathery branches, but faintly, from the main road they had left, came the distant impatient hoots of cars, and the muted drone of traffic.

Standing in the sunshine, K felt, with a sudden,

agonizing awareness, the nearness of death; and not death in the abstract, but his own. The scent of pines was sharp and clean in his nose: life seemed unbearably sweet. Was there really no means of escape, no hope of rescue? While time remained, hope still lived; and so did he. It was this eternal, unquenchable optimism when all seemed lost long since that had made him so good at his job.

'There's something we need in that box over there,' the man said, nodding towards a brown wooden box marked Carlsberg Lager - This Way Up. 'Get it for me, please.'

'That box?' K repeated in surprise. What the devil could he mean?

The man nodded.

K started to walk towards it with short, careful steps. At the third pace he jumped to the right, seized a lump of plaster from the ground and flung it back at the two men.

But the manoeuvre came too late: they had already drawn their Lügers from their jacket pockets and as he jumped, they fired together. Through the thick throats of the silencers the shots sounded like dry twigs breaking.

For a moment K stood upright, then, like a straw man, he crumpled and fell awkwardly, his legs turning to rubber beneath him. Red stains grew across his shirt.

They fired again into the back of his head. White brains flowered within the splintered bone; the blood ran out through his thin grey hair and down his neck under the collar of his shirt. Only then did they put away their guns.

One of the men turned and signalled to the driver. Through the window he handed out a small sponge roller on the end of a long stick, part of a do-it-yourself decorating kit. Walking backwards towards the car, the two men rolled away their footprints from the dusty ground.

The driver lowered two rubber flaps hung behind the back wheels so that these could drag through the dust, obliterating any trace of their tyre treads. Then the two men climbed back into the car with their roller, and they set off slowly back to the Tajrish road. At the end of the track the driver wound up the rubber flaps.

They turned left towards Teheran, one of a dozen other nondescript cars speeding past the country buses and the motor scooters and the gaudy tin signs advertising Iranian Airways and Coca Cola and the big new air-conditioned hotels.

Under the cypress trees in the clearing, the tide of thick, dark blood moved slowly across the dust to the merciful green shrubs. A few hooded crows and vultures spread their dark wings against the afternoon sky and called the news of death from the tops of trees.

Soon it would be night, and then nothing would disturb them. They could finish what the bullets had begun.

***

It was that hour of evening in Covent Garden when the business of the day has died and the traffic of the night not yet begun.

Already, on the roads from the west, the north, the east and the south, the heavy diesel lorries were trundling towards the market piled with crates of dates, boxes of apples and oranges bursting like breasts in tissue paper. But it would be several hours yet before the first of them reached the cobbled streets of the market.

The day workers had gone home from their offices to their telly and bingo and their narrow suburban gardens with the chicken-run fencing and clipped privet hedges in Penge and Orpington and Herne Hill. The cars of the night people, the diners-out, the parties for Drury Lane and the Royal Opera House, had not yet arrived. So for ten, fifteen, maybe thirty minutes the market seemed deserted and empty, almost as quiet as when it had indeed been the garden of a convent.

A lamp-lighter, long pole over his shoulder, cycled skilfully from lamp to lamp, pulling down the taps. Gas mantles flared behind the globes like the bright white wings of captive moths.

Outside the Boulestin, a doorman manoeuvred two handcarts to make space for a taxi. Here and there, cats prowled among boxes of fruit and cabbages piled behind wire net screens in the market.

MacGillivray stood in his office watching the scene through the double glass windows and not seeing any of it. He was a tall man with a hard face and reddish hair gone grey above his ears.

He wore tweeds, a check shirt and woven tie; he might have been the managing director of any successful public company, with the olive-green S2 Bentley, the town house in Charles Street, a thousand acres outside Newbury. Or again, he could have come in from a day's salmon-fishing in Callander.

In fact, he wore the clothes because he would have enjoyed the open-air life they represented. They were

11

evidence of a chameleon wish for another background, an escape from the frustrations of reality; for which his job gave him little time or chance. MacGillivray lived in a seven-roomed flat off the Brompton Road, had a bank overdraft, and a Civil Servant's salary, with some expenses for which he need give no account. He was the deputy head of the British Secret Service.

His office had white walls, a low ceiling with a five-bulb candelabrum and was decorated and furnished in an impersonal Ministry of Works way. Across one wall ran built-in wooden cupboards. They concealed the steel filing cabinets with the treble locks and magnetic catches: these cabinets contained the list of agents past, present, potential.

The pile of the fitted lime-green Wilton carpet was trodden down by too many feet, but then, since no one below the equivalent rank of captain was allowed inside MacGillivray's room, it was never properly cleaned. This accounted for the dust on the shelves, the grey mounds of cigarette stubs in the ashtrays, the general clutter of papers. It had the look of a room looked after by a busy husband when his wife is away.

This general air of impermanence always characterized MacGillivray's office; for every few months, usually in the early hours of Sunday morning, all the cabinets, the desk and chairs were packed and moved.

In the previous autumn his office had been part of a travel agency in a block of flats off the Marylebone Road. Now it was above a fruit exporting firm, Sensoby & Ransom, in King Street. By midsummer they could be somewhere else; just as they might need some new cover; anything that could be a plausible excuse for frequent visitors and unlimited overseas telegrams.

They moved regularly because it seemed only a matter of time before the other side discovered their whereabouts. Then the opposition, as they called them, would book rooms across the street and set up their delicate Japanese infra-red cameras that could photograph a meeting through curtains and their ultra-high-frequency transistorized microphones able to filter the noise of traffic.

Once adjusted to the tones of three or four voices, these could pick up voices clearly at a distance of up to forty feet through walls and windows and, rejecting all other sounds, could thus monitor the most secret meeting. MacGillivray would let them establish themselves, for it helped to be able to recognize your enemies' faces, to photograph them and their callers, and to monitor some of their meetings as well; then they would move on again.

Here, for the time being, MacGillivray's office was safe. The thick curtains contained aluminium foil woven into the cloth; it could screen the most inquisitive microphones, and defeat the most sensitive cameras.

All the electronic devices, all the mechanical safeguards were perfect, MacGillivray thought sourly as he watched a man making a hash of backing a Morris Minor into a space by the silver bollard beneath him. Every prospect pleases and only man is vile; and he is bloody vile.

MacGillivray had long ago given up any shred of belief in the dignity of man. For fear, for money, for

13

lust, or simply, to feel important, people would do almost anything against their country, their family or themselves, and in that order. When others showed shock at his theory that all men had their prices, they invariably thought in terms of money. But other currencies could be far more attractive: the use of a girl and a flat in Half Moon Street; an amenable boy who lived in a pretty mews; or even simply school fees paid; the loan of a house in Antibes for a family holiday. These were the prices that bought carelessness with a secret key; the file of unlisted telephone numbers left in an unlocked drawer - 'After all, everyone must know the damn things already. I mean, what about the printers, for instance?' This rationalization, plus the old, familiar levers of blackmail, the sudden threat of exposure to a wife, a superior: all were means to the same result.

MacGillivray knew the answers to such questions; he realized why people did what they did. But what was the answer to this Teheran business?

He searched in the capacious pockets of his jacket for his cigar case, took out a thin Burmese cheroot, lit it and stood gazing out into the darkening street.

The trouble with espionage, he thought, was that there were no supermen. They belonged to the myths, the folklore, the father figures of M. and Richard Hannay. In reality, you knew only a fraction of the puzzle, and when you discovered the whole ramifications, you weren't believed. Who would have credited the story that the British War Minister could share the mistress of a Russian spy? You took two steps forward, one step back, half a step to the side. The only consolation was that the other side was probably equally in the dark.

And MacGillivray drew wry satisfaction from the knowledge that every head of the Soviet spy system, from the time of the October Revolution to Beria after the death of Stalin, had died in a violent way, often at the hands of those he had once controlled.

Even so successful an executive as Colonel Zabotin, who had controlled the massive spy net in Ottawa, that resulted in Russia learning the secrets of the atomic bomb, had been eventually brought back to Russia to disgrace and eclipse.

At least in Britain the results of failure were less drastic: you might only miss your 'K', and be palmed off with some junior honour, but the sense of defeat and frustration remained at least as sharp. And in this case, the consequences were unthinkable.

MacGillivray went back to his desk, sat down under the two green-shaded reading lights, and examined the last message he had received from Teheran. It had reached him in a roundabout way from a cover address of a dealer in oil equipment in Khartoum, on to a drilling engineer in Darwin, then to an importer of diesel machinery in Vancouver, back across the Atlantic to Durban in the form of a message requesting details of cut-rate South African holidays and so to Sensoby & Ransom in a cable offering a special prize for Cape apples. Decoded, it read simply: 'Oil treaties seriously endangered stop details following sixteenth.' But now the date was March the eighteenth, and still nothing had followed this cryptic warning. In MacGillivray's experience, only death or some other almost equal disaster could be the reason for such a delay. His agents had their regular daily calls to make with codes that varied at unequal intervals. Two days was too long to be overdue.

The Foreign Office had asked the British Embassy in Teheran whether they knew the whereabouts of a British subject, one Mr Peter Offord, in which name K. had had his passport. The Embassy had, of course, no inkling of his real activities. He was described as a former professor who had a job with a local oil exploration firm. Back came the reply that his room was still booked at the Park Hotel, and according to BOAC booking office records, he had not taken up his open return ticket to London. So where the hell was he? And how were the treaties endangered and which treaties?

Until a year or two ago, it would have been a simple routine matter to dispatch another agent to find him, but since the treachery of George Blake, the entire British Middle East spy network of agents lay in ruins. Of all his professional agents, full-time and part-time, MacGillivray knew of only one - a woman in Rome - he felt he could trust; and he did not want to use her on this case for reasons of his own. It looked as though he would have to use an amateur, some businessman, some traveller, and hope he could find out something on the side.

MacGillivray loathed this idea. It was unprofessional, a leftover from John Buchan. And in only two cases, those of Somerset Maugham and Sir William Stephenson, could he recall it ever being used with real success - and both these occasions had been in time of war.

The usual end to such an episode was the sudden announcement by Tass that a British export manager had been arrested for Imperialist-Fascist espionage in Prague or Warsaw. Then came his removal to Moscow, the extracted confession, the hypocrisy of a 'trial', then years rotting away in Lubyanka prison, the jail built ironically in the basement of the headquarters of the Russian Secret Service.

But if MacGillivray had no pro he wasn't certain was still unblown, what else was he to do?

He glanced through the list of names his adjutant had prepared for him.

Who the devil were these people, anyway? Samuel Abramson, export manager of Northern Breakfast Foods, Preston, Lanes. Six years ago he had helped, almost by chance, to discover a link in the chain of narcotic smuggling during the Cyprus emergency. Now he was sixty-one. No good. Too old.

David Culross, ex-Kenya Police. He seemed a possibility until MacGillivray looked at his photograph. A blind man could see the policeman in the round face, the short, cropped hair, the jug-handle ears. Impossible to use him. What could he pretend to be? A copper on leave?

There were half a dozen others: the European service manager of a motor company; the chief foreign correspondent of a Sunday newspaper; a retired country parson who supplemented slender private means by running tours to East German cathedral cities.

MacGillivray sifted through them, answering his own objections. Why should a motor firm suddenly send their man to Teheran when it was out of his area?

What cathedral could the cleric consider worth

visiting in Teheran? For the matter of that, what was happening in Teheran?

He pulled another file towards him. A team of Russian scientists had discovered some ancient relics in a dig at Persepolis. A Russian Ilyushin Aeroflot airliner was due tomorrow on the second stage of a round-the-world peace flight. Odd. Could there be any connection? Possibly, but what could he discover in his office in Covent Garden when even the clerks had gone and the telephone switchboard had closed?

The fourteenth post-war International Malaria Conference was being held in Teheran University. Thirteen British doctors were attending. That seemed to be the sum of events in the city of the Peacock Throne.

A malaria conference. Was there any specialist he could use? He went through more files. The only possible chance was a neurologist in Cardiff. A naturalized Czech. He had been useful in 1948 at the time of the Communist *coup d'etat.* His British citizenship was part of the price they had paid for his usefulness. MacGillivray consulted more filing cards. The most recent entry was written in red ink: 'Dead 17-8-58.' So he was back where he started.

He began to go through the cross-indexes in the steel cabinets. Surely there must be *someone*, out of the scores who had been associated with the Service, knowingly or unknowingly, over the last twenty years? Many had placed only one minor piece in the vast mosaic of British Intelligence, and then moved on; some had not even known they were being used. The tourist at Nice airport, for instance, who was suddenly asked by another Englishman to take home a letter and post it to his girlfriend in London because he had forgotten to. do so and it would be quicker than all these confounded foreign postal systems, had no idea what the letter contained.

But the registers of all such people were kept up to date. From time to time, local area representatives of MI5 were asked to fill in some details about a few residents for unspecified purposes; this was one of the purposes.

What about the war? Surely some of the people he'd used then in the Middle East and Burma for little unimportant jobs must have taken up medicine as a career? Several must have been undergraduates before they joined up. Hell, he only wanted one.

It was nearly half past ten before MacGillivray discovered the one he wanted. He studied the card for a long time, checked it against the Medical Register: this one was still alive, and he was a doctor. This seemed his best hope so far. He had used him once, very briefly, in Chittagong during the war.

Dr Jason Love. Parents (deceased) Dr and Mrs T. J. Love, The Meads, Old Bexley, Kent. Served war of 1939-45 in India and Burma. Enlisted as private soldier, June 1942: Royal East Kent Regiment (The Buffs). Commissioned: Royal Berkshire Regiment, attached 1st Lincolns, Arakan. MC, Buthidaung, March 1944. Studied medicine, Oriel College, Oxford, and St Bartholomew's Hospital, London, MB, BS, 1949.

In general practice. Address: The Old Vicarage, Bishop's Combe, near Taunton, Somerset. Telephone, Bishop's Combe 11. Unmarried.

Hobbies: Judo (Brown Belt); Cord cars. Clubs: East

India and Sports, Oxford and Cambridge, Auburn-Cord-Duesenberg Car Club (USA).

MacGillivray put down the card and lit another cheroot. He studied a railway timetable. Then he pressed a button on the desk. The duty officer entered.

'I'm going to Taunton,' MacGillivray told him. 'On the late train. It gets in at about three in the morning, so lay on a taxi.

'I'll be away tonight and possibly tomorrow night. You can't ring me, but if I want you I'll reach you through the cut-out.

'Get me a warrant to Taunton, and book me a room. Then ask. the Quartermaster to fix up a few medical gadgets - hypodermics that shoot gramophone needles; a couple of fountain-pen guns: that sort of thing. Stuff a doctor could conceal in what he usually carries in his bag. We may need them.'

'Very good, sir.' The man turned to go.

'Oh, and another thing. Find me as much gen as you can in the time on the Cord car, whatever that may be.'

CHAPTER TWO

As Dr Love turned his white supercharged Cord roadster between the steep grass verges of the old Quantocks road the echo of his booming exhaust beat back so pleasantly from the wooded hillside that he sang against the masculine growl from the four-inch tail-pipe, revelling in the emptiness of the sky, the freshness of the morning air.

He usually chose this rough, lonely road with its quaint Edwardian warning, "Unfit for Heavy Motor Cars", when a call took him over the Quantocks towards Bridgwater. Timid motorists feared the long winding hill behind Crowcombe. Thus he invariably had it to himself and could turn back the years to the heroic age of motoring when roads were empty, and only the wind and not the mimsers got in a driver's hair.

Officially, Love was off duty, beginning a three-weeks holiday, his locum already engaged and in the guest room. But at half past two that morning his bedside telephone had awakened him. A passing motorist was ringing from the AA box near Holford, where his number was listed as being the nearest doctor. There had been a bad accident. Could he please come quickly?

Two old beat-up Yankee cars, a Plymouth and a Dodge, speckled with chequer tape and paper pennants and packed with Teds on a booze-and-birds outing from Bristol, had collided with a cider lorry. The highway was awash with blood and oil and cider. Young men in tight black jeans, pointed shoes and black leather jackets squatted with green faces at the roadside. Their greasy dark hair hung like oiled worms over their narrow, voles' faces. The injured lay, still and pale as wax dummies, under the headlamps of another car. The air was hot with oil, sharp with the smell of petrol and vomit.

Love reached this scene of chaos and gloom in half an hour. He should have been home long ago, but there were complications; there always were. Neither of the Teddy boy drivers had a licence; both cars were uninsured. Worse, the lorry-driver's skull was fractured and it was doubtful whether he would live: spinal fluid was already seeping from his right ear. Thus, with police statements and travelling into Bridgwater behind the ambulance, it had been four hours before Love was free.

Now, in the early morning, with larks soaring above the bracken like tiny VTO aircraft, he was going back to breakfast. That afternoon he would pack; tomorrow at this time he'd be off to Hurn. Within a matter of hours he'd be beetling down south to the sun, the wine and whatever the night might offer.

He kicked down the throttle and accelerated through Crowcombe village and out towards Bishop's Combe, on the main Minehead road that stretched ahead invitingly, empty as a dead man's eyes. As 2,400 revs came up on the tachometer, the supercharger engaged with its high whistling whine and the huge car took wing.

This was the nearest thing to human flight Love ever experienced, and at ten miles to the gallon nigh on as expensive. But to hell with it: he had no ties, no old father to support, no wife with a charge account at Harrods, no children at boarding school. He was on his own and, after Maureen's death, he meant to stay that way.

Being single meant more than just being alone: it meant being an entity, a complete person, without ancillaries, without anchors or any encumbrances. Every morning he felt a special almost clinical pleasure when he awoke in his bedroom overlooking the wide lawn that stretched to the slopes of the Quantocks, and lay in that warm, drowsy half-world at the frontier of sleep and wakefulness, hearing from somewhere, far away, what he called the Somerset Sound.

This was simply: *U-r-r-r.* He never knew whether it was made by man or beast, and it didn't matter a damn, because both were friendly, living at their own intended pace, away from the false, frenetic activity of town.

With a wife, he was sure there would be complications, pointless, boring involvements with dinner parties and friends of hers who weren't necessarily friends of his; and gradually what had at first joined them would end by simply tying them, strangling individuality. And although he liked children he did not think he liked them well enough to be perpetually surrounded by them.

Sometimes, when friends of his year at Oxford or hospital were driving along the Minehead road, either to or from a holiday, often towing caravans behind their staid Rovers, they would drop in unexpectedly to see him.

That in itself showed one value in being single: how

many wives genuinely relished unexpected visitors who arrived unannounced?

Some expressed surprise that he should like to bury himself away in the country when he might be an honorary at a London hospital, or with a far larger suburban practice. And then he looked at their faces, pale from too many hours indoors, maybe furrowed by worry, with mortgages and school fees to pay, plus their wives' second cars (because everyone else's wife had a second car), and he had several unassailable reasons for staying where he was, as he was.

There was also the attraction of knowing everyone in the village, and liking most of them, or some of them; and, in any case, he had no intention of surrendering the citadel of his independence. At least, not yet. QED.

At twenty-five to eight Love turned in at the stone gates of his house, past the low windows with their pale-blue shutters, and parked in the yard cobbled with grey pebbles placed on their ends like stone eggs, the traditional Somerset approach to paving.

Originally, his house had been the home of the local parson in the time of hunting parsons, but then the new vicarage had been built - new in the country sense, meaning about a hundred and fifty years ago - and from that date the local doctor had lived in what became known as the Old Vicarage.

His surgery had been constructed in what had formerly been the gardener's cottage. The ground floor was divided into a waiting-room and consulting-room, with an office upstairs.

Outside, a hitching post for horses still remained. The Cord lived in a converted stable with a loft above; the rafters were useful when he had to winch out the engine.

In another, loft Love had made a flat for his housekeeper and her husband. Odd how he always thought of her as being the more important, but then Mrs Hunter was the dominant personality. Her easy-going husband David was glad to accept her decisions, her pronouncements made with oracular authority, thankful to escape argument in the shelter of the garden where he laboured to produce the best asparagus beds in the country; and had nearly succeeded.

Love lifted his emergency bag from the seat beside him and went into the hall. From the black beams hung his collection of car name-plates of forgotten makes. All, like his Cord, were the epitaphs of dreamers, of forgotten individualists, out of place in a world of volume production and conformity: Ansaldo through Hispano; Lammas-Graham through Marmon; Schneider and Squire to Voisin and Vale and Vernon-Derby. Altogether he had nearly forty plates, of most of which no one seemed to have heard. Yet why should one succeed and the other fail; why on the face of it and with similar specifications, had the Clyno gone under and the Morris triumphed? The underlying psychological reasons interested him.

The smell of eggs and bacon frying on the Aga welled out satisfyingly from the kitchen. He walked through the low-ceilinged passage towards it. On a blackboard above the dish-washing machine Mrs Hunter, his housekeeper, had chalked the calls that had come in so far. Mrs Banes at Vicarage Farm wanted a new packet of her red pills. A drug company traveller was coming at ten. A Mr MacGillivray had telephoned. Ah, well, for the next three weeks they were his locum's responsibility.

His passage on the ten-thirty Silver City flight to Cherbourg next morning was already booked. He had no concern with drug travellers, red pills or Mr MacGillivray, whoever he might be. Probably some insurance man trying to flog him a policy. To hell with him.

Love picked up the morning papers and went into the dining-room. The daily glut of violence, sex, envy and rumour leapt from the pages. Two young men in Chelsea had killed a night watchman for ten shillings in his wallet; a homosexual dress-designer was explaining to an ingenuous woman columnist why he had never married; the life story of a Mayfair whore was to be filmed. He threw the pages to the floor; to hell with all that rubbish, too. It would be good to be away: his temper was growing shorter, always a clear sign that he needed a holiday.

As Love sat down at the table Mrs Hunter had laid for him, the telephone began to ring. Instinctively, he picked it up. The action was as automatic in a doctor's house as the salivation of Pavlov's dogs. Only when the voice at the other end asked for Dr Love did he remember that he was technically on holiday. The caller's rich, dark brown, fruit-cake, port-wine accent awoke echoes down the long aisles of his recollection. It nearly, but not quite, opened a door to the past.

'Sorry, but I'm not on duty,' said Love. 'If you'll hold on a minute, I'll put you through to my locum.'

'Please don't. This, isn't a professional matter, Doctor. I want to speak to you. I don't know if you remember me - it's nearly twenty years since we met. My name's MacGillivray. Douglas MacGillivray.'

Love's mind dredged for a link between the name, but still the groping antennae of memory could find nothing beyond the name chalked on the blackboard in the kitchen.

'Sorry,' he said. 'The name's familiar; but then I believe you rang earlier What can I do for you now, anyway? It's not insurance, I hope?'

'Good Lord, no. It's simply that I'm in Taunton and I'd like to, see you if I could. It's a personal matter. An urgent one.'

'But what sort of personal matter? I'm off tomorrow to France for three weeks. How can it be so personal and urgent if we haven't met for twenty years? And I can't remember when or where or why we met then. Won't it keep until I'm back?'

After his session with weeping, maudlin Teddy boys, Love felt out of sympathy with other people's problems: they should consider the consequences of their actions before they took them. What did a personal matter mean? It could be anything from a request for an abortion to the loan of a fiver.

'I'd rather not say much on the phone,' said the caller. 'But I can tell you when we met. I was in Chittagong. Forty-three. November. *Now* do you remember?'

Now he remembered. Chittagong was the key that unlocked a dozen half-buried memories. Burma. The war. The smell of rotting mangoes piled at street corners. The background jingle of tired tonga ponies' harnesses; at night, the roar of naphtha flares above the stalls in the bazaar. The bored British troops, too

27

long away from home, over-cynical, corroded by indiscipline and inefficiency, their morale festered by retreat and defeat: Hong Kong, Singapore, Rangoon.

When would Chittagong fall - and then Calcutta, Delhi, Bombay? Why not pack it all in now? What were they fighting for, anyway, apart from tea-planters' profits - planters who wouldn't even invite them into their homes when they were on leave? And in remembering all this, he also remembered MacGillivray.

As a second-year medical student, Love had suddenly volunteered for the infantry in a moment of quixotic lunacy, brought on by reading too much Rupert Brooke and Sassoon when he should have been busy with *Gray's Anatomy*. In Chittagong he was in charge of a draft of British troops just out from England on the way to Bawli Bazaar, the next staging post in their long, dusty journey to the Arakan front.

He was packing his kit by the light of a hurricane lamp in one of the upper rooms of the filthy old house taken over as a transit camp, when an orderly came in with a message to report to the Camp Commandant. This simply meant walking down the slimy stone stairs to the Commandant's office - the ground-floor front room - where he sat behind a wooden trestle table covered in traditional Army style by a grey blanket.

The Camp Commandant was a major, long over retiring age, First War ribbons up, the armpits under his KD jacket dark with sweat. A pressure lamp hissed above his head. On the whitewashed wall behind him, beyond the dancing night moths and mosquitoes that fluttered within the halo of the light, hung coloured front- and side-view posters of Japanese soldiers in KD jackets with leather belts and peaked caps. These were headed 'Know your Enemy'. Beside them was pinned a map of the Arakan dotted with arrows and coloured pins, denoting British and Indian formations. All the arrows moved one way. West.

'Ah, Love?' asked the Major hopefully, screwing up his eyes against the glare of the unshaded light. His breath smelled slightly of Carew's gin.

'Yes, sir. I understand you want me?'

'That's right.' The Major fussed with some message forms on the blanket. 'I've been informed that there's a spy in this camp.'

'A *spy?* Whatever can he spy on here?' asked Love in amazement.

'I agree it does sound damn odd,' allowed the Major. 'I don't mean a spy in a Mata Hari way - countesses and false beards. All that sort of thing. I mean an Indian with a transmitter, and the wish to do us harm.

'Let me put you in the picture. As you probably know already, thousands of Indians in Malaya and Burma went over to the Japs during the retreat. Now they call themselves the Indian National Army.

'They've even got what they call a provisional Indian Government under this fella Subhas Chandra Bose, who escaped from our chaps in Calcutta.

'I don't know what you think of the civilian population here in Chittagong, but the Security people's opinion isn't very high. Remember, they probably think the same of us. They've seen us retreat from every other bloody place. Now they're just waiting to see if - or when - we're going to move on from here.

'Now, if the INA thought things here were much worse than they are, they might try to make something of it. And you don't have to be Liddell Hart to realize that one more crisis here would be one too many.

'Right. Well, I'm told that an Indian in this camp somewhere - probably a bearer or a *bhisti* - has this transmitter. He's pouring out a lot of rubbish over it about the number of Congress wallahs and INA sympathizers and so on in Chittagong.

'Our Security people pinpoint the source of the messages to an area of thirty yards around this house.'

'I see, sir; but where do I come in?'

'Like this. Take your men and search the place and find him.'

'But we're off to Bawli at about four in the morning.'

'Exactly. That's why I want to use 'em. It won't matter if they talk about it, for they won't be here tomorrow. Okay? Right. A colonel's here from Security. He'll brief you.'

The Major stood up and opened a door beyond his desk; Love followed him through into the next room. It contained a camp bed with a khaki blanket and a pillowcase, dyed jungle green; the mosquito net was neatly tucked in all round it. As an old soldier, the Camp Commandant did not believe in taking risks.

A long, lean man with red hair lolled in a seat taken from a fifteen-hundredweight truck. To Love's surprise he was not in uniform but wore a crumpled linen suit. Surely it was odd in wartime for a colonel to be in mufti? But then, the whole set-up was odd.

'Colonel MacGillivray. This is Lieutenant Love, sir,' said the Major. Love saluted.

'Well, I expect the Major has explained as much as you need to know?' said MacGillivray easily.

'We've given a *burra-khana* for all the sweepers and *bhistis* and bearers, the whole damn boiling of them. You and your fellows can go through their rooms and find this transmitter without much strain, I should say.

'You'll probably find it hidden in a suitcase or a cardboard box, or maybe even in a biscuit tin. Any odd bits of wire you see lying about should give you a clue. When you spot what you're after, don't tell the men what it is, but come and tell me. Any questions?'

'No, sir.'

'Right.'

Love went back to his room. It would be much quicker to, nip through the Indians' huts himself, instead of bringing along half a dozen privates, all muttering and resentful at being disturbed on their last evening when they still had kit to pack. He could search more easily on his own, anyway; Love picked up a pencil torch he had bought in Calcutta, strapped on his Smith & Wesson 38 in its webbing holster and checked that it was loaded.

The *bhistis* and sweepers lived in what had been the servants' quarters when the house was privately occupied. These were single-storeyed stone huts, some without glass windows, others with holes in the roof which served as crude chimneys.

The first hut smelled strongly of ghee and Bidi cigarettes. On a groundsheet the unknown occupant nearest the door had made up a crude bed with strips of blankets. At its head stood an empty square ration-tin with a handful of wire twisted across it to make a handle. At the foot was a tin suitcase, painted in brown grain to simulate leather, with cheap brass locks and hinges.

Love opened the lid. It contained two fusty sets of vests and underpants dyed jungle green, a few pairs of bid socks, a medicine bottle of ink, a pen. Some letters written in a spidery Bengali hand were tied with a piece of string. But there was nothing that remotely resembled a radio transmitter. Most beds had similar trunks or suitcases near them, but none contained a radio.

Love came out into the warm night that twittered with the croaks of lizards and frogs, paused for a moment savouring the fresher air, and then went into the next hut. The first sleeping place yielded a supply of East Indies rum in a Brasso tin. The second bed had nothing unusual about it, nor did the third. At the head of the fourth bed, under a piece of mosquito netting, he saw a square ration-tin. It looked the same as all the others, and he prised up the lid with a two-anna piece and shone his torch inside, expecting to see a few personal trinkets. Instead, the narrow beam lit up an ebonite panel with three switches, a tuning dial and a socket for an aerial. A piece of paper, with some numbers written on it - wavelengths or frequencies - was gummed inside the lid.

Love stood up, switched off his torch and left the

room. He knocked on the door of the Camp Office. There was no answer. He went inside; the room was empty. He tapped on the door behind the table.

'Come in.'

MacGillivray opened the door for him.

'You're quick. Did you find it?'

'Yes, sir. In a ration-tin.'

'Where?'

'Near the head of the fourth bed on the right in the second hut.'

'Thanks. I'll remember this.'

'So will I. Anything else you want me for?'

'No,' said MacGillivray, holding out his hand. 'Just forget it ever happened. You've done your whack. Goodnight.'

And he closed the door, leaving Love on his own, with his packing still to do...

'Yes,' said Love slowly, nearly twenty years later. 'Chittagong. *Now* I remember you. Tell me, whatever happened to that Indian with the radio?'

'God knows. He's probably a member of the Indian Cabinet now, the way things are. But I didn't ring up just for that. I want to see you urgently about something else. Can I come over this morning?'

'Well, as I said, I'm off tomorrow, so I'm a bit pushed. But come all the same. Come to lunch. You have a car?'

'No, but I'll hire one.'

'See you here, then, around one.'

Love replaced the receiver. Damn this fellow, he thought. What could he possibly have to discuss that was either personal or urgent after all this time? And however had he discovered he was practising in the

West Country?

He finished breakfast, and sauntered into the walled garden under the great cedar of Lebanon that gave shade to the north side of the house, to stand looking at his car. Long, low and white, with the March sunshine glittering on its four polished outside exhaust pipes, and the chromium mesh ventilators on either side of the bonnet, the sight of the Cord always gave Love an absurd thrill of pleasure.

Here was a car built not as a means of transportation but as the fulfilment of a dream. The fact that the venture had failed commercially could not detract from the braveness of the attempt or the beauty of the result. Although made in 1937, the Cord contained so many ingenious ideas still accepted as revolutionary that its attraction among enthusiasts remained at a peak. The few Cords left in circulation changed hands at more than they had cost when new; they were of an age, but somehow ageless.

Love had planned to do a few final adjustments in preparation for the run down to Antibes on the following day, but the knowledge that the work would be interrupted by MacGillivray's arrival dissuaded him from changing into dungarees. Instead, he did some desultory packing and then spent the rest of the morning reading in the sun in the courtyard behind the house.

The morning's mail contained the usual mass of circulars from drug manufacturers, free and unsought samples, offers of encyclopaedias at cut prices. These he put under a stone at the side of his chair to be thrown away.

One letter had a Taunton postmark; it was from the

chairman of the local British Legion branch. Once a week Love took a class in judo for some of their younger members. This had the combined merit of keeping down his weight and also keeping him in contact with a generation whose views so often seemed at diametric and inexplicable divergence to his own.

The letter was a stencilled copy of his syllabus for the new session, beginning after Easter.

Lesson One. Breakfalls, then *Tsukuri*, the breaking of balance; *Kesagatame*, the scarf hold, and *Osotogari*, major outer reaping.

Lesson Two, *Hizagurma*, the knee wheel; then *Chugaeri*, the rolling breakfall; *Ogoshi*, the hip throw, and *Namijuji-jime*, the cross strangle.

Odd, how the familiar Japanese names always seemed to awake some response in him. How long ago it was since he had seen a Japanese - a *real* Japanese with square teeth and baggy KD trousers and a star in his cap; not the smooth Americanized ones he occasionally saw at airports. They didn't seem like Japs at all: they were only actors playing Japanese parts.

Ah, well, this little programme would wait until his return. He put the letter in an inner jacket pocket, and looked at the only other envelope of interest.

It had come by sea-mail from America, and contained the previous month's issue of the Auburn-Cord-Duesenberg Car Club Newsletter. He turned over the pages: a dentist in Alabama had discovered one of the 1935 Auburn 851 Speedsters being used as a breakdown wagon at a country garage and was restoring it. A real-estate dealer in Tampa, Florida, had bought an L-29 Cord with a Chapron body, surely one of the few ever made, while on holiday in Cannes. And in a suburb of Teheran had been located one of the rarest Cords, a Le Baron, with a wheelbase of eleven feet, four and a half inches, which sold pre-war for 8,600 dollars. It had apparently belonged to some court official, and had been stored for nearly twenty years.

Also in the post was a copy of the original edition of Sir Thomas Browne's *Hydriotaphia,* that curious discourse on all the different forms of burial the seventeenth-century Norwich physician could call to mind. Love had ordered it from a bookseller off the Strand.

Turning the thick, yellowing pages with their ragged edges, he wondered idly how Browne would have treated National Health patients who threatened to change to another doctor if he would not give them chits to confirm they were unfit to work, when all they wanted was a day off without losing any pay.

The thought caused Love a wry smile; no doubt Browne would tell them to do just what he told them to do. He was in full agreement with Browne's views on the mass expressed in his *Religio Medici;* 'If there be any among those common objects of hatred I do contemn and laugh at, it is that great enemy of Reason, Virtue and Religion, the Multitude: that numerous piece of monstrosity, which, taken asunder, seem men, and the reasonable creatures of God; but, confused together, make but one great beast, and a monstrosity more prodigious than Hydra.'

That lot wouldn't get him any votes at the local elections; but then Browne wouldn't have cared. He wouldn't have been standing as a candidate, in any case.

The stable clock had just begun to whir before striking the hour when Love heard the crunch of wheels on gravel. He walked out to meet MacGillivray. He had aged and his hair was greying, his face more spare and lined, more cynical, than Love remembered it; but that was to be expected. He himself had changed; after all, they were both nearly twenty years older.

The two men shook hands. MacGillivray's grey eyes took in the stone yard, the whitewashed house with its blue shutters, the rose garden and the paddock beyond.

'This must be about the last outpost of the old English way of life,' he said appreciatively. 'Not bombed by Jerry or ruined by the Jerry-builders.'

'I've heard it called other things,' said Love. 'You might have a different way of describing it if you'd to pay all the bills. But at least it's a bit better than that camp office at Chittagong.'

They sat down in the courtyard. Love filled two glasses with his own favourite drink, Bacardi rum, lime-juice and crushed ice. He handed one to MacGillivray.

'To the memory of INA,' he said.

'An imperishable memory, indeed,' replied the older man.

MacGillivray took out his cigar case, offered a cheroot to Love, who refused it, lit one himself. Then they sat back in the aluminium-framed garden chairs.

Both started to speak and then stopped at the same time, bowing for the other to continue. Their attempts at conversation had barren beginnings. Do you remember that drunk at Cox's? What happened to that old Major at Maungdaw? Was it true that the Japs had kept 'comfort girls' in the Tunnels?

Love poured two more drinks.

'Well,' he said at last. 'I'm delighted to see you, Colonel, Brigadier, General, Field-Marshal or whatever you are now, and to talk over Burma days. But let's not horse about. After all, we only met twice before for about five minutes altogether. What's the urgent personal business that brings you here now?'

MacGillivray leaned back in his chair.

'You mentioned the Indian on the phone,' he said. 'You toasted INA just now. I'm no psychologist, but I'd say that both these subjects must be fairly close to the surface of your mind. The personal matter I mentioned is this. I want to ask your help in something not unlike that Indian affair.'

He paused for a moment.

'When we met last, I was a colonel in Military Intelligence. Now I'm a civilian in another branch of the same net. I won't go into all the ins and outs, but now and then we have to appeal for help - just as I did in Chittagong. I'm doing that now. I'm looking for a doctor who'd like a free ticket to attend a malaria conference in Teheran.'

'Well, you're not looking at him now,' replied Love sharply. 'You're looking at a doctor who's bought his own ticket to France.'

'I know. You told me.'

'So you'd better look elsewhere.'

'I get the message, loud and clear,' said MacGillivray. 'But as I've come this far I might as well explain why I wanted such a doctor. And why I thought - quite wrongly as it now appears - you might be the man.

'We had a message from one of our people in Teheran the other day. He said he was sending us some absolutely vital news about our oil treaties. But we heard nothing more. Not a peep. Not a whisper.

'We checked on him. He hadn't booked out of his room in his hotel. And he hadn't used his BOAC ticket. So presumably he's still in Teheran. And I want to know just where in Teheran he is.'

'But why pick on me? Can't you send someone else out to find him? One of your own people?'

'No,' said MacGillivray bluntly.

'Why not?'

'Here's why not:'

He pulled out a photostat of an article from the *Daily Express*, dated June 20th, 1961. Some paragraphs had been underlined; Love read these first.

'George Blake, the Secret Service agent who spied, for Russia, betrayed the names of at least forty other British agents to the Communists...

'Many of these agents have disappeared and several are believed to have been executed...

'As a result, some of the most important sections of the Secret Service behind the Iron Curtain and in the Middle East have been ruined.'

'Almost the entire British Intelligence network in the Middle East, built up over years, had to be withdrawn...'

'But that doesn't answer my question. Why come to me?' asked Love, handing it back. 'I know nothing of agents and spies and so on. I only got involved in that ludicrous business at Chittagong presumably because you hadn't anybody else to do it.'

'Which is exactly why I'm here now,' said MacGillivray.

'I've been through the list of people who've helped us in the past - people Blake would know nothing about - but there's no one else I could use for this. One has to have a reason for being in Teheran. I thought that the malaria conference might give you enough reason. But if you've made up your mind, I'd better be on my way.'

'Stay for lunch, though. It's all ready.'

'Thank you, no. I've got to try and find someone else quickly. We should have heard on Friday from our man. Today's Monday.'

'The lost weekend. What do you think's happened?'

'God knows.' MacGillivray shrugged. 'Maybe he's had an accident, been knocked down, lost his memory. There's no reason to think there's any mystery about it. I just want to *know*, that's all.'

'Who will you ask now? How many other doctors have you on your list?'

MacGillivray examined the glowing end of his cheroot.

'None. You're the only one. I only got you because I remembered your name from Chittagong. Ah, well, Love's labour's lost. But don't let me persuade you to change your mind.'

'You haven't tried very hard,' said Love. 'You don't offer much. What's in it for me if I did change my mind? How long would it take?'

'Three days. Maybe four. And what would you want

to be in it for you?'

'I don't know the rate for the job,' said Love. 'But I'm on holiday. What's the bidding?'

'As a basis for discussion - if you *were* considering it - which I know you aren't, how would it be if we paid all your expenses to Teheran, and your expenses to France as well?'

'That's not a bad basis for discussion,' admitted Love. 'At least it's better than a kick in the nuts with a hobnail boot.'

'Or even a hand-sewn shoe,' said MacGillivray.

'Even so, I'll settle for the fast run down the N7 tomorrow. That's all been arranged for months.'

'Ah, well,' said MacGillivray philosophically. 'There it is. Well, thanks for the drinks.'

He held out his hand.

'You're sure you won't stay for lunch?'

MacGillivray stood up.

'Much as I'd like to,' he said. 'I can't.'

They walked out of the courtyard into the garden. The taxi was still waiting. So he must have anticipated my reply, thought Love. He must have guessed. I'd say no, or else he'd have sent it away. The thought depressed him. Was he becoming so predictable, so set in iron ways that even before a request was made his refusal was definitely expected?

As he stood, hand outstretched to say goodbye to MacGillivray, he felt a sharp, almost overwhelming remembrance of his years in the East; he savoured again that lost, unreturning feeling of being young and free in a far country.

Here was a chance - perhaps a last chance - of trying to turn back the pages of the past and once more to be on his own, with no bills to pay, no health committees, no unsatisfied patients to see.

And what about that Le Baron in Teheran? That was another reason, surely? Four days, the man said. Hell, it would be worth it for a free holiday; worth it almost just for his expenses.

The hire car's engine spluttered; the Austin began to move slowly towards the gate. When the car had gone, Love would have no means of contacting MacGillivray even if he changed his mind. He had no address for him, no telephone number. He would vanish into the past with all the other memories, going out of his life as swiftly and quietly as he had entered it; and when he had gone some part of his dreams would go with him.

Balls, thought Love in elegantly. I'll have a go. He ran after the car and beat on the roof with the palm of his hand. The driver looked around in alarm; MacGillivray motioned him to stop.

Love wrenched open the door.

'All right,' he said. 'You win: Promise me a new booking to France as I've lost my present one, and you've got a deal.'

MacGillivray grinned.

'We're in business,' he said. 'As of now. I was going to give you to the gate to change your mind, and then I'd have come back and asked again. For if you won't go, there just isn't anyone else I know I can ask.'

'Don't think I'm going because I want to find your man, and all that cloak-and-dagger stuff,' began Love.

'I don't care a damn why you're going,' MacGillivray interrupted him. 'I just want you to go. And I promise you a lot more warmth and sun than you'll find in France this time of the year.'

They went back to the courtyard; Love filled their glasses for the third time.

'Now give a bit on the details,' he said.

'There's very little I can tell you. And it's best you don't know too much, in any case. Let's leave it that we just want to know where our man is. We'll take it from there ourselves.

'Now, if you'll come back to London this evening, we'll fix you up with a visa and money. We'll book you a room at the Park Hotel in Teheran where our man's staying, get you an invitation to this bloody conference, and the rest will be up to you. Know anything about malaria, by the way?'

'No more than any other GP, except as a patient. Can't remember having even one case here.'

'I can imagine. So we'll give you a handbook about it. Be useful to read on the plane. I'll also show you photographs of our man. His code name with us is K, because he works mostly in Kuwait. Our people take the initial letter of their territory as their own. He's in Teheran simply because we hadn't anyone else. K's passport, in the name of Peter Offord, describes him as a university professor, by the way.

'We've been using an organization called the Oil Exploration Centre in Teheran as a cover. They actually do prospect for oil, and so all kinds of people - scientists, geologists and chemists and the like - come and go every day. Thus the odd extra man wasn't noticed: Or perhaps he was. But we've dropped that cover now, so don't contact them. They won't be able to help.'

'What's K's real name?' asked Love.

'It doesn't concern the issue,' said MacGillivray easily. 'You'll know him as Offord when you meet him.'

'If I meet him.'

'Have it your own way.'

'What's his background, then?'

'Quiet, scholarly fellow. Widower. Getting on for this type of work - he'll be sixty in May. Took a First in classics at the House in the twenties. Professor in Rangoon University. Then moved to Calcutta. Held the chair of Roman Studies. A keen amateur geologist, too. When he retired he went to Kuwait. He's been working for us off and on since thirty-three.'

'Am I armed?' asked Love. It seemed a point to clear up.

'Do you want to be? Wouldn't it be difficult for a country doctor at a foreign medical conference to explain away the presence of a nine-millimetre Beretta in a briefcase or inside a book? What if the Customs found it? Or if someone in the hotel went through your cases? It'd be a strong case of physician, heal thyself, then, surely?'

'I thought you said this would be an easy job?'

'It's because I want it to be easy that I think you shouldn't be armed.'

'And who's on the other side? Who are they?'

'Everyone who's not with us is against us,' said MacGillivray pontifically. 'But about being armed. We'll compromise. We'll give you some bits and pieces. Do you remember the escape gadgets the RAF had in the war?'

'I've heard about them vaguely, that's all.'

'Well, the reason so many of our people escaped from German prison camps was that they literally took the keys of freedom in with them. They had flexible sawblades in bootlaces, maps sewn in jacket linings, compasses in buttons and so on. We even issued the Maquis with fountain pens that shot needles. Very effective. Quiet. Clean. We'll fix you up with a few items of this kind.'

'Well, I hope they don't find them on a country doctor, either. What about another drink?'

Love uncorked the bottle.

'By the way, how fit are you?' asked MacGillivray. 'I see you're a Brown Belt.'

'Yes. Better than being a brown hatter, at least, but not as good, of course, as being a Black Belt. I help a British Legion thing in the village, and I'd say I'm a pretty good medical risk, even if I do have to sign my own health certificate for the insurance company. But is there any strain involved in this?'

'There shouldn't be. That's why we're kitting you out with these gadgets.'

'You mentioned oil treaties earlier on,' said Love. 'Don't they run on for years and then get renegotiated and so on? What's the worry there?'

'The fact that they may not be negotiated. With each bit of the Empire we give away what we still hold on to grows more important. For instance, Kuwait, where K operates, is a tiny place, barely as big as Sussex. Yet it contains one-fifth of all the known oil deposits in the world. For this we pay the Sheikh a royalty of £400 *every minute* of every day and every night. He's deposited about £300 million of this through London. If he withdrew this money suddenly, the market would drop as badly as in twenty-nine.

'But worse than that, if we lost that source of oil we'd be finished as a country with any pretence to power.'

'Is there any suggestion that we will lose it?'

MacGillivray shrugged.

'There wasn't much warning at Abadan in 1951 when Mossadeq squeezed us out of Persia - with a bit of connivance from America - was there? Eventually, we were allowed back into Persia - but only as junior partners in a consortium'.

'We built up Kuwait to compensate for this. But now there's nowhere left to build up. If Kuwait goes, that's our lot.'

MacGillivray contemplated the Cord through the amber rum.

'But why should there be anything wrong with the treaties, any kind of danger?' Love asked him.

'When you find K, that's the first question I want answered,' MacGillivray replied, holding out his glass.

CHAPTER THREE

Churchill, Manitoba, Canada, March 19th, 09.05 hours {local time) Teheran, March 19th, 19.35 hours (local time)

LATER, after lunch, when MacGillivray had duly admired the Cord and paraded what few facts his duty officer had been able to glean about the marque's short history, two apparently unrelated events that would be of importance to them both were taking place on opposite sides of the world.

In room seven of the Hudson Hotel in Churchill, Manitoba, on the edge of the Canadian Arctic, a man propped himself on his elbow in bed, looking out of the window. The cold had frozen a frame of white frost around the glass, but he was not thinking about that, nor even of the homely snow beyond, punctured by buildings and telegraph poles and hoardings. He was thinking of other endless, empty, alien snow he had left behind him; so similar, so different: the snow around Vorkuta. His thoughts made him shiver, although the room was stuffy and overheated.

Beside him, still asleep, lay a girl, her dark hair spread like a wide fan over the pillow, her lips slightly parted. He looked from the window down at Irina, wondering, not for the first time, whether the bondage of the present was much lighter than that from which he had escaped. But at least it was more comfortable.

He was a dumpy, sad-faced man with dusty hair and lugubrious, spaniel eyes. His barrel chest, legs like tree roots, as much as his stolid acceptance of whatever hand fate dealt him, marked him as a peasant born to carry the can for cleverer people he would never meet, whose names he would never even know.

His passport in the pouch beneath his pillow gave his name as Axel Lukacs. It was not his own, but it seemed as good as any other; his superiors at the spy training school in Kuchino, outside Moscow, had decided this for him with the same care that they had built up a false background for him to remember.

He lay thinking about this now, these thoughts superimposed on other deeper, more dangerous thoughts of freedom. Just feet away, beyond the window, lay escape and a life without chains. In that free world, so near, so far away, silvery grain elevators, oil storage tanks, the bare masts of ships towered in the frozen grey distance. Then came the shanty town of tin huts and shacks where the Indians lived with their noisy dogs. Their squalor was infinitely better than the best in Vorkuta: they had the priceless gift of freedom.

Flocks of tiny snow birds, speckled black and white, fluttered around the deep drifts on either side of the road. Here and there, American cars with flamboyant fins and two-tone paintwork lay half-buried in the snow, their roofs forming bright glittering islands of red and green and vermilion.

To the left stretched overhead power wires, so heavy with snow and frozen rain that the poles stood together in threes to bear their weight. Taxis waited outside the hotel, fronds of smoke at their exhausts, drivers huddled inside with the heaters. To Lukacs, the cold was like a fourth dimension, just as it had been in the prison camp at Vorkuta. Cold conditioned your mind, your actions, he thought. In the end, it marked your whole life. You became like a frog, a fish, with blood like ice; all your human feelings muted and numb.

Although the central heating in the room was turned up to its maximum, no warmth could ever completely cauterize the cold from his bones. Despite the double windows, wind blew in from a pinhead bored in the frame for a radio aerial. For Lukacs it held the sharpness of a knife, the pain of many memories.

The air felt heavy with the smell from sewage that should have flowed away through a vast conduit into the sea. But part of the Bay was frozen and the pipe was blocked.

For Lukacs, too, the smell also recalled the vast, unspeakable miasma from a hundred unwashed bodies; the rush into the huts from their daily work norm for the tiny bowls of fish soup; the frantic search for a piece of flaking fish floating in the oily urine-coloured liquid.

Beyond Vorkuta's cluster of wooden huts, 1,200 miles north-east of Moscow, forests stretched to the Great Arctic Plain. Only in July and August was the climate bearable; but even so the political prisoners worked through all the other ten frozen months of each year. Day and night had no difference, for both were equally dark in the mines; and shifts of men and women, harnessed to coal trolleys, toiled like blind ponies: ageless, sexless, beyond hope and without desire.

Between the wired fences that ringed the camp roamed watchdogs. Like the slaves inside, the dogs were always hungry. Thus, they did not only kill and mangle anyone foolish enough to try and flee: they ate them.

How had he ever escaped from that frozen death-in-life? Truly, God had helped him. Automatically, in a reflex action, Lukacs crossed himself as his mother had taught him to do in a lost, happy world of childhood innocence and belief.

One afternoon, the commandant at Vorkuta had sent for him. Would he like a month's release from hard labour? But of course he would. Well, it could be arranged. He had been selected, with some others, to tour the work camps, to go to Rostov, Krasnouodsk, even to Kara-Kala, where spies for Persia and the Middle East were trained. These selected few would lecture new recruits to the camps on the glories of hard work for the Communist cause. The commandant did not add that it was difficult to find captive Albanians still with strength for such a task. Nor did Lukacs raise the point; he had no wish to push his luck. So the little group, given warm clothes, boots and an adequate escort, set off on their tour.

At Bukharden, near Kara-Kala, their train broke down. With the rest, Lukacs spent the night chained by the ankles in a local police cell. During the night, some began to vomit: the food was strong for their ruined stomachs.

In the morning, the police doctor - a woman - examined them all in case they carried infection. Lukacs's papers gave his birthplace as Tirana, in Albania. The woman doctor looked from the printed words to his naked body, to his muscles, the mat of dark hair on his chest; the message was clear in her eyes. She was thick-bodied, in middle age, with large breasts that even her bulky uniform could not hide; her lips were moist. She turned to the other prisoners who also stood naked before her and dismissed them.

The police guards marched them away.

'There is a saying that Albanians are made for death and love,' she said, when she was alone with Lukacs. 'Is that true?'

' "What is truth?" asked Pilate,' said Lukacs, wondering whether he was reading the signs aright. It was so long since he had spoken to a woman on more or less equal terms that he suddenly felt afraid. Was this a trap, some further excuse for his humiliation and punishment? Or could this be the chance to escape, to drop out of the draft, the first step on the march to freedom and dignity?

He looked at the doctor: her face was sallow, with a few wispy hairs on her upper lip. Even her fingernails looked none too clean. He despised her for her obvious need, but he despised himself more.

She stood up and slipped the bolt on the door. Then she moved towards him, one hand already at the buttons of her jacket. There was no risk of discovery with a prisoner: he was no more than a human toy, to be discarded at a whim. This was not the first time, nor would it be the last. She pressed against him, rubbing her body against his lightly, like a cat.

'There is no time,' Lukacs said hoarsely, the unexpected nearness of a woman, of even so unattractive a woman as this, the unaccustomed food and warmth working their own alchemy in his blood. But the stakes were too high for any error: he had to bargain, in the only way he had left, for delay; for the best possible deal.

'I can make time,' she whispered. 'Please. I can have you taken off the draft. I'll say you're too ill to travel.'

He reached out then, cupping the firm warm breasts

in his hands, feeling the nipples harden against his palms. She covered his mouth with hers, her lips wide and warm. But still he resisted. He must have his part of the deal agreed first. Afterwards might be too late.

'Say that, will you?' he asked hoarsely. 'Promise?'

She nodded, beyond speech, as his hands moved about her body, unzipping her skirt, smoothing her thighs. Lukacs allowed himself to be propelled to the couch and then forced her back on it roughly, arousing the fierce sharp appetite of her longing until she writhed in an agony of want for him.

To him it was simply a commercial transaction: the exchange of sex for the hope of delay; for with delay he might somehow avoid returning to Vorkuta.

That afternoon, when the rest of the draft went on their way, Lukacs stayed behind: she had kept her promise; he was declared medically unfit to travel. He would follow under guard when he was able to do so. Lukacs stayed in the little police hospital for several weeks, fed on extra rations that should, have gone to other patients. Then his papers were conveniently mislaid. He was entirely dependent for his life on the pleasure he could give to a woman who desired him.

Then the doctor was posted elsewhere. But before she left she arranged for him to be given a new set of identity papers. She also introduced him to a friend, a girl in her twenties married to a man twice her age, an assistant commandant at the spy school in Kara-Kala. Again and again with this new companion, more sophisticated in her desires, Lukacs proved his manhood. But still he was no nearer freedom; his life still hung on his sexual ability.

Finally and unexpectedly, the assistant commandant sent for him: he was to be posted abroad, for the greater glory of Russian Communism. So far as the assistant commandant was concerned, the farther Lukacs went, the better; he had his own suspicions about his relationship with his wife, for Lukacs was not the first. But he did not want a scandal or to become the object of masculine pity. And of course he had no knowledge of Lukacs's real background; the doctor's papers described him as an orphan, a loyal Party worker, and he had no reason to doubt this.

So, after training at Kara-Kala, Lukacs received new papers as a Hungarian, memorized a new past, and travelled to East Germany. He 'escaped' to the West and within six months he was in Canada, not quite clear as to the exact nature of his duties, only knowing that he was at least alive and nearer freedom than he had been since boyhood in Tirana.

His first assignment seemed simple. He was to remain in the Hudson Hotel for a fortnight. Within this time other instructions would reach him, how or from whom he knew not, but he would recognize their authenticity by certain identity signals. While he waited he had to forward any messages he received to a Madame Eugenia Lukacs at 117b Brodski-Allee, Budapest, Hungary. He had never met Madame Lukacs, and doubted very much whether she existed in that name, although on his immigration papers he had written that she was his mother.

So far he had only received one message to forward to her. It made no sense whatever to him, but he remembered the wording, simply because he had so little else to remember: 'PLEASE ADVISE MOTHER THAT JACK IS SAILING 27TH STOP HIS NEW OFFICE IN STOCKHOLM OVERLOOKS PARK WHICH SHOULD PLEASE COUSIN PETER AND UNCLE OFFORD.'

The message was meaningless; but then so was his job, so far as he was concerned. He knew that his superiors preferred to send their messages in clear because they sounded harmless that way and so were safer than using a code which shouted out that it contained secrets of some kind; otherwise why use a code at all?

Who was Jack and Peter and Offord? Were they three men or one? Who, for the matter of that, was Mother? Nothing was ever as it seemed, and the incredible was credible in the end when measured against the other unbelievabilities of his own experience. After all, six months ago, who would have imagined him in Canada?

Irina stirred and turned on her side, and stretched luxuriously, like a cat. She gave a child's small sigh of content. Lukacs looked down at her sleeping form, at her firm parted breasts with the nipples spread like dark flowers, seeing her without love, without want. She was there for the purpose of watching him. They wouldn't trust so raw a recruit alone abroad for the first time: there had been too many cases when such people working on their own had used the opportunity to flee.

Thus Lukacs was untouched by the nearness of her nakedness, unmoved by her warmth. To him she was simply his guard; the fact that she demanded him with the fierce, roaring urgency of nymphomania was a possible key that might eventually open some further door to freedom. But where and when were questions to which he had no answer. He had travelled a long way since the train broke down at Bukharden; he was determined to go the full distance if he could.

Irina's eyelids fluttered, and when she saw him watching her she was immediately awake, listening.

'What's wrong?' she asked, one hand already feeling under the mattress for the Lüger she kept on her side of the bed.

'Nothing,' he said. 'Relax. I was just thinking.'

'What a waste of time: to think,' she said dreamily, stretching her bare arms above her head.

'It's almost an insult to be in bed with a man who says he's thinking.'

'It *is* an insult,' agreed Lukacs, and slipped down against her.

'Now,' she said. *'Now.'* Her voice was thick with longing. But when it was over, no more than an immediate and soon returning appetite had been slaked; nothing final whatever had been solved.

Yet if he could satisfy Irina, if she imagined he was fond of her, might there not eventually arrive a moment long enough for him to attempt to choose his own future?

She lay half across him stroking his hair, kissing him lightly, lifting her head to look at his face as though she had never seen it properly before, already beginning to want him again. He shut his eyes lest his inner thoughts should show in the windows of his mind.

At the same moment they heard footsteps in the corridor outside, footsteps that passed the door and then returned. Lukacs seized Irina firmly by her shoulders and lifted her to her side of the bed. He stood up, grabbing a towel to cover his nakedness. Irina gripped the Lüger under the sheets, watching him, wariness displacing warmth in her eyes.

They both could hear breathing on the other side of the thin wood panels. Someone knocked so heavily that the door, trembled in its frame.

'Why!' Lukacs called out. His command of English in moments of stress was not so colloquial as he had led his superiors to believe.

'You Mr Lukacs?'

The voice sounded foreign. But in this country he could never be sure whether the owner was Canadian or not.

'Yes,' he called out. 'What do you want?'

'A cable for you.'

At last, a message. He slid back the bolt on the door and opened it a few inches. A stocky man of his own build, possibly even from his own country, stood with a telegram in his hand. Lukacs spelled out the name and address. There was no doubt: it was for him.

'Thanks,' he said, taking the envelope and closing the door in. one movement. He sat down on the bed - after years in prison camps with only beds in the huts you lost the habit of using chairs when a bed was near - and ripped it open.

'What does it say? Who's it from?' asked Irina.

'It's in code! In English.'

Lukacs began to read it slowly for her.

'Dear Alex stop have heard that Uncle not expected

to live the night stop please cable Mother this news writing regards from all here stop.'

'What's it mean?' she asked.

'How do I know? My instructions are not to wonder what it means. Only to pass it on.'

'Of course,' she agreed sharply.

Lukacs opened the little dressing-table drawer where he kept his paper and envelopes, and started to write with the Parker 61 he had bought at the local Hudson's Bay Company shop the previous morning.

He copied the message in capital letters onto a telegram form, the tip of his tongue between his lips with the effort of concentration. He added his first code recognition 'Letter following Monday', and signed it with the second identity phrase, 'Your loving son Alex'.

Now that he actually had a job to do he felt more cheerful, more resolute. He pulled on his clothes and his brown lumber jacket, his gumboots, then tied his scarf in a knot and pulled on his fur hat.

'I'll take it to the post office right away,' he said.

'I'm coming with you,' said Irina, kicking her long legs out of bed. He watched her as she dressed. The Canadian underwear was infinitely smarter and more alluring than the clothes she had bought in GUM, the Moscow department store.

They went out of the room. Irina locked the door behind them and slipped the key into her handbag with her Lüger. Then she took his arm, squeezed it and smiled up at him; they might have been in love.

In the hotel entrance-hall, a long red-leather settee stood against one wall near a green-painted self-dispenser for Pepsi-Cola. You tipped up the lid, put twenty-five cents in a slot; this released a hidden catch and a bottle came out. A foolish Western idea, of course, with no social value; and yet it intrigued him. There was nothing like it in Vorkuta.

Three engineers from a local construction company stood about, smoking cigars, waiting for a truck to arrive. Big, burly men in plaid jackets, peaked caps in huge hands, they were obviously workmen; and yet they had dignity and authority. Alex remembered seeing such men in Tirana when he was a boy. Would he ever again count himself of their company?

The men followed them with their eyes, mentally undressing Irina, wondering what sort of pants she wore, assessing her as a potential lay. They passed the Midnight Beverage Room, the Frontier Bar, and went out through the double doors into the bright cold morning, where their breath hung on the air like fronds of mist.

Lukacs sent off his message, put the receipt in his pocket, and returned more slowly with Irina. After the urgency of action, he felt the slackness of anti-climax. He dreaded returning to the small room, and the inevitable, mechanical lovemaking she would demand. That would come soon enough but for what was left of his self-respect he felt he had to delay it as long as he could.

And what happened when this assignment was finished? Where would the next one be? And what if Irina tired of him?

The thought of a return to Vorkuta cast a shadow over the pale sunshine. The cold was reminding him of it all again. Maybe he had a fever?

'Let's have coffee,' he suggested, with a brightness he

did not feel. She nodded, pleased that he had made the suggestion. Usually she had to take every initiative. It showed he really did like her; in his own odd way.

She felt rather mean that she had put in a negative report about him to her controller in Winnipeg. Lukacs was quite sweet, really, but just not very bright. Also, he talked in his sleep, and what he said sounded dangerous. Perhaps they'd let him stay, though. But if they didn't, it would be fun to see who replaced him, and how he made love. She hoped he showed more imagination than Lukacs.

They turned up a side street near the hotel and went into a cafe, all bright strip-lights and chromium beading and plastic walls, with a juke box blaring a twist. They sat at the bar and the coffee became steak and chips for two with farm-fresh, new-tossed lettuce and Thousand Islands dressing.

While it was being prepared, while the Gaggia coffee machine hissed and spluttered, and a man in a chef's white hat chewed spearmint and flung the chips in a pan of roaring fat, Lukacs puzzled for a way out, a move in the game that could somehow bring him the keys of freedom.

The meal took all of half an hour to eat, and so they were not in the hotel when two men in heavy overcoats of a kind not common in Churchill came to visit room number seven. They arrived at the Hudson unannounced and entered by the back door, walking through the kitchens near the private apartments of the manager, on through the empty restaurant to the stairs, with a sureness that suggested prior reconnaissance. They ignored the notice above the reception desk - 'Only patrons and guests are allowed upstairs at this hotel; others must inquire at the office' - and walked up the stairs with a lightness unusual in two men so heavily built, and neither patrons nor guests.

One of them knocked on Lukacs's door in a strange tattoo but there was no answer. Then they tried the handle, and the man who had knocked was about to slip a strip of mica around the edge of the door to cheat the lock when an Indian cleaning woman came slopping down the stairs in her loose moccasins, carrying a bucket and a mop. They stepped back into the washroom across the corridor until she had gone, and then they also went away, in the silence with which they had arrived.

Afterwards, no one, not even Lukacs or Irina, knew that they had ever been there.

While Lukacs and Irina sipped their scalding coffee and cut their steaks; while Love stacked his cases into the Cord boot and prepared to set off with MacGillivray for London, another event was taking place several thousand miles to the east, in Persia.

Outside Teheran, on the Daraband road, where the air feels as sharp as iced wine, and waterfalls tinkle like bells in the hills, the rich Armenians and Parsees have their magnificent homes. These are set well back from the thoroughfare, screened by cypress trees, and guarded by watchmen with Doberman Pinschers. Some also have guns, but they are discreet about this; they don't like the fact to be widely known.

The thick wall of trees, like the rich Bokhara carpets and tapestries within, soak up sound and throw back silence. Here the owners have all that money can buy, except, sometimes, peace of mind. Behind one of these houses, on a terrace of veined pink marble, where fountains pumped their tireless silver spray and fish moved in the ornamental pools like plump gold cigars, a man lay on his back in a wicker chaise-longue.

He was tall, with bread shoulders, a narrow waist, a hard flat stomach. His hair grew thick and black and curly; for a man of all but fifty he was proud of his magnificent physical shape.

He lay at ease, basking in the sun, hands clasped behind his head. Now and then, as he moved, the sun caught the Rolex Oyster on his left wrist and the thin gold chain and name-plate he wore on his right. On the plate his name was inscribed, in delicate script: Andre Simmias.

On a table by his side stood a bottle of dimple Haig, a bowl of ice-cubes, a soda-water syphon in gold mesh. Yet, although his body lay apparently relaxed and uniformly brown, uniformly fit, one tiny tremor of tension flickered in his face. A muscle twitched intermittently by his left eye, and the calipers of cruelty tightened on either side of his ' mouth.

Simmias stood up, wrapped a thick towel around his middle, and pushed open one of the french doors into the wide, high-ceilinged room. The thick curtains held back the sunshine, so that it was almost like coming from day into night. He blinked for a moment to accustom his eyes to the darkness; then he took in the familiar ornaments, the baroque clock, and the girl standing by the marble table and the pale slender rod that lay across it.

The girl was small, and through the thin stuff of her cotton frock her breasts pressed with the firmness of youth. He walked across the soft carpet and faced her.

She looked up at him for a moment, almost fearfully, and then lowered her eyes, like someone expecting punishment; and yet her face was slightly flushed, her eyes bright with expectation. As he faced her he wondered, not for the first time, who enjoyed these sessions more, the giver or the taker of pain?

So far as he was concerned, the act of cruelty recharged the batteries of his confidence so that for the moment he felt invincible. He needed this reassurance more and more, for beneath the outward, bland patina of confidence there lurked a tiny canker of fear: the unthinkable thought that one day all this might crumble and he would be back where he began, a lonely figure in the empty endless wastes of snow.

Then he seized her and, mouth on mouth, tongues touching, he reached out for the thin cane. He drew back and looked at her; she did not meet his gaze.

'So you've been naughty again,' he said softly, almost gently. 'So you need the punishment that fits the crime.'

The cane rose and fell and rose again.

Outside, in the hard, hot sunshine, the little yellow and black Vauxhall bazaar taxi carefully threaded its way between the huge stone posts that supported metal eagles on either side of the entrance gates into the long, shaded drive. The driver read aloud: 'Doctor Andre Simmias, Medecin-Chirurgien, Rayons X, Medecine Generate.'

This must be the place. He was surprised that two such nondescript fares as the men who sat behind him should have the cash to pay the prodigious fees such a doctor must charge to live in this sumptuous style.

He did not know that Simmias was rather more

62

than a general practitioner. But then, why should he? Only a handful of people in Teheran knew that; and they were scattered in the Soviet and Rumanian embassies.

Dr Simmias did indeed maintain a small clinic in his house, which explained arrivals and departures of all kinds of people at all hours. But only some of the ambulances contained patients. In others sat men of various nationalities and names who wished to consult him on matters entirely unconnected with medicine. For Dr Simmias controlled all Communist espionage in Persia.

As is the custom, he was not a Russian. If he should be caught and accused of espionage then, because he held a French passport, the guilt would point towards France. Surely he must have been spying for his own country? The French were up to their colonial tricks again! Down with Western Imperialism!

Old raw hatreds would erupt, half-covered wounds of pride would open, and the real culprit would escape all censure. They might even heap rebukes on the wicked French for so abusing the hospitality of a friendly country.

As is also the custom with professional Soviet spies, Simmias had no outward link with the Russian Embassy in Teheran where, in the usual way, two completely separate staffs had completely separate jobs.

One staff, comprising the Ambassador and his secretaries and attaches, was concerned with orthodox diplomatic duties. The second - under such disguises as a valet, a chauffeur, a maintenance man - were professional spies; and in matters affecting his work the Ambassador's valet was in fact senior to the Ambassador.

Simmias dressed and glanced at his watch: his guests were late. Then he heard the expected, diffident crunch of tyres on the gravel chips in front of the house.

'Wait here,' he told the girl. 'I have to see two people. It's best they don't see you. I'll be with you in twenty minutes at the outside.'

He felt larger than life, but then, in a sense, he was; for he was not one man but two, and he always extracted a kick of pleasure from the thought. He was a success both as a capitalist and a Communist: he was in business on both sides of the street. And how many other rich men could say as much?

As Simmias walked between the high mirrors that made the hall seem even larger than it was, past the gilded angels that stared sightlessly at the ceiling from their plinths in each corner, he knew he was indeed one of the immortals. Love-making always had this effect on him; and it would be even sweeter after he had seen these two men, provided they could report the success of their mission.

Although, as a doctor, he was used to blood and broken bones and scarred tissue in the course of his professional calling, his pulses still raced when he heard a story of violence and murder. There was nothing sweeter than life except death, and the red raw pain that preceded it, the sweat of another man's fear, the empty agony in his dimming eyes.

He saw the shadows of the callers against the frosted glass of the front door, etched behind the black wrought-ironwork. Let them wait: he knew the psychological importance of keeping underlings on edge, unsure of themselves. He went into his study; it was his custom always to meet subordinates on his own ground, where it was obvious he was physically, mentally and socially their superior.

There was only one man to whom he in turn showed an equal and abject respect, a man he knew .as Stanilaus. A direct telephone line ran from his house to the villa in Baku, on the Soviet shores of the Caspian. He had never met Stanilaus and probably he never would, for this was only one name of many, one identity, one code-sign out of a dozen the man possessed; but something about his cold, impersonal voice, never raised, never hurried, made the sweat bead at the roots of Simmias's hair.

For Stanilaus would hear in silence his arguments, his reasons for not doing something the way Stanilaus wished, and then would quieten and quell all impatience with two words: 'Remember Kem.'

And Simmias, standing on the sea-green carpet of his study, at the heart of luxury and wealth, remembered Kem. He had first seen the place in 1929, when he was in his teens. He was with more than 35,000 Kulak families - peasants who refused to enter collective farms - who were deported from South Ukraine and shipped to this convict colony on the shores of the White Sea. Their task was to build or re-build a whole series of towns in northern Russia - Hibinagorsk, Nevastroy, Murmansk, Archangel - working for their food alone.

With them went thousands of political prisoners, victims of the almost annual purges of those days. Simmias's parents, both French Communists expelled

65

from Algeria, had gone to Russia intent on finding the promised land. Instead, they found their deaths at Kem within a year.

They lived in leaky tents, where their thin summer clothes could not mask the perpetual agony of cold. Typhus and typhoid, plague, diphtheria and dysentery raged among them until the living had scarcely strength to bury the dead. And by the time they had stripped the bodies of clothes to wear themselves, the corpses had frozen as hard as marble.

Then, in 1933, the purgers had themselves been purged. Hundreds of the original prisoners - there were only a few hundred left - were inexplicably released.

Simmias, and the handful of, others still young and fit enough to absorb learning after their experiences, were sent to school and then to college. He qualified as a doctor, and was allowed to practise in France, until the Soviet should have need of his services elsewhere on more serious matters than the problems of individual lives and deaths. He was known, in the language of spies, as a sleeper: he would take no part in espionage until the orders came. Thus, he worked for years, attracting sympathy and rich patients, and no suspicion whatever.

But his experiences in Kem had laid their indelible mark on his character. He lived now for luxury and warmth and ease and all the soft pleasures that enough money can buy.

Then, five years after the war, a man came to see him who was not a patient; he brought details of a small job Simmias was to do for the Soviet fatherland. One of Klaus Fuchs's controllers needed urgent plastic surgery on his face to change his appearance and help him to cross a frontier where the guards were watching for him. Then, in the following year, he organized a larger job for one of the men who had helped Burgess and Maclean to leave Britain. Soon Simmias was so hopelessly compromised that he had no road back and, worse, no wish to escape even if he could find a way. The excitement, the scent of danger, the whole fever of espionage had infected him like a virus in his veins.

He opened a cedarwood box inlaid with mother of pearl, selected a black Russian cigarette; lit it from the pale silent flame that burned endlessly from the torch of one of the figures in a statuette group on his desk.

He blew the smoke from the strong dark tobacco through his wide nostrils, and paused in his walk to press together the delicate wings of a tiny bird carved in silver that stood on his desk. It contained a hidden bell-push: a servant appeared soundlessly in the doorway.

Simmias nodded towards the windows. The man bowed, and pulled -the tasselled ropes that closed the curtains, although it would not be dark for hours.

'Now let them in,' Simmias told him. Within seconds, the servant was back again; behind him walked the two men who had arrived in the Vauxhall taxi. They were stockily, almost squarely built, in badly cut alpaca suits and square-toed shoes. Their felt hats had been pulled down so tightly above their ears that when they removed them, their bristly heads still wore red rims. They stood in the doorway, uneasy in the presence of so much power, so much elegance, on the threshold of a world of influence to which and in which they were completely alien. They had no wish to linger in it; they hoped the doctor would find no fault with what they had done, and then they could be on their way.

The servant withdrew. Only then did Simmias speak.

'Well?' he asked.

The two men exchanged a quick nervous glance as though to decide who should reply. The man on the left cleared his throat and, standing to attention, he began to speak. At first his voice was thin with nervousness, but it gathered strength as he continued.

'We went twice to the Park Hotel, sir,' he said. 'On the first occasion our person was not there. At about sixteen hundred hours, I received a telephone call from our contact - the barman - who said there was a message for our person in the pigeon-hole. He was expected back shortly.'

He paused, looking at his companion as though for reassurance and confirmation: the other man nodded, turning his hat round and round with both hands in his unease.

'He arrived at about sixteen fifteen. We were waiting for him. He came with us.'

'Anyone see you go?'

'No, sir. It was Friday. A holiday.'

Simmias felt in the box for another cigarette. He did not offer one to his visitors; neither did they dare to offer him a light. Even in a classless society, they knew their place:

'Was there any struggle? Any argument?'

'No, sir. He came quietly. In fact, at first we were a bit suspicious. But we weren't followed.'

'How do you know?'

'There was no one behind our car.'

'What precautions did you take? Did you change cars? Did you double back?'

The two men stood staring at him awkwardly, like birds mesmerized by the presence of a snake; sweat began to glisten on their foreheads. Their silence answered the question. Simmias's contempt showed on his smooth, dark face. How the devil could you run any kind of operation successfully with people like this?

How many times must this simple necessity of going through the motions of routine procedure have been drummed into them during their time at Kuchino? How *could* they forget such a thing? But what was the use of arguing? They had either been followed, or they hadn't; no amount of talk would alter that.

'Well?' asked Simmias ominously.

'We took him up the Tajrish road.and along a track to the right some way out of town. We'd reconnoitred it thoroughly last week. We spent two days there.'

'Do you mean to say that you waited on two separate days *together* up there?' asked Simmias tonelessly. 'Didn't it occur to you that someone might have been suspicious? That they might have thought you were waiting to break into a house or something, and reported you?'

The two men were silent. Behind them, an antique clock began to whir and then to chime, filling-the room with its tiny melody.

'Go on,' said Simmias in a voice of resignation.

'Well, we turned the car, sir, and got out. We shot him through the back of the head as in our orders. He died immediately. We covered our prints and tyre marks and left him.'

As the man spoke, his voice suddenly trailed away. A fearful vision of K falling had flashed through his mind; fearful not because of the manner of his death, but because he remembered an elementary point of detail he had somehow overlooked in the haste of murder. He had left the roller with which he had removed his footprints in the back of the car. Something of his thoughts showed in his face. Simmias saw the alarm in his eyes, but said nothing. What was done was done. Recriminations could alter nothing.

'Which of you drove?' he asked, looking from one to the other.

'Neither of us, sir. We thought there might be trouble collecting our person, so we used Kaposki.'

'Who's he?'

'An Iraqi. He's in Teheran from Basra. He's sound. He was in Baghdad when Feisal was murdered. Kassem used him. He had a very high opinion of him.'

'And look what happened to Kassem! Where is Kaposki now?'

'In a house in Teheran.'

'His being here at all seems too dangerous for my liking. So get Kaposki out of it. Quickly. And make sure he doesn't talk. And don't you be seen together again. And throw away those ludicrous hats and buy something different.

'And you' - he pointed to the man who had spoken most - 'buy a pair of spectacles with plain glass and wear them. It's a simple disguise, but effective. Don't come here again, together or alone. You'll only have a few more days until the plane leaves, so keep out of sight in case someone recognizes you in Persepolis. It's only a small risk, but it is a risk and you've taken enough already. Any questions? No? Then that is all.'

He squeezed the silver wings of the bird, the distant bell rang, and the door opened. The interview was at an end.

Simmias stood for a moment listening to the noise of their taxi's tyres on the drive, and then he crossed to the bookcase. In the fourth row of the white shelves was the collected edition of Churchill's *History of the Second World War*, bound in dark-green leather. He touched the author's name, tooled in gold, just beneath the title of volume four.

At once, one of the dummy spines of Romain's *Men of Goodwill*, sprang open in the far end of the case and revealed a telephone. He picked it up. The man he knew as Stanilaus - answered immediately. Simmias gave the identity phrase and pressed the scrambler button.

Now it was his turn to appear ill at ease and nervous as he heard his orders issued tonelessly, dispassionately, from someone who knew there could be no dispute, no argument, no turning back.

As he listened, Simmias could picture the room in the house in Baku on the Caspian where Stanilaus was staying, and for an instant he thought of the empty mountains that separated them: the snowy peaks, the deep lonely forests where silence was broken only by the roar of waterfalls, the howl of wolves.

Over all this desolation, over the border posts with the barbed wire, the searchlights, the guard dogs, stretched the telephone wire, connecting them like an electronic umbilical link between master and man, the giver and the taker of orders. It would be cold in the hills as the mist grew first thicker and more milky and finally deepened into dusk and darkness. Already the sheep in the fields on the lower slopes would be standing huddled together for comfort and warmth and safety. As Simmias listened, he thought he knew how they felt.

Then Stanilaus ceased to speak; there was no farewell, no good wishes; simply an end to the orders.

Simmias was left holding a disconnected telephone that crackled in his ear. He replaced it thoughtfully and lit another cigarette. But even its expensive Russian tobacco tasted, sour and comfortless on his tongue. At times like this he weighed the risk, the danger, against the wild exhilaration that violence induced in him; he was remembering Kem.

He poured himself a whisky and smoothed back his hair, and as the alcohol ran in his blood he remembered the girl in the other room: the job had compensations, too. He walked through the hall soundlessly in his sambur-skin shoes with their thick soles, and opened the black-lacquered door.

She was waiting for him as he knew she would be; it was as though he had never been away. Her need of him, her wish to be humiliated, to be hurt, was as strong and deep as ever: and in overcoming her, he overcame the niggling shadow that the thought of the task ahead of him had cast across his confidence.

'Why are you smiling?" she asked afterwards, looking up at him with her large dark eyes.

'I'm not,' he lied, smoothing her hair back from her

forehead.

But he was.

He was thinking how infinitely exhilarating it was to have heard that a murder you'd arranged had been carried out one moment; and then to make love to the dead man's daughter the next.

CHAPTER FOUR

London, March 20th, 16.35 hours (GMT) Rome, March 21st, 21.00-01.45 hours (local time)

THE GREEN LIGHT flickered twice above the door. The middle-aged secretary in the severely cut tweed suit looked up at MacGillivray. She was an arts graduate of St Andrews, class of thirty-six. She approved of his Scottish name and clothes; equally, he approved of her sexless efficiency.

'Please go in,' she said. 'He's free now.'

MacGillivray put down his copy of the *Financial Times,* knocked once at the panelled door out of habit, and went into the farther room.

Behind and below the double windows, Whitehall traffic moved like distant toys; the wind blew spray from the fountains in Trafalgar Square across the shining flanks of Landseer's lions. Wet or dry, they remained as unruffled by national conflicts and foreign ideologies as by the droppings of the pigeons. Oh, to be a Landseer lion.

Across the street, the radio antennae above the Admiralty trembled in that same afternoon breeze from the river. Would they be bringing any news from Teheran?

The head of the British Intelligence Service sat at his desk, under an undistinguished portrait of James the Second dressed incongruously as a Roman senator. He wished, not for the first time, that he had held his post in James's reign, for by the time messages arrived from distant outposts the problems would mostly have resolved themselves.

The top of his desk was completely cleared save for

a blotter and two telephones, the green one with the scrambler, and a green glass paperweight with a seahorse imprisoned within.

He was a tall, white-haired man in an elegant dark suit. A puff of silk handkerchief showed in one sleeve; the thin black thread of a monocle round his neck. His face was tanned: he had spent the previous day on his farm in Wiltshire. His neighbours there, if they thought at all about his infrequent appearances, believed he had something to do with running an ex-Service charity in London. The charity put it about that he was in the country when anyone dropped in to see him there in a social way.

He was also known to have taken some nebulous appointment at the War Office when he retired from the Army two years earlier. Then he had been General Sir Robert L —. *Who's Who* was curiously reticent about his career. Now, in his official capacity, he was known as C. This stemmed from the early days of MI5 - Home Security - and MI6 - the overseas branch of British Intelligence - in the First World War.

It became the custom then for the heads of these Services to sign reports and memoranda with their initials in an attempt to conceal their identity. The head of MI6 at that time was a naval officer, Captain Mansfield Cumming. He signed his papers as 'C'; the initial is still used although Captain Cumming has been dead for many years.

'It's about Teheran,' C said, lighting a Turkish cigarette. 'I understand that nothing more has come in from K?'

'Nothing at all, sir:'

'I've been on to Air Intelligence, and they've no one in the area who could help. The DNI has a man coming back from Singapore who knew K. He's dropping off in Teheran for a couple of days on the off-chance he can do something, but he's not much to lean on. He's had jaundice very badly, and the medical people say he's not fit for anything taxing. Anyway, I'd rather keep this to ourselves. Too many people will only make a balls.'

MacGillivray nodded agreement. The idea of one cohesive organization, gleaning and sifting Intelligence on Britain's behalf, was simply a public myth. In fact, the Army, the Navy and the Air Force all maintained their own sources of information; so did the Atomic Energy Authority. Interpol fed information to Scotland Yard, while the Special Branch was not always at one with MI5.

The result was that operatives often spent more effort jealously safeguarding leads and clues, anxious to channel any credit to their own department, instead of finding leads to safeguard.

These interdepartmental jealousies, the ancient feuds, the rat races for a 'K' or at least an OBE to carry into retirement were as fierce and ruthless as anything in business. And in the last analysis, all too often the Intelligence executives were simply axed naval officers who wanted a pleasant part-time job with good expenses convenient to their club.

'What arrangements have *you* made?' asked C. 'I take it you've been through the files to find someone else who's unblown?'

'Yes sir. I've got a man. A doctor from Somerset. He did a tiny job for me in the war. He's off this evening to Teheran. As a delegate to a medical conference there.'

'Hmm. Doesn't sound wildly hopeful. How much did you tell him?'

'Just the bare bones. We were expecting grave news about oil treaties. We hadn't received this news and the man who should have sent it has disappeared. I thought it best to let him know as little as possible. In case things don't go too smoothly.'

C nodded.

'Quite. But I must say it's a bloody poor do when we've got to use some country quack on a job like this.'

'Perhaps the situation needn't arise again, sir,' suggested MacGillivray hopefully.

'It needn't, but it will,' said C grimly. 'You know that as well as I do. Now, I'm off to Washington on Thursday. I'm in direct touch with the Prime Minister over this business, and he's asked that you inform him immediately if anything definite comes in.

'It takes at least thirty-six hours to get the Strategic Reserve alerted and the fire brigade into action, so don't hang about. If you have *any* firm gen, let him know. By the way, how's this doctor fellow keeping in touch?'

'Through Darwin. We've had a surgical instrument firm registered there for some years. We're using it now for the first time. He's got a simple code.'

'Not too bloody simple, I hope?'

'If it is,' said MacGillivray dryly, 'it'll be the only simple thing in this business so far.'

***

As MacGillivray announced this bleak and

inescapable conclusion, Love's aircraft was coming in to land at Fiumicino, outside Rome.

The whole airport turned on its end, a sparkling riot of red and amber lights, as the Comet 4B came down on Number Three runway.

Through the oval window at his side, two parallel strips of blue landing lights stretched to infinity. To the right, Rome wore its nightly halo of millions of candlepower. But Love was thinking not of the beauties of the eternal city, but of the gadgets concealed in his luggage, in such unlikely places as his electric razor; between cut-out pages of *Tropical Medicine;* in his watch; even in a drilled tooth. What plausible explanation could he have if the Customs discovered them? But then why the hell should they? Let's cross that bridge as and when.

The bump of landing, the crescendo from the jets as the pilot braked, drove all twinges of apprehension from his mind. One by one, the engines died. Steps were wheeled out, doors opened. Love let the passengers stand and coagulate, clogging the centre aisle and small oval doorway in a thrombosis of pointless haste and frustration in their eagerness to be first out. The seconds they saved then would be lost again at Immigration. The last shall be first, etcetera.

Thus he was the last off the plane, breathing with pleasure the warm Italian air laced with centuries of heat and wine and olives: the night-time smell of a sunshine land.

He caught up the other passengers and waited with them in the Customs hall near the little boutiques of over-priced souvenirs and ceramics and rubbish that clutter every airport. Bells chimed, loudspeakers chattered about unknown flights in half a dozen tongues, and then their suitcases came up on the conveyer belt.

The bored Customs official nodded him away, chalking the hieroglyphic mark without even asking if he had anything to declare.

Love moved through the glass doors that opened automatically as he approached the wide entrance-hall. He paused for a moment, looking about him, wondering how he would be recognized. He had no name, no address for the person he was seeking.

In fact, the whole arrangement seemed rather vague, and the more he thought about it, the less plausible it appeared. This was the Army all over again: well-meaning amateurism, the old pals' act, a tie with the right stripes on it. If this was the way the British Intelligence system worked, it was no wonder they made so many mistakes; the wonder was surely that they didn't make far more.

What happened, for instance, if no one turned up to meet him? He felt as he had often felt in the Army, twenty years ago, arriving with a draft of men at some remote railway junction in India. The train had steamed out and they were left disconsolate, muttering, hungry, tired, dirty and wretched in the noon-day heat because the trucks that should have picked them up had gone to the wrong rendezvous.

A line from a half-forgotten signal he had read on one such an occasion, during the transport of trucks full of bullocks for some unremembered purpose, filtered through his mind. It had read: 'Bollock dropped at Itharsi Junction.' Next day had come the emendation: 'Re earlier message. Correction. For bollock read bullock.'

'Dr Love.'

The voice was low: it stated a fact rather than asked a question. Love turned. A girl in a crisp linen skirt stood by him, holding a huge raffia bag. Instinctively, his eyes dropped to her left hand. She wore an opal ring on her third finger; so she was engaged, presumably. Her face had that grave, composed look he had only seen in one other person. The similarity hit him like a blow, and the years rolled back as rapidly as the pages of a book.

He was meeting Maureen after the news that he had qualified. They had booked a table in advance at The George, in Dorchester, where they could either commiserate or celebrate, according to his examination results.

How strangely alike was this girl with her dark hair, her full mouth, the breasts firm and round through the thin stuff of her blouse, the hint of laughter and tenderness in her eyes.

For a second the hall seemed to whirl around him, a kaleidoscope of people and marble pillars, and then it steadied.

Maureen had died three years ago, and part of him had died with her. The past belonged to the past. By a freak of lighting, a chance way of standing and dress, this stranger had suddenly reminded him of her. But as she moved the spell was broken like a splintering mirror.

'Yes,' he said slowly. 'I'm Dr Love. For a moment you reminded me of someone else.'

'Oh, I'm Simone. Business hardly warrants keeping me here,' she said, giving him the first part of the phrase by which he was to recognize her. 'It's been a bad year.'

'A bad year everywhere,' replied Love, in the answer by which she would know his identity.

'Well, that's over at least,' said Simone in a matter-of-fact way. 'My car's outside. I'll run you back to my flat. You've nearly six hours to wait before the plane goes. MacGillivray's told you of the firm's dislike of hotels?'

'Yes,' said Love.

She led the way to a grey Fiat 600 parked behind the airline buses and the Lancia taxis. Love threw his case into the back seat, held the door open for Simone, and climbed in beside her. They sat very close together in the dark interior. Bracelets on her wrists jangled as she opened her handbag for the ignition key. He had the quick impression of a girl at the edge, of nervousness, a whiff of Or by Coty, then the car started.

Simone drove fast, overtaking the Lambrettas, the heavy lorries festooned with coloured lights, the other little Fiats, and Abarths.

'You've got something for me?'

'Yes,' said Love again.

MacGillivray had given him a parcel of several travel books tied with string, the gay dustcovers visible, the ends left open to discourage any Customs search. Love guessed that probably one at least had its inside hollowed to contain something; but what it was did not concern him.

He looked out at the warm night through the little sliding windows of the car. Beyond the high sodium lights, beyond the huge hoardings for Campari and

Cinzano, a forest of poles supporting telegraph wires and electric cables marched over the countryside into darkness. Here and there stood groups of stucco-faced villas. Broken, terracotta gods gazing sightlessly at each other across the Via Appia Nuova, like stone extras waiting for the film to start.

They ran past a clutter of small farms, petrol stations with the Agip lion, shuttered shops, ancient tombs, brick ruins and, all the while, to the west, the flowing line of the old Appian Way, the familiar dark shape of the pines, kept pace with them.

Here and there, in arches of the aqueducts, near pillars coruscated and corroded by centuries of sand blown on biting winds, squatted the homeless - and the hopeless. What difference did it make to them who won the dark and secret unknown battles of espionage and treachery? They would be on the side that could offer food, a job and hope.

Soon the countryside surrendered to suburbs. Blocks of concrete flats, windows ablaze, flowered in piles of debris and rubble; and then came the green tramcars, the hooting buses. A fountain flung its white arms despairingly to the velvet sky.

Simone turned off the road through an ancient stone archway into a mews. Gargoyles leered down at them stonily with eyes the size of tennis balls. Several cars were already parked close together as though for company. In long peninsulas of darkness doorways opened, music played, a party was in progress. Love looked at Simone questioningly.

'My flat's on the right,' she explained. 'There's a party going on next door. Always reminds me of Queen's Gate - except it's so different.'

She switched off the engine. Love followed her through the doorway, carrying his suitcase, up the stairs to the unexpected marble floor above. She led him into a bedroom with a painted ceiling, three easy chairs covered in cheerful cretonne. A vast eighteenth-century mirror, framed in gilt, filled one entire wall. In its reflection he saw stubble on his chin, tiredness around his eyes. He'd be glad when he was on his way back to London and his holiday: would he call here to see how he looked in the mirror then?

Love dumped his case in a corner, washed quickly and went into the living-room. Simone poured out two Camparis. They clinked glasses and were suddenly without conversation, looking at each other, a little warily, actors without a script.

She was the first professional Love had met, apart from MacGillivray, who somehow didn't count, and he didn't quite know who or what to expect. Perhaps someone with a hard face, a nervous twitch, the eyes straying towards a handbag where she kept the pep pills, the boosters, the stabilizers?

Instead, this delicate-seeming Dresden shepherdess of a girl in her linen skirt seemed altogether incongruous, as out of place as someone asking 'Who's for tennis?' in a Lionel Bart musical. He glanced around the room, seeking clues to her personality in the red damask curtains lit by wall brackets, the gilt angels supporting clusters of candles. Their tiny flames trembled as though afraid of the dark. But there was something in Simone's eyes, in the bone structure of her face, the determined tilt of her chin that made him think she would not scare easily. Would he ever grow to know her well, or would they simply remain people whose lives had touched briefly and then branched apart? Did she want it to be like that, or didn't she?

A middle-aged peasant woman came in to say dinner was ready; they followed her into the dining-room, still dredging for small talk, their thoughts elsewhere.

Did you know so-and-so? No, but I shared a room with his brother in the Iffley Road; Have you been in Rome long? About a year. And before that? I was in Beirut - the Foreign Office language school. Wasn't Blake there too? Yes, for a time.

They opened a bottle of Chianti. It had a short life. Simone suggested they open a second; Love thought this an excellent idea.

'This your first job with Six?' Simone asked him casually.

Love held up his glass to the candle. The flame glowed deep red through the wine: the colour of danger.

'Is it yours?' he asked.

She shook her head.

'You know it's not.'

'Then you must surely know the answer to your question. Here, I'll open that bottle - you've broken the cork.'

Why was she so anxious to know about his background? Did she know anything already and so was checking on him - or was there some other reason? Surely this curiosity was unusual in an agent where the less that was known about other people's tasks the less chance there was of something going wrong? The thought cast its shadow on his face, for Simone smiled at him reassuringly.

'I'm not being nosy,' she said. 'I just wondered. Hadn't seen you around before.'

'The same goes for me. I've not seen you. I'm just passing through. A convenient messenger boy for MacGillivray. But how did you become involved, anyway?'

She blew a smoke ring.

'Drifted into it, I suppose. Like most of us. You do one thing in this business, and that leads to another. And then there's no going back.'

Simone paused. Love said nothing. She went on:

'I shared a flat with another girl off the Fulham Road. She knew someone in the Special Branch. They wanted some gen on a poetry-reading group that met in a basement cafe in the King's Road. It all seemed innocent enough, but it was really a cover for drugs. People would bring in manuscripts and music cases with their poems and so on. But when they got up, they'd somehow take out different cases. You follow?

'A friend took me along, and it wasn't very hard to find what was going on. Then I told my flat-mate. She told her friend. Later, he asked me to meet him for lunch. He even paid me.

'A couple of months afterwards, my girlfriend asked if I'd help with another cover-up place in Chelsea.

'Politicians were being blackmailed through a little paper shop that sold pornographic photographs. It was all very simple, really. The man behind it got seven years.

'Well, after this, the character in the Special Branch thought I'd better join the staff. He said it would be cheaper than to pay me by results! I didn't fancy the police, but I was quite keen on the Service. So I joined Six and well - here I am.'

Here she was. A code number, a secret agent, part of an international equation, an entry in some unknown profit-and-loss account. But who were the accountants? And to whom would the final reckoning be presented?

Simone glanced at her watch, put down her glass.

'Excuse me,' she said. 'I've a call to make.' She left the room. Love heard her speaking on the telephone, and stood up to shut the door; he did not wish to be thought listening. Then he paused at the window, looking down into the mews. Beneath him, two young men in tight jeans, sweaters and suede shoes were leathering a red Alfa-Romeo Spyder under one of the lamps. The sight of the slotted silver wheels sent a small arrow of nostalgia through his memory: his Cord had similar wheels. He wished he were back in Somerset, driving it with the hood down, the hum of the supercharger in his ears, the wind in his hair.

He moved restlessly across the little room, seeing and yet not seeing the ebony ornaments, the walls papered in sackcloth, the Canaletto reproductions. The gap in the hands of the ormolu clock widened; the time was ten past nine. He picked up an *Elle*, flicked over the pages put it down again; the pictures of skinny models leaning against balustrades did nothing to him. He began to thumb through some other magazines, killing time. In an *Oggi*, he saw the red and blue edging of an airmail envelope slipped between two pages. He opened them; the letter, already stamped and sealed, was addressed to Mrs I. Welcombe, Station Road Newsagency, Ashton-under-Lyne, Lancashire, England.

He picked it up for no reason at all and turned it over: the sender was Maria Franklin, care of American Express, Rome. An odd place to keep a letter, he thought. Perhaps she had forgotten it, perhaps it had been slipped in there by mistake, perhaps half a dozen reasons. Anyway, it was none of his business. He replaced the magazines on their pile. When Simone returned he was standing by the window.

'I've been seeing your bed's OK,' she explained. 'You've a long wait. Might as well have a rest. Be a horizontal man.'

He followed her into the bedroom. The sheets were already turned back invitingly.

'Oh, it's not worth it,' said Love. 'I'll stretch out in a chair with a magazine. I can sleep on the plane.'

'Another drink, anyhow,' she said, speaking almost nervously.

Ice clinked in the glasses. In the cobbled yard outside, car doors shut and the crack of the Alfa's exhaust beat back from the grey walls. A faint smell of oil smoke blew in at the open window, reminding him of home.

'How long do you expect to be in Teheran?' she asked.

Love looked at her quizzically as she poured another drink. Why should she assume that his journey finished in Teheran? MacGillivray had assured him that no one outside his own office knew Love's destination: his ticket for the conference had been arranged through two intermediaries, or cut-outs as MacGillivray called them, to minimize discovery.

Also, his ticket was to Karachi and Bombay. The reservations might never be taken up, but they had seemed a common-sense insurance. Was Simone simply assuming he was staying in Teheran? Or did she have definite information?

Love decided she was guessing, probably just making conversation to pass the time. Before he could reply, the telephone tinkled faintly in the hall. For a moment their eyes met, and then Simone went out of the room to answer it. Love poured himself more wine.

He still felt vaguely uneasy; doubt rang warning bells in his subconscious mind. Something was wrong somewhere - but what, and where, and why? He drank the wine, and poured some more. Red for Chianti, red for danger. Then everything fell into place, message received and understood: that letter.

He took two paces across the room and opened the magazine. Who was Mrs Welcombe? And Maria Franklin? If he didn't know, perhaps someone else would. He copied the names and the addresses into his diary, replaced the letter in the magazine, the magazine where it belonged.

He felt tired, on edge, wishing he had not been persuaded by MacGillivray. Simone's suggestion of rest seemed suddenly welcome. Six hours was longer than he thought.

He went into the bedroom, kicked off his shoes, hung his jacket over the back of a chair, and lay down under the coverlet, hands behind his head. Usually, Love took any chance of rest he could, believing, like many doctors, that it is foolish to stand when you can sit, or sit when you can lie. Thus, between planes on other overseas trips, he had slept as easily as Napoleon before Austerlitz, secure in the knowledge that his Juvenia wristwatch alarm would waken him on time.

But on the previous day MacGillivray's gadgeteers had removed the alarm from the inside of the watch. In its place they had fitted a tiny transistor transmitter. Now, instead of activating the alarm, the knurled knob near the winder operated this set, which was automatically tuned to one of the RAF distress wavelengths.

Should he be in difficulties, then he could switch on and some RAF station somewhere should pick up the continuously repeated emergency signal, and calculate his position.

This had seemed an absurd idea to Love when MacGillivray explained it to him. After all, what risk was he running? What difficulties could he encounter that could be solved by the RAF? The whole thing seemed ridiculous, a pointless cloak-and-dagger outlook, echoed in the other gadgets he had brought. And now, lying on the bed, he saw no reason to change this view. All that the transistor meant, so far as he could see, was that he could not fall asleep confident he would wake in time to catch his plane.

But even had his alarm been working, he would still have felt too tense to sleep easily. He was on the first lap of a journey to a new experience, and while it had all seemed simple enough back in England, now the doubts began to grow.

Why had Simone asked him about Teheran?

Was it possible that MacGillivray had told her of his destination - maybe after his assurances to him - and she was testing him to discover how discreet he could be, whether he could keep a secret? Or was there some other explanation?

Questions chased answers through his tired mind

like painted horses on a fairground roundabout, never catching up with the one in front. Then, slowly, gradually, Love's muscles relaxed, and he drifted into a light, uneasy semi-sleep.

He was suddenly, instantly, entirely awake.

His left arm prickled with pins and needles, and he lowered if cautiously to his side. But, although a contributory factor to his sharp awakening, this was not the main cause. An old, half-forgotten sixth sense, an automatic reflex of approaching danger, a legacy of the war, was working again.

Love lay, eyes half closed, still feigning sleep. The door began to open slowly, a narrow fan of light from the hallway widening on the thick grey carpet. Simone came into the room and shut the door silently behind her. She was wearing some kind of housecoat. He could not move his head without giving away the fact that he was not asleep, so he sensed rather than saw the housecoat fall to the floor. Then Simone slipped into the bed beside him, under the coverlet.

For a moment, she lay on her elbow looking at him. Then she snuggled down against him. He could feel the warm nakedness of her body through the thin stuff of his shirt. It was an invitation, obvious and in clear. Message received and understood. RSVP. Still he appeared to slumber. Simone put up a hand and stroked his cheek gently and then nestled down on his shoulder, her hands exploring his body.

Hell, he thought, they're not selling it, they're giving it away. Is this a part of the Service, too? There might be some more pleasant way of spending the hours left before the plane departed, but off-hand he could not think of one. Nor on-hand, either.

'Are you still asleep?' Simone whispered to him.

Love smiled.

'Remember what Sir Thomas Browne wrote?' he asked, equally softly, ' "The huntsmen are up in America, and they are already past their first sleep in Persia." That goes for me.'

'Never mind Sir Thomas Browne.'

'I wasn't, particularly. I was more concerned with you.'

He moved against her.

'Why all these clothes?' she asked dreamily, her fingers already at the buttons of his shirt.

Then, suddenly, all desire drained away. He was acting like an idiot with a girl he had never seen before; would probably never see again. Surely this was the classic mistake in his new role, the most obvious pitfall to avoid, as so many had discovered, from Samson onwards?

It might be diabolical to turn up such an open invitation, but then life could be diabolical; was indeed frequently so. His wisest motto now was business before pleasure. But, if he had an hour to spend on the return journey the encounter could have a different ending. But he had to act instantly, or he would reach the point of no return that would be the death of good intentions.

He sat up under the coverlet and snapped on the bedside light. Simone blinked in the sudden glare.

'No,' he said gently. 'Please. Another time, another place. I can't explain now.'

He reached out to touch her hand; but she turned away from him, hiding her face in the pillow,

'Don't try to explain. There'll be no other time.

Ever. I thought you were a man. Not a boy.'

Looking down at her, so small and slight and furious in the bed, he saw for the first time the dark bruises on her bare shoulders, and her back.

He put out his hand and touched one of them, smoothing the outline of blue marks.

She shook herself free.

'Don't dare to touch me,' she said, her voice muffled by the sheets. He swung himself out of bed and went into the kitchen. Hell, what a fool he was to turn up such an invitation. Already he cursed his caution. After all, he had no secrets to conceal: he was simply trying to solve one. He'd acted like an idiot. As you grew older, you only regretted the opportunities you hadn't taken, the women you hadn't laid. The wheel of fortune never stopped at the same point a second time; the lost chances were never found. He sighed.

'Mind if I make some coffee?' he called through the door as cheerfully as he could, which wasn't very cheerfully.

She did not bother to answer; he hadn't really expected her to, but he had to say something.

He busied himself with the electric coffee mill and Caff-express, and searched in a cupboard until he found some brandy. He took a couple of deep swigs from the bottle. He needed it, he thought. Overcoming shock to the central nervous system. Then he waited until the water bubbled and boiled in the machine, poured out a beaker of black coffee, added a dash of brandy, and carried it back into the bedroom for Simone.

She had dressed and was making up her face. Coming up behind her he saw in the mirror that her eyes were red. She had been crying.

She looked away from him.

Why the devil was she crying, he wondered? So you didn't make love. You let the moment go. But there would be others: there always were. Surely she wasn't so desperate for a man? Then he remembered the bruises, and wondered.

Women: not a different sex, a different race. He looked out in the mews, seeing and not seeing the parked cars, the lamps by the gaily painted front doors, the cobbles that unexpectedly reminded him of his pebbled yard in Somerset.

They went out together in silence to her little Fiat. The eyes of the gargoyles stared with stony contempt at them as they turned under the arch. Well, did you? they seemed to ask. No, you didn't. Because you're too cautious, too careful You haven't the wit to open the door when opportunity knocks. To hell with you.

Love switched on the car radio. Endless waves of sugar-crested Puccini billowed over them, submerging them. They did not speak all the way to Fiumicino, and although Love looked from time to time at Simone, she did not once look back at him.

The airport was busy in its tireless, timeless way. Some of the airline booths were shut, but at other counters queues of people waited for their luggage to be weighed.

'Are you coming in to say goodbye?' asked Love.

'No,' she said. 'I've said goodbye.'

They were standing at the side of the car. He held out his hand. She made a move with hers and then withdrew it. She did not meet his eyes

'I'm sorry,' he said quietly. 'More than I can say.

More than you know.'

He bent down to pick up his suitcase and saw once more, in a trick of the lights, the mouth, the eyes, that were so alike, and yet so unlike: the eyes and mouth of someone he had once loved.

Simone's face seemed to tremble, as though she was near to tears, and then her lips tightened. He stood up to watch her climb into the car. The sodium lights glittered on the metal roof, and then she was gone down the concrete road, under the lamp standards, towards Rome. She did not look back; not even through the mirror.

Love went through the glass doors. At the airline desk, the girl in the blue uniform looked at his ticket, and checked it against the passenger list.

'Ah, yes. Dr Love,' she said brightly. 'Would you weigh in your baggage, please?'

'I'd like to. But could you do me a favour?'

'If it's possible,' she said, rather more coolly. Men had made the request before; she was bored by it. But this man seemed different. Or, apart from the queers, was any man different? They had so many devious routes to the same destination.

'Not what you think,' said Love with a grin, reading her thoughts, 'much as I would like it to be. Some other time, some other place. Right now, I'd like you to book me on a later plane.'

She laughed. The English. You never can tell with them.

'That's easy. We've another one going at oh four fifty which reaches Teheran at nine. Would that suit you?'

'Perfectly,' said Love.

The girl lifted the telephone to confirm the booking and then altered his ticket. He went back to kill five hours, looking at the American paperbacks, at the inferior tourist rubbish with their superior prices.

Perhaps he was being foolish in delaying his departure.

But if MacGillivray had told Simone about his destination and the reason for his journey, then others less well-disposed might also know and be waiting for him. Or, indeed, they might have found out about him some other, way, just as perhaps they had found out about Offord.

Better, he thought, lighting a Gitane, to be ten minutes, or even ten hours too late in this world than to risk being twenty years too early in the next.

***

Exactly on time, at 02.45 hours, the silver Boeing 707 bound for Teheran, Karachi, Bombay, New Delhi, Calcutta, Rangoon and Singapore, roared down Number Six runway at Fiumicino and up into the paling darkness of the dawn. Love watched it go, tail- and wing-lights winking its departure.

As the huge aircraft climbed into the lambent sky, its undercarriage folding like the hands of a child in prayer, the drowsy passengers settled back in their seats, coats and collars loosened, determined to recapture their interrupted sleep.

Up front, the pilot and the co-pilot checked and re-checked their instruments, their course, their engines. Blue, violet, amber lights winked reassuringly from the dimly-lit dashboard. The stewardess doused the main lights in the passengers' compartment so that only the deep-blue night bulbs remained glowing in the smooth curved ceiling.

On up to the clouds, through the clouds and then beyond, the Boeing soared, where the moon still shone, cold and bright and, in the distance, the pale birth of a new day etched the horizon with a blush of pink.

The aircraft turned towards the east and held course. Outside, moonlight glittered on the polished silver fuselage, the long wings that dipped and trembled slightly in the endless, unseen eddies of the air.

In her little kitchen, the stewardess began preparing hot drinks for two passengers who wanted them. The rest fled thankfully back to the shores of Lethe, mouths open, eyes shut, their faces waxen arid unhealthy in the strange light, the filtered, pressurized air. And on and on, up and up, the plane soared, the only noise within being the sad singing of its jets, the occasional snore or grunt of one of the sleepers.

Down in the forward hold, amid the tartan-covered airline baggage; the expensive glass-fibre luggage of the tourists, and the cheap fibre suitcases tied with straps of two Pakistani seamen flying to Karachi to join a new ship, beneath the portable typewriters and the Japanese cameras in their imitation leather cases, was a box marked *Venetian glass with care, this way up.*

Stamped on the side was the silhouette of a wineglass, so that even those who could read no English, French or Italian, in which languages the notice was printed, could see from the picture the imperative necessity of keeping the box upright. But, in fact, the only glass the box contained was the glass

96

dial of an alarm clock.

It rested within a cocoon of wood shavings and glass wool, wrapped in a pouch of blanket to muffle its ticking.

Two wires led out to a small battery tied to it with a rubber band, then on into holes pierced in the lid of a cocoa tin. Thus cushioned, the clock ticked away, minute by minute, measuring out the lives of the pilot, the co-pilot, the radio officer, the stewardess, the business man from Birmingham, the embassy typist from Milwaukee, the honeymoon couple holding hands in sleep in seats M5 and 6, the Pakistani seamen and all the others in the aircraft.

At 4.17 by this clock, the hour hand touched a small bolt that protruded from the face. It pressed against this with all the strength of its coiled spring until the ticking slowed and stopped. Impulses from the cell ran through the wires, bridging this switch, into the detonator. The moment when the ticking stopped marked the moment when the mists of eternity opened up for everyone in the plane.

With a roar, the explosive burst its way out into the morning sky, ripping through the fuselage, the nets of wires and hydraulic tubes, the whole complicated nervous system of the aircraft. Wheels, undercarriage, wings suddenly fell away. Luggage cascaded from the heavens, fuel poured out into the air like some apocalyptic deluge.

In the control cabin, the pilot frantically moved levers that slid without resistance, without meaning, without contact to the ailerons, the rudder, the engines.

Most of the passengers died instantly, blown to pulp,

their dead pummelled flesh wrapped in tattered fragments of torn nylon shirts and slips and expensive suits. The rest had barely time to struggle back from sleep before a deeper sleep engulfed them.

The ruined, shattered shell of the aircraft hit the Persian desert and burst across the brown, cracking ground. Terrified sheep fled from the noise and the smell of burning, for within seconds the reserve fuel tank took fire and blazed with a fierce masculine hunger, lighting up the scene of disaster for miles around.

In a police post five miles away the local constable, hearing the explosion, struggled to the roof of his square, mud-walled house, and focused his night glasses on the scene. And then, still in pyjamas, he fled downstairs barefoot to turn the handle of the crude telephone that would link him with the outer world; the world which those in the aircraft had left for ever.

***

Love settled back in his seat, eyes closed, mind relaxed, the piped music floating from the loudspeakers, as the French stewardess welcomed the passengers aboard, giving them the usual unheeded information about the altitude of their flight, the time of their arrival.

Engines began to hum; Love's thoughts turned towards the end of the journey. With a bit of luck, he could find K or Offord or whatever he was called, and be back within thirty-six hours, say forty-eight, at the most. K must either be alive or dead, and if he was alive, he couldn't be so far away; Teheran was not a very large city. No doubt there was a simple explanation. He might even have surfaced before Love reached Teheran. In that case, he'd have the best of the bargain. A quick visit to the owner of the Le Baron Cord, and then back on the first available flight. Gradually, lulled by the muted murmur of the jets, he dozed; and then he slept.

He awoke with a sour taste in his mouth: The stewardess was shaking his shoulder.

'We're coming in now at Mehrabad Airport, Teheran,' she said. 'Please fasten your safety belt.'

He looked out at the scrubby brown grass far beneath, the desert wrinkled like a mummy's face, then at the rippling hills like a dappled beach magnified a thousand times. Here and there a thin river glinted in the sunshine like splintered glass. A shepherd shielded his eyes as the shadow of the. plane, a travelling cross, grew larger and larger as it descended.

As they came down, past the other parked aircraft with crews working on them, Love saw that the airport was decorated with thousands of little paper pennants, all emblazoned with Picasso's Dove of Peace. To one side was parked a Russian Ilyushin jet liner, also decked out with flags; the red flag of Soviet Russia fluttered from a mast.

White ropes were tied to posts around the plane, and beyond them a crowd waited expectantly. A man stood on a wooden platform, facing them, speaking into a microphone. He punched one fist into his other open hand as he spoke to emphasize his points. Love guessed the sort of speech he would be making.

The Customs were uninterested in opening Love's bags; the description in his passport - physician and surgeon -seemed harmless enough. He was through the Customs hall and the Immigration Office within minutes. Outside the airport, entrance stood a yellow bus for the passengers, and a handful of brightly coloured Chevrolet taxis. Love hailed the nearest; no need to waste time and save a few government shillings when he was in a hurry. The driver put his suitcases in the cavernous boot, held open the rear door. Love climbed inside.

'The Park Hotel,' he said.

He sat back on the wide expanse of unpleated plastic engrained with silver threads, watching other American taxis, horns blaring, jockey for pole position through the airport gate.

Under the awnings of open-fronted shops along the road towards Teheran, housewives held children, some of the older women still wearing the black veil of Islam. On the outskirts of the city, shimmering in the heat, surrounded by wooden scaffolds and pulleys lashed with ropes, skyscraper blocks of offices were going up. Soon every city in the world would look much the same: the huge buildings as featureless as up-ended matchboxes, the same international chain-stores selling the same plastic-packed frozen food to the same piped music.

The driver turned off the Khiaban Karadj into the Khiaban Simetri, and then into the Khiaban Hafez and through the rose-hung trellised arch outside the Park Hotel. To the left lay a cluster of new buildings, and Love wondered idly where K had stayed. *Had.* Was he already so sure he belonged to the dead? To the right was the older building, shaded by palm trees and trellises hung with creeper. The cab turned past the pond where water trickled over green-encrusted rocks, and fish moved with golden languor under lily leaves.

A porter opened the door for him. Love climbed out, and paid off the taxi. Then he followed his bags through the glass doors of the reception lobby.

On the right was a glass-topped counter with a miniature BOAC flag on a pole, a calendar for Iranian Airways. Behind the counter an Armenian booking clerk attempted a crossword.

The lobby felt cool and welcome and pleasant after the arid heat outside. The clerk looked up at him questioningly, his mind elsewhere: what was a four-letter word meaning arquebus?

'I've a room here,' said Love. 'Booked from London.'

He pushed his passport towards the man. The Armenian peered at the name on the front as though he had never seen a British passport before, and then went to a table behind the counter. He turned over some pages in a loose-leaf book and returned, pulling his chin.

'I'm sorry, sir,' he said. 'But there seems to have been a misunderstanding.'

Love looked at him in irritation.

'What do you mean, a misunderstanding? I've got your confirmation of the booking in my bag.'

As he spoke, he began to rummage in his briefcase.

'No, no, sir. I quite appreciate that,' the clerk agreed. 'I sent you the telegram myself. But since then we've had other instructions.'

'Other instructions? Who from?'

'Only an hour ago, sir, a gentleman telephoned. He said he was speaking from the airline office. He said you wouldn't be requiring the room after all: You'd been killed in the air crash last night, sir.'

'The air crash? What do you mean?'

'You can't have heard, sir. But the night plane from Rome to Teheran - the one I thought you'd be on, as the telegram from London said you'd be arriving very early in the morning - came down in the desert. I understand it was completely burned out. There are no survivors.'

CHAPTER FIVE

Teheran, March 21st, 13.35 hours (local time)

HE WAS in the annexe, a modern building with tessellated floors and walls, of black marble veined in green. Somewhere, an air-conditioning machine hissed and vibrated. He climbed the two flights of stairs behind the page, followed him down the long, cool corridor to his room. The page unlocked the door and stood to one side to let him pass, hand cupped for a tip. His fingers closed over a handful of rials.

The outer door opened into a small hall. To the right was the bathroom, fluorescent-lit, without a window, heavy with the smell of polythene shower-curtains. Beyond was a bedroom with fan turning lazily in the ceiling, a double bed, and the usual Middle Eastern hotel furniture of unpainted wood. The windows beyond the nylon curtains opened on to a small balcony with a wrought-iron balustrade.

Love crossed the grey carpet and looked out. Beneath the window a narrow alley led to the Khiaban Hafez; half a dozen cycles and shabby grey Isettas were parked in it. A little boy made water against the hotel wall. The sound of the window opening made him look up. He appeared neither embarrassed, hostile nor friendly: simply aware.

Love locked the door behind the page, leaving the key in the lock to prevent anyone opening it with a duplicate. Then he hung up his jacket, kicked off. his shoes and lay back on the bed, hands folded under his head. He lit a Gitane, and looked up at the pink ceiling through the pale haze of smoke, letting his mind free-wheel. Should he ask the receptionist whether he had seen K - or was that altogether too crude, too direct? Once he declared his interest so openly he could be marked; and if anything had happened to K, perhaps watched. He'd scout around a bit on his own first; it seemed a basic precaution to conceal his own interest until he had to reveal it.

According to the details MacGillivray had given him, the conference didn't begin until eleven on the following morning. The first meeting was to be held in the audience chamber of the Shah's Summer Palace. After that, the meetings would be in Teheran University. But with any reasonable luck, Love would be able to find out what had happened to K that same evening, and then he would be on his way home. He could be in Antibes by the weekend. Could be.

He picked up the telephone; a girl answered in English. I've just arrived,' he explained. 'I saw a lot of flags and a Russian plane at the airport. What's it all in aid of?'

'Peace, sir. The plane is flying round the world with messages of peace from the Soviet Union. From scientists and professors and so on. It only arrived yesterday. From Jakarta, Indonesia. Next stop is Leipzig.'

'I see. Well, good luck to them. Now I'm on the phone, I'd like to send a telegram.'

'Just one moment, sir. Your room number?'

'Seventeen.'

'Right, sir.'

Love put on a pair of specially tinted sunglasses and looked at the centre pages of the Diner's Club booklet with which MacGillivray's gadgeteers had supplied him. At once the cable address, otherwise invisible, came to life on one page. He checked the code on the other; it seemed straightforward enough.

'It's to Surgical Supplies, cable address Scalpel, Darwin, Australia. It reads: '"Kindly forward your brochure on folding invalid chairs to Mrs I. Welcombe, Station Road News agency, Ashton-under-Lyne, Lancashire, England, and to Miss Maria Franklin, care American Express, Rome, Italy, stop." Sign it Dr Love.'

The girl read back the message. Love replaced the receiver, undressed, took a shower. The message meant that the two people should be investigated: he knew no reason why they should be, but they were the only names he'd found. He could imagine MacGillivray's face and comments if they turned out to be British agents. The thought made him smile.

He towelled himself vigorously, put on a pair of dark-blue Italian trousers, cut close, with a short-sleeved sports shirt and rubber-soled shoes. He locked his case, slit the bar of soap in the bathroom into two pieces, as MacGillivray had advised, to provide a simple hiding-place, scooped out a small hollow, put his keys in it, and pressed the two slices together. Then he went downstairs and took a taxi to the University to sign the register for the conference.

He had to admit that he was enjoying himself. Here he was in the sunshine, booked in at a first-class hotel at someone else's expense, playing what was really a grown-up variant of hide-and-seek. The thought - almost the hope - that others might conceivably be against him added zest and piquancy to the game. He had not felt so free from care since he was 6300414 Private Love J. in The Buffs at the depot in

Canterbury, more than twenty years ago. The vague hint of secrecy and danger, the business of pretending to be someone he wasn't, appealed to the actor in him. He paid off the taxi and followed the paper arrows pasted on the doors to the registry.

A notice, pinned to a blackboard in the hall, gave the times of the lectures. They did not add up to a very arduous schedule. Love felt that he could cope.

Besides the lectures and discussions, the British and French Ambassadors were to give receptions for the delegates; and an outing had been arranged to Persepolis, the seat of the legendary Achaemenean kings: Cyrus, Darius the Great and his son Xerxes. The Shah was inspecting an archaeological 'dig' that Russian scientists had just finished; special places had been reserved for any delegates wishing to attend. Love didn't think he'd be in on that; with any luck at all, he should be on his way home by then.

He found a small restaurant and had lunch - caviar from the Caspian, an excellent *shish kebab,* and *ekanjedeen,* a cool mint drink flavoured with sugar and vinegar. Then he walked back to the hotel, buying a guidebook and street map on the way, savouring the warmth of the sun. The weather in France would have to be very good to equal this. MacGillivray had certainly kept his promise about a warm climate.

When Love reached the Park he went into the entrance hall, but the reception clerk was not at his desk. Love leaned on the counter for a moment, and then spun the visitors' book towards him. Most of the hotel guests seemed to be German oil-engineers, with one or two American geologists and tourists. He saw Offord's signature against room No. 27. Assuming that his own room, No. 17, was the seventh room on the first floor, then No. 27 should be the seventh on the second floor, right above his.

He turned back the book and went into the bar. Taped music played softly, endlessly, one tune merging into another; muted saxophones moaned together; a piano scattered single notes like drops of water.

Love sat on a leather-topped stool, drinking Bacardi rum with fresh-squeezed limes, hoping that someone might come in who would turn the conversation towards K and give him a lead. But nobody did.

Presently, he went into the lounge, opened a copy of *Motor Sport* and glanced through the small ads. 'Patter of tiny feet - my bank manager's - makes me sell mint SS100' ... 'Stork dropped in so must drop out of running my Bugatti Royale'... 'Anybody here seen Kelly? Stop me if you do. He promised to buy my Austin Healey but didn't ...'

Soon, his head nodded and, stretched out in the armchair, he dozed. He had not realized how tired he was; for when he awoke, early evening had moved in on Teheran.

Love stood up hastily and walked through the hotel, flexing his cramped muscles. If he was to keep to his own schedule, he'd have to move himself. The reception clerk had changed into a dinner jacket and was making out a bill under a shaded desk-lamp. Waiters carried piles of plates, kicking open the swing doors of the restaurant with their right feet.

Outside, the air felt cooler, washed with the scent of jasmine. The courtyard smelled like something from *A Thousand and One Nights:* one of the more interesting,

107

sexier, summer Nights.

Love crossed the courtyard, pushed open the doors of the annexe and climbed to the second floor. Now seemed as good a time as any other to see whether he could get into K's room; now is always the best time to do anything. He walked along the corridor until he came to room 27. It was, as he thought, exactly above his own room.

He shook out his pocket handkerchief over the door handle to conceal any fingerprints. There was no reason why he should conceal them, he supposed, but he had seen people do this on television so often that it made him feel vaguely professional and less of an amateur. Although, wouldn't it look odd if someone saw him doing this?

To hell with this play acting. He pushed his handkerchief back into his pocket, beat imperiously at the door, and then turned the handle. The door did not move. He stuck his own bedroom key into the keyhole, but it wouldn't fit. He bent down and peered through the keyhole, thankful the corridor was still empty.

There was a good reason why the key didn't fit, quite apart from it being the wrong key. Another key was already in the lock, on the inside.

Love put his key back in his pocket, went down the staircase to his own floor and his own room. He let himself in, locked the door behind him, and pulled the curtains before he turned on the light.

Why should K's room be locked on the inside? Was it possible that he could have fallen ill - had a stroke or a seizure? Or could he be dead behind that door? If there were no other involvements, Love would simply ask the reception clerk to open the door. But the last thing he wanted was to draw attention to K. And what if the reception clerk started to ask questions?

The easiest thing was to search K's room himself and see whether his suppositions were true. And since he could not enter through the door he'd have to go in the only other way - enter through the window. He prised the piece of soap apart, removed the keys and unlocked his suitcase.

He bundled out his shorts, underwear and his second suit on to the bed, and then lifted the false bottom of the case with which MacGillivray's gadgeteers had provided him. Underneath were revealed a bewildering display of ridiculous objects, like a junk-tray of bric-a-brac marked at five shillings each on a stall in the Portobello Road.

Now what would he need for the job in hand? The choice was wide. He could have-a sword stick, for example, or a couple of thunderflashes, like plastic marbles. He had told MacGillivray when they handed him these that if they had only given him three balls he could have set up as a pawnbroker to hock the rest of the junk. MacGillivray had not been amused.

There were fountain pens that were more than pens - one was a hypodermic; there was a black leather case containing two hypodermic syringes that shot gramophone needles under compressed air. What a lot of chat, he thought, looking at them. Boy Scout stuff, everyone's own Instant Superman Kit. Even so, which or what should he take - if anything?

He settled for a pair of surgical rubber gloves - there was no good excuse for leaving any prints that might

109

need explaining away - and a signet ring with a phoney ruby which he slipped on the little finger of his left hand.

He put a pencil torch in one trouser pocket and the passport photograph of K in the other, so that if he found him dead or alive he could check he was the right man, although God knew the picture was bad enough. It could have been of almost anybody.

Love wrapped his money and his passport in his pyjamas and put them under the pillow, locked the suitcase, and replaced the keys in the split bar of soap. Now he was ready for action, whatever the action might be. If K were not behind that locked door upstairs, then maybe he had left some clues as to his plans or whereabouts. Maybe he would find a diary or an, engagement pad with his appointments, maybe there was nothing at all: but he had to find out. He had to begin somewhere and this seemed the best (and only) place.

He turned out the bedroom light, pulled the curtains and opened the long windows on to the balcony. Beyond the city, the Alburz mountains lay to the north like the huge dark spine of a crouching beast. The night air felt unexpectedly warm on his face as he looked out. The alleyway beneath was deserted; across it, horizontal slats of light showed through shutters. Taxis sped up and down the Khiaban Hafez, blowing their horns, and groups of people strolled past the shop windows.

Love leaned out of his window and gripped the drainpipe that ran from the gutter to the road. It was made of rough, unpainted concrete. At least this would give him more grip than a metal pipe. He looked up and saw with relief that K's window was open.

Once more into the breach, dear friends. Standing on the sill, he gripped the pipe and began to climb. It seemed harder than he remembered from such exercises in the Army. Maybe they built the walls higher these days.

The side of the building was dashed with sharp pebbles that cut through the thin stuff of his trousers into his kneecaps. Also, the drainpipe itself proved more difficult 'to grip than he had imagined: it was fixed so close to the wall that he could not get his hands right round it. Slowly, his muscles knotted with his efforts to control his breathings Love edged up towards the window of K's room.

Whenever he heard an unusually loud blast of car horns, or any cry from a passer-by, he froze into immobility, head pressed against the wall. Then no one could see him because the wall was in shadow.

Finally, he hoisted himself on to the sill of K's window, balanced for a moment, and went through it. He landed with a small creak of springs on a settee beneath the window, and sat there gratefully, feeling the rough moquette through the thin rubber of his gloves.

As far as he could see from the dim reflected light of a street lamp at the end of the alley, the furniture occupied roughly the same position as in his own room. On the little table by the side of K's bed a seven-day leather travelling clock still ticked. The dim green luminous hands pointed to five minutes past nine.

Love stood up, edging himself slowly towards the

111

suitcase stand, holding his breath. Here, if anywhere, he would find K's diary - if he kept a diary - which, of course, by all the rules, he shouldn't have done. But then neither should the Chief of the Imperial General Staff during the war; yet he had. You had to have a break somewhere.

Love had nearly reached the suitcase when he heard a tiny click behind the bathroom wall. He stopped and held his breath, head on one side, listening.

In a room farther down the corridor a radio was playing. A trumpet fanfare ended with wild applause from a studio audience; a man began to tell funny stories in French. Then the voice died and there was no other sound. He must have imagined the noise; or maybe it had been an air bubble in the tank or a hot pipe creaking.

Love took another cautious step forward to the suitcase, reached it and began to raise the lid slowly. One hand went into his pocket for his torch.

At that moment, the room exploded into light.

Love swung around, his right hand still in his pocket.

A man was standing at the bathroom door: a broad-shouldered, dumpy man in flannel trousers and a light short-sleeved shirt. Like Love, he wore a pair of flesh-coloured gloves. His face was sallow, with grey shadows under his eyes.

'Stay where you are,' he said flatly. 'Take your hand out of your pocket. Raise 'em both above your head, palms open to me. And don't try any smart stuff.'

Love did as he was told. The man sounded English and as though he was used to being obeyed. The Smith & Wesson magnum that pointed unwaveringly at Love's navel was an added argument in favour of obedience.

Time, Love's heart, his thoughts, stood still. The curtain from the open window flapped behind him like the wing of a frantic bird. But, with the rush of accelerating cars in the Khiaban Hafez, it belonged to another world that had never seemed so pleasant.

Love looked at the man's cold eyes, then at the black mouth of the gun and back again to his face. Finally, he found his voice.

'Are you Mr Offord?' he asked.

'I'll take the questions,' said the other man, crossing the carpet towards him. He was heavily built, but surprisingly light on his feet. His body. Love noted professionally, was fit and hard, belying the colour of his skin. Who the devil was he - a house detective? Surely not, with a gun - and English. But what excuse could he give for entering another man's locked room through the window? What would MacGillivray's advice be now - and his comments on this pathetic performance?

Christ, what a balls he'd made of this! Here he was, in his own thoughts, a combination of Superman, von Rintelin, The Spy in Black, and James Bond, and all he had achieved was to be held up by a stranger - the first stranger he'd met, apart from the hotel clerk and Simone, neither of whom really counted. Clearly, he'd never graduate in this way. MacGillivray's report about him would read: 'Could do better if he tried.' But the odd thing was that he had tried. He'd even thought he was rather superior to all this sort of thing. It had - seemed so childish and unbelievable from the safe homeliness of Somerset. Now it seemed too believable for comfort.

Of course, he must have been imbecilic to imagine the search for K would be easy. No government department would subsidize a holiday in the south of France for nothing.

Love's mind whipped back over the years to that time - April 1944 - when he had seen his first Japanese in the Arakan, with the sudden almost unbelievable realization that strangers with whom he would never speak, whose names he would never know, would shoot him on sight. Unless he shot them first. But now he had no gun. Now he was on his own, a long way from home.

'Call the manager,' he said. 'He'll tell you who I am.'

The man ignored his remark.

So presumably he had no authority to be in the room, either. If he had, he'd be on the telephone at once. Possibly he had also climbed in unobserved, and no doubt one of them could climb out in the same way. But which one would it be? Love had no wish to be left behind, a body for the police to find; and no intention of fulfilling that role. Possibly this character felt the same way.

'Turn round,' said the man roughly, and frisked him for a gun. He found K's photograph and put it in his own trouser pocket without seeming to look at it.

'Now face me. What do you want here?'

'I'm a friend of Mr Offord,' said Love!

'And you don't even know what he looks like? Don't give me that chat.'

The man took a pace closer to Love; the muzzle of his revolver did not waver. Love's eyes did. He was thinking what a mess a magnum bullet would make of his lower digestive tract.

'Who are you?'

A phrase from *Religio Medici* passed through Love's mind: 'I dare, without usurpation, assume the honourable style of a Christian.' He let it pass through.

'Well?'

Love cleared his throat to cover the fact that above his head he was drawing his hands together so that the palm of his right hand was behind the left. He shifted his weight from one foot to the other. The second and third fingers of his right hand touched the smooth red stone of the ring with which the gadgeteers had provided him. If twisted, the magnesium compound it contained would explode with a violent flash, like a photographer's flash-bulb.

'Well?' The man moved nearer.

'Well,' echoed Love, and turned the stone.

The ring flared like a bright comet in the room.

The gunman stepped back half a pace, blinded, not immediately associating the blaze with Love. One hand went up instinctively to shield his eyes; his Smith & Wesson wavered for a moment.

In that moment, Love pivoted to his right in the judo movement, caught his opponent's wrist in his left hand, kneed him in the groin, and as he came forward dug the knuckles of the first two fingers of his right hand in his eyes.

It was all simple, routine stuff, the sort of thing he would teach the British Legion fellows in Lesson Seven under the general heading 'Protection against attack by man with a revolver'. The only new twist was the magnesium ring. Love had to give MacGillivray marks for that. He did so, willingly.

The stranger writhed on the floor, one hand held against his face to shield the agony of his eyes, the gun uselessly on the floor by his side. Love picked it up, broke it, slipped the rounds into one pocket, the gun into the other. Then he closed the window behind him, drew the curtains and turned on the light.

He sat on the bed watching the man on the floor. The gunman crawled to a sitting position. Suddenly, he gathered his strength and leapt at Love.

This boy is tough, thought Love: he wants to learn it all the hard way. He brought the edge of his right hand across the bridge of the man's nose in the *atemi* blow (Lesson Eight: advanced methods of self-defence). This time he went down and stayed down. The blow was so strong that Love had actually seen Black Belts break a piece of wood with it. He had often demonstrated it in the village hall at Bishop's Combe, but this was the first time he had ever used it with any intention to hurt. Well, it certainly worked. He couldn't grumble about the results. He'd recommend it to his class. He only hoped it had not worked too well and the man was dead, because then he would be in a worse position than ever.

The dominant emotion he felt was surprise, almost wonder, that after teaching judo moves for so long he had suddenly put the theories to the test, and they worked. This was the first man with whom he had dealt in anger or danger. The thought that all had gone so smoothly gave him a curious, rather pleasant, feeling of power and superiority.

He knelt down beside the body and felt his pulse. It was a professional reflex action. He might have been kneeling by the side of someone injured in a motor

116

accident. Now that the danger to himself was past, he was just someone else in pain and trouble.

The pulse was irregular but strong; he'd live all right. And at least he wouldn't have to send out for a doctor. How strange it was to be on the side of violence again, after so many years spent in trying to ameliorate its effects'!

His heart thumped slightly with reaction, but otherwise he felt calm. The search had started; something was happening; but how to take it from here?

The first thing was obviously to discover who this character with the gun might be. Was he working for the Other Side, as MacGillivray would say? It sounded almost like a spiritualist's meeting to use such a phrase, he thought, as he began to go through his pockets, watching his face warily, in case he should pounce again. But he stayed where he was, still. His nose was bleeding badly. Love hoped he had not broken the bone. No, he hadn't. Next time he'd hit a little higher, just to stun.

So there would be another time? Of course. There always was another time. The wheels turned, the clocks chimed, the days passed, and another chance would come up again. The strange thing was, he rather looked forward to it. He would like to try his luck, and his judo, on a few more people. There was something about violence that begot violence, so long as the violence was your own.

In an oilskin pouch in the back of the man's trousers he found a British passport issued to Richard Mass Parkington, described as a salesman. Parkington had been born thirty-nine years before in Enfield, Middlesex; his height was five feet eleven inches and he had blue eyes.

In another pocket were some air letters, addressed to him at a post office box number in Singapore. Love opened one of them. The notepaper had an embossed address of a wine-exporting firm in Cape Town. The letter dealt in business terms with consignments and prices of grapes. This meant little to him; but it looked the sort of letter that could mean different things to different people.

Another typed letter from 'Your loving aunt, with a Durban postmark, had a postscript: 'I have not been able to find the book you asked as a present for Angela, but I am substituting instead Plato's *Dialogues*. It is full of good sense - especially page 334.'

Love felt inside the book flap of the wallet. As he now expected, it contained a single page, numbered 334. He read some words that had been underlined: 'And he who allows himself to be taken prisoner may as well be made a present of to his old enemies; he is their lawful prey, and let them do what they like with him.'

Mr Parkington, he thought, should have taken Plato's advice more to heart. Love recognized the page with its red edge: he had a Pocket-Book edition from which the same page was missing in his briefcase downstairs. It was a part of the means by which one British agent could recognize another. He replaced the papers and the letters, went into the bathroom, filled a toothglass with cold water, took a drink, filled it again, came back and threw the water into Parking-ton's face.

Then he sat on the edge of the bed watching him struggle back to consciousness. Parkington's eyes opened. He. shook his head, and drips of water scattered like beads. Then he reached into his trouser

118

pocket for a handkerchief. Love let him do so; he knew he was unarmed. He wiped the blood off his face and lay back showing no wish to move, watching Love look down at him.

'Who exactly are you?' asked Love gently. 'I know your passport says you are Richard Mass Parkington, and that you were born in Enfield, but that doesn't take us very far. What are you doing here?'

Parkington said nothing.

Love began tapping on the bedside table with the edge of his right palm. Parkington watched his hand go up and down, mesmerized by the movement. He got its message loud and clear and alarming.

Love saw him set his teeth, expecting another blow. He was tough, all right, but he didn't look healthy. Why was his skin so yellow? He might be a jaundice or a malaria case, after too much mepacrine. It was nearly twenty years since Love had seen someone with that yellowish parchment skin, faintly green around the eyes, as though permanently seasick. Then it had been his own face, seen dimly in a shaving mirror at the CCS in Bawli Bazaar.

'Well, if you won't tell me anything about yourself, I'll tell you who I am,' he said, still keeping up the business of the tapping hand. 'I'm a doctor from Somerset. I'm over here for a conference. Plato also happens to be my bedside reading. Like you, I carry a page of his *Dialogues* with me, Pocket-Book edition, page 334.'

Parkington looked at him. He showed no sign of interest or comprehension.

'I also deal with Sensoby & Ransom in Covent Garden. We could have friends in that firm or again we couldn't. I'll give you three to prove it either way.'

He took Parkington's revolver out of his pocket, slipped in one round and aimed it at his face. Then, his finger on the trigger, he began to count.

'One.'

'You'll never fire that thing,' said Parkington, trying to convince himself.

'Two.'

Parkington stood up shakily and undid his wristwatch. He placed it face down on the bed. Still covering him with the revolver, Love did the same. On the back of each was the identical inscription: 'From your dear father, in memory of the boy you used to be.'

It was the second part of the recognition signal MacGillivray had given him. The torn page was changed every ten days, the wording on the wristwatch every month.

Love stopped counting. He put the revolver back in his pocket.

'I don't know who you are,' Parkington said slowly, feeling the back of his neck carefully with one hand. 'But we both seem to be fighting the wrong man. Who are you after here?'

'K,' said Love simply: 'For MacGillivray.'

'Are you really a doctor?'

'Surely.'

'Then thank God I'm not one of your patients.'

Love handed him his cigarette case; Parkington lit a Gitane from his lighter. They strapped their watches on their wrists.

'But I'm not a pro in this business,' added Love.

'As a pro, I can say you're learning. I'll give you a

testimonial.'

'Are you after K, too?' asked Love.

'In a sense. I'm on my way back from Singapore to London on leave. I'm not with your crowd. I come under the DNI. But I've been sick with jaundice and so I've six weeks' leave ahead of me.'

That would explain the sallow skin, thought Love.

'K and I used to be together in Penang when all the Communist trouble was on in North Malaya a year or two back,' Parkington continued. 'I knew he was here, so I called in to see him. A purely social call. Nothing else. Well, not much else. But the reception fellow here didn't know where he was. Or so he said. Apparently he hadn't been around for some time. That's unhealthy in this business. We pros have our regular radio calls to make at set hours, you know. If we miss one, we get a rocket. If we miss two, we're in trouble. If we miss three, we're written off. K had missed four, so I heard through Durban. So in I came to have a look around.'

'Where did you get the key of this room?'

'Made it.'

'Made it? How?'

Parkington put his hand in his pocket and pulled out a flat key with a blue plastic tag numbered 2471.

'This fits a safe-deposit of the Melli-Iran Bank,' he explained. 'In it there's an envelope with another key that unlocks a second deposit box in the Export Development Bank in the Khiaban Saadi.

'That contains outline photostats of keys of all the major hotels in Teheran. I simply found out the number of K's room, went to the safe deposit, traced the key-shape of Room 27 at the Park Hotel on a

121

piece of bog paper, had a key cut in the bazaar - and here I am. We've got similar arrangements in most big cities.'

'Oh. Well, where do *you* think K is?'

'In heaven or hell,' said Parkington bluntly. 'You're too near the Russian border here to be taken prisoner unless they want to get something out of you. And no doubt they knew all about him. Maybe Blake gave him away. Maybe someone else did. But I'd say he was rumbled.'

'But how do we start finding out? MacGillivray assured me that it'd be a very simple matter,' said Love. 'I thought I could do it in thirty-six hours - forty-eight at the outside.'

'I'm sure you did. No doubt the way MacGillivray sold it to you, you thought you were getting the best of the bargain, or you wouldn't have come at all. But let's take this business step by step. We know K *was* here, but as he's not here now, he either went off on his own account, or he was taken off. Right?'

'Right. Brilliant deduction.'

'Don't extract the urine just yet. I've been through all his stuff here. There's no diary, no engagement pad, not a hint anywhere of his intentions. Not even an air ticket home. Possibly he had that on him. So it seems to me that our only chance is to find someone who saw him last Friday.

'There's usually a crowd of taxi-drivers hanging around, the hotel for a fare, or chauffeurs waiting for their masters and so on. Maybe one of them did see him, though why they should, I don't know. I'll try the driver who brought me over here, for a start.

'In the meantime, let's get a drink. And don't give

me all that chat about it being bad to drink with jaundice. I know it's bad. But the way I feel after your unprofessional horsing about, it's worse not to.'

They went out of the room, switching off the lights behind them, walked along the marble corridor, down the stairs, across the courtyard. Water still tumbled into the pool and lights from the restaurant glittered on the shining bonnets of a dozen parked taxis.

As they approached the glass doors of the main hotel building, Parkington clicked his fingers. A driver materialized from the dusk like a genie. Parkington passed over a 100-rial note folded into four, the size of a postage stamp. The man took it without his eyes leaving Parkington's face.

'There's as much again if you can help me,' Parkington told him in Arabic.

'If I can, sir,' replied the driver in the same language.

'A friend of ours, a Mr Offord, left this hotel last Friday. He's not very well and needs treatment, and we think he may have been taken ill somewhere. He's a grey-haired man, about sixty, my height. He has room twenty-seven. Can you find out if any of the cabs gave him a lift?'

'I'll do my best, sir,' said the man.

'We'll be in the bar for half an hour.'

They walked on through the doors and the piped music welled up at them: they might never have been away.

They sat on the red-topped stools drinking rum and lime-juice, waiting for thirty minutes to die. Then they went out into the courtyard and sat talking on one of the white-slatted benches behind the pool.

Cars and taxis arrived, deposited their guests and went off, leaving only the echo of their engines and the smell of their exhaust. Then someone coughed behind them: the taxi-driver was standing in the shadows.

'Sorry I've been so long, sir,' he began in English. 'But I had to wait till all our drivers came back. None of them had your friend as a fare. He went off with two men in a private car - not a taxi - on Friday afternoon, about half past four.'

'How do you know?' asked Love.

'My cousin was driving his taxi from the airport, sir, and he came in through the entrance just as this car was leaving. In fact, he had to back to let him through. He saw Mr Offord then, sitting in the back seat. He has often taken him down to the Oil Exploration Centre. He knows him well by sight.'

'Who was driving the car?'

'No one we know, sir. A stranger.'

'What sort of car was it?'

'A black Packard Eight. Quite an old model. Probably pre-war.'

'Do you know who owns it?'

'No, sir. I don't know the car at all.'

'Thank you very much.'

Another folded note changed hands; the driver melted away into the darkness.

'Well, back in square one,' said Parkington gloomily.

'Not quite,' said Love. 'Come up to my room. I've got an idea.' Once inside, he locked the door.

'Do you think this place is bugged?' he asked, anxious to sound professional. 'I mean, hidden microphones, and so on?'

'Could be. Come into the bathroom. That's the easiest way to fox 'em.'

Parkington turned on, the bath taps and the shower; the water poured like a miniature Niagara.

'If we speak against this background it's impossible even for a selective microphone to pick up our voices. What's your idea?'

'This.'

Love went into the bedroom and brought back the Newsletter of the Auburn-Cord-Duesenberg Club that he had received on the morning MacGillivray called to see him.

'Listen to this.'

He began to read.

'From Teheran, Iran, site of the Peacock Throne, comes word of a car to make even the peacocks green with envy. Wisconsin enthusiast, real-estate man Randle B. Cross, currently vacationing there, sends us details of what must be one of the few Le Baron Cords made.

'The body is aluminium, but the hood and fenders are steel. Those at the back are a little longer than in the standard model. Original price was $8,600.00 as against $2,500.00 for the standard 1937 Sportsman.

'Doors are panelled in mahogany, the dashboard is upholstered in leather from the windshield to the instrument board.

'Enthusiast Cross says he spotted the Cord's unusual frontal treatment in an open shed off one of Teheran's main streets, the Khiaban Ferdowsi. This suspected Le Baron is owned by a Mr Hossein Ali Shah, who has been rebuilding the car since he bought it from its first owner, a former Palace official of the Shah's father, Reza Shah the Great.'

'Very interesting,' said Parkington insincerely against the rush of water, 'I don't understand a word of it. And where the hell does it get us?'.

'Maybe a step along the way. Cord cars are my hobby. Any enthusiast for these huge old beasts is bound to know the whereabouts of other American cars about the same age - such as the Packard that collected Offord.'

'Well, it's worth trying. Let's go down the Khiaban Ferdowsi and have a gander at this distinctive frontal treatment.'

'Just a minute. I've got a box of toys that MacGillivray gave me. I think I'll take one along. The one I tried on you – the ring - seemed to work quite well.'

'*Touché.* Though the only time I used one of his fountain-pen guns, the spring inside came apart, and I nearly killed myself with the bloody thing. I've never gone much on them. They seemed a bit forced, a bit artificial.'

'"All things are artificial",' said Love, quoting Browne again as he rummaged in his suitcase, ' "for nature is an act of God."'

'After you with the act of God,' said Parkington dryly. 'What I'd be more in favour with now is an act of love. And with a small "l".'

They walked the length of the Khiaban Ferdowsi, but they saw no Cord cars. But between the Bokhara Emporium, its windows full of enormous carpets draped over a beam, and the First Iranian Photographic Supplies, bright with Leicas and Fujitas, a narrow alley stretched into the darkness. The opening was uninviting, lit by an unshaded bulb high up on a whitewashed wall.

Wires from the bulb ran to a post near some sheds. The air smelled sour with stale urine. Mosquitoes hummed and a thin cat scratched hopefully in the debris of an overturned dustbin.

'This is the only place it could be,' said Love. 'Let's try it.'

They walked slowly up the alley, a yard between them, in case anyone rushed them. About fifty feet away from the Khiaban Ferdowsi the alley branched into a shabby, cindered courtyard. Lights on the walls of the houses that ringed it showed a handful of abandoned cars with flat tyres, paint bleached by the sun, roofs spattered with bird-lime. Directly ahead of them was a shed with double doors. A light glittered between the doors and hinges. A radio played 'La Mer', beating the night with sad, soft music.

Love banged on the door; Charles Trenet reached a crescendo. Nothing else happened. Love bent down, picked up a piece of concrete, and banged again on the door with it. This time the music stopped suddenly. They heard the sound of breathing behind the wood.

"Who's that?' called a man in Arabic.

'Two friends. Two car enthusiasts,' replied Parkington in the same language.

A bolt slipped behind the door and it opened a few inches. A man of about fifty looked out at them. He was short, bald-headed, with a ring of black hair he had cropped to his skull like fuzz.

'Come in,' he said, 'whoever you are.'

They moved into the flood of light from the door.

127

'Ah, two Englishmen,' he said, breaking into English.

The garage was large, but hardly larger than the enormous gold vehicle, a Cunarder among cars, that stood with its rear bumpers touching the far wall, its front bumpers half an inch from the door. On the gear-box cover beneath the radiator was the familiar black and white Cord badge with its vizored helmet, three arrows and three hearts.

'Obviously we've come to the right place,' said Love, pointing to this. 'You must be Mr Hossein Ali Shah. Correct?'

'Indeed. And your name, sir?'

'Dr Jason Love. I read about you in the A-C-D Newsletter and thought I'd drop in and see you. I've an 812 supercharged Sportsman in England.'

He passed a small photograph of his own white Cord to Mr Shah, who looked at it appreciatively.

'Ah,' he said. 'A very large car, Doctor. But, if I may say so, not as large as this Le Baron. I had an American tourist here some weeks ago and he told me he'd never seen anything like it.'

'I'm not surprised. Neither have I. I think there are only two other Le Barons left in the world, in any case.'

'You are right, my friend, you are right.'

Delighted at the prospect of an audience who had actually sought him out, the little fat man walked round the car, pointing out the difference between his enormous car intended for maharajahs and millionaires, and Love's standard Cord.

'Well,' said Love, when Mr Shah had finally paused for breath, enraptured with his own property. 'We're staying at the Park. You must join us for dinner tomorrow night if you're free. We've a lot to talk about.'

'I would love to,' said Mr Shah, 'but unfortunately I'm leaving for Ahwaz in the morning. I'll not be back for a week. Perhaps we could meet then?'

'If we're still here, of course,' said Love. 'But in the meantime, I wonder if you could help me with one small point?'

'If I can. What is it?'

'I'm trying to trace the whereabouts of a black Packard. Not a new one, probably a pre-war model. I believe it's a Packard Eight, but I'm not quite sure.'

Mr Shah stroked his chin reflectively.

'A pre-war Packard Six coupe I know is owned by one of the young Counsellors at the American Embassy. But a Packard Eight. Ah, I *have* seen one, but I don't think it's owned locally.

'I've seen it going into the garage of a house on the airport road. It's a new house beyond the petrol station. I don't know the number or the name, but the walls are painted cream, and there's a white roll-up door like a bureau door on the garage.

'But the car's not registered here. As far as I remember, it had an Iraq number-plate.'

'Is that the only one you know of?'

'Yes, sir: positively the only one. It's not quite my type of motor car, but naturally I keep an eye out for any of the older American models. Well, gentlemen, it's been a privilege meeting you, and I'll most certainly telephone you when I come back.'

He bowed in a courtly way, and Love and Parkington were out in the yard once more.

'Let's have a look at that house,' said Love.

They hailed the second taxi that came by, letting the first go past in case it had been planted. It dropped them a hundred yards beyond the petrol station, ablaze with fluorescent lights, in the airport road. They watched its tail lamps twinkle away into the darkness, and then walked back towards the house.

The windows were shuttered and the folding slatted door pulled firmly down in front of the garage; the whole place seemed deserted. They walked past it and the next house and round the side to the back yard. They crossed the fence behind the middle house and so came up behind the garage of the house with cream walls.

A window looked out over its garden - a small undug patch walled in by half-sections of terracotta drainpipes. Love peered in: the dim shape of a car was just discernible. He flashed his pencil torch; it showed the familiar Packard hexagon on a wheel. He nodded to Parkington.

'This is the place,' he whispered. Parkington slid a knife blade beneath the catch; the window opened easily. They climbed inside and pulled it shut behind them.

'Well, we've found *a* Packard, but where does that get us?' whispered Parkington. 'So far as I can see, all we've discovered is the back way into this garage.'

Love didn't answer; he was shining his pencil torch inside the huge, dusty old car. The interior handles had been removed from the rear doors, and the carpet was white with powder, like cement dust. In one corner lay a pole with a do-it-yourself decorator's roller at one end.

At that moment they heard a door opening. Love snapped off his torch. Footsteps crossed the concrete path to the garage. Then the slatted door rolled up suddenly and they were looking out at the moon and stars. Silhouetted against the ambience of the evening stood a fat man wearing a fez, with a revolver in his hand.

He spoke rapidly in Russian. They said nothing. This was partly because they didn't understand what he was saying, and partly because to speak would give away their position. The fat man repeated his remarks in Arabic. Again they held their breath. The second reason for silence still obtained. Parkington's right hand came up slowly and silently to the Berns Martin shoulder-holster under his left armpit.

'I will repeat in English what I've said,' the fat man said slowly. 'I know someone is there because the alarm sounded. If you are not just local thieves, you may be friends of the English spy. I will give you three to come out, with your hands above your head. Otherwise I will kill you as you stand. I'll start counting now.

'One.'

They stood, holding their breath.

'Two.'

The man moved his Lüger slightly from left to right, as though gauging in which direction he would fire first.

'Three.'

Crack.

The silenced pistol shot sounded like a stick breaking. For a moment, the fat man teetered on his toes and then sank forward, his head striking the back of the car with a noise like a hammer hitting a bell. The fez rolled away under the mudguard. Love looked across questioningly at Parkington, but his revolver was still in its holster. Parkington held a finger to his lips. They stood, waiting.

Around the side of the garage came two stocky figures in linen suits with panama hats pulled down over their eyes. They picked up the fat man's body and pulled him into the mouth of the garage. One man held a silenced Lüger in his hand.

He looked down at the body and then stooped to rearrange it so that when the police discovered it they would assume he had disturbed some thief who had shot him. Then he opened the rear door of the Packard and pulled out the roller on the pole. He nodded to his companion, who walked away down the road.

Love raised the hypodermic syringe he had taken from his suitcase; a quick touch on the plunger and the concealed needle, thin as a hair, would carry for thirty feet before it began to sink. At least it had carried for nearly this distance across MacGillivray's office when he had taken a few practice shots at a dart board on the wall.

He took aim at the man silhouetted against the moonlight, looking along the barrel using nicks in the serrated rings as sights. He aimed at the triceps muscle of the stranger's right arm, between shoulder and elbow. Then he fired twice.

The syringe spat out two long needles with a tiny sigh of escaping air. The stranger gave a grunt of pain and surprise and dropped his gun. It fell with a clatter against the rear bumper of the Packard, as his left hand flew to his arm in the sudden sharp agony of the two tiny tufted needles embedded in the tortured muscle. For a second he stood, half hunched up, and then he bent down to find his gun.

Parkington was waiting for this. His left knee came up into the man's face with the expert smooth precision of a drill movement. The stranger went down in an untidy heap.

Parkington and Love dragged him inside the garage and rolled down the door.

Love put away his syringe and knelt at the man's side, feeling his pulse. This was the second stranger he had downed within hours: the habit could be catching.

His pulse was strong: the man would live. He examined the Lüger, but its numbers had been filed away. Then he went through the man's clothes. Under his left armpit was a light-weight shoulder-holster of unfamiliar pattern. In a pocket inside his jacket, under a. button-down flap, Love found an oilskin pouch. It contained a yellow International Health Certificate and a British passport. From the pale blue page, K's face, younger than he remembered it from the photographs in MacGillivray's office, and with darker, thicker hair, looked up at him.

There was no tailor's name in the man's suit. He carried no passport, no papers, no card of identity, only a bunch of rial notes of different denominations in a cheap Japanese spring-clip, and half a dozen spare cartridges in a cigarette packet.

Love propped him up against the car door and smacked him twice across the face with the open palm of his hand. He moaned slightly and his eyelids began to flutter. As his mind swam back to consciousness, his right hand jerked instinctively towards his shoulder-holster. Then the pain took him again. He winced and feigned unconsciousness to give himself time to regain his strength.

Parkington hit him with the edge of his hand above the bridge of his nose. The pain forced open his eyes. Love pointed to K's passport.

'Where is he?' he asked.

The man said nothing.

Parkington hit him again. A thin sliver of blood crept down his nose. He stayed silent. Then his jaw began to work.

'Look out,' said Love urgently. 'He's chewing something.'

Parkington wrenched open his mouth. A white powder lay on the man's tongue. He had bitten through a capsule concealed over a tooth.

Parkington pulled him up and kneed him in the stomach. He slipped forward retching, hands tearing at his groin. In his giant agony, the veins in his neck stood out like great purple cords. Then the vomit came. They had caught him just before he was able to swallow the L-pill.

He leaned weakly against the sloping wing of the car, gobbets of sickness sticking in a streaky yellow mass to the front of his suit.

'You'll never get him to talk like that,' said Love. 'I've a better idea.'

He unscrewed the top from one of the fountain pens the gadgeteers had given him, pulled up the left sleeve of the man's jacket and lifted the little lever as though

134

to fill the pen. The tiny needle concealed beneath the nib pricked the artery. At once the man's knees became hinges on which he folded up quietly in front of them on the soiled concrete floor.

'Now can you hear me?' asked Love slowly, holding up the man's head. He moaned softly, like an animal being disturbed by nightmares of torture in its sleep.

'Do you speak English?'

The man nodded, his head moving up and down gravely; like a marionette.

Where is K?'

The man said nothing; possibly the name K meant nothing to him. Love rephrased the question, adding, with guesswork of his own:

'Where did you take the Englishman you collected in this car from the Park Hotel?'

The man's fingers scrabbled in the gritty dust and sticky vomit on the floor.

'North,' he said slowly and thickly, as though the voice belonged to another man.

'We drove north.'

'How far north? Over the border?'

The man gave a little negative grunt and shook his head.

'The Tajrish road.'

'Where on the Tajrish road?'

'On the right. A track. We went there.'

'Did you kill him?' asked Love, prodding him with his foot.

The man nodded.

'Why?'

'Orders,' he replied, and repeated the word as though he liked it, his tongue rolling round the two

135

syllables. 'Orders.'

'From whom?'

But the few beads of pentathol, the truth drug with which Love had been able to inject him, were already losing their effect. The only answer was a moan, and then a snort as his mouth fell open slackly and he began to breathe through it.

'That's all,' said Love to Parkington. 'Let's go.'

He let the unknown man slip to the floor. He lay relaxed, near the ruin of his panama hat. Love replaced the cap on the pen, and the pen in his pocket. Then he put his gun back in the man's hand. He had killed K with it; now the police would find him asleep, gun in hand, next to the body of another victim.

There seemed a certain irony about it: one life for two, the first down-payment of the debt.

Parkington summed up his thoughts as they climbed into a passing taxi to the Park.

'Die now, pay later,' he said.

CHAPTER SIX

Churchill, Manitoba, Canada, March 22nd, 05.45 hours (local time)

London, March 22nd, 12.15 hours (GMT)

Teheran, March 22nd, 13.00 hours (local time)

LUKACS LOOKED down at the silent figure beside him, paused for a moment to reassure himself that she was indeed dead, and then began to slide slowly out of bed, as though she was only asleep and would awake at the sound of movement.

The air in the room felt fuggy and stale, but soon he would be out in the cold, clear morning and this horror, with so much else, would belong to the past.

His plan was simple: it had to be, for he must put his side of the case to the Canadians before they found Irina. He would run to the nearest station of the Royal Canadian Mounted Police and explain who he was, what he had been doing, and ask for political asylum. Surely they must accept him, just as they had accepted Igor Gouzenko how many years before? He would tell them what his orders had been, where his codes and his recognition signals were. With all the information he could give them, surely they would hot, could not, refuse to help him? He hoped they could ignore the fact that he had murdered his guard to get away. After all he had been through, one more death was of little account.

Lukacs dressed quickly, pulling on his string vest, his long pants, his thick woollen socks, unable to keep his eyes away from the still body, unable to believe that never again would Irina turn around half raised on one elbow, and face him, her hand already reaching for the Lüger beneath the pillow.

Just to reassure himself, Lukacs touched her bare shoulder with the back of his hand. The flesh felt chilly, for already her body was stiffening. Soon, even in that warm room, she would be as cold as marble, or the inside of a prison hut in Vorkuta. He pulled the sheets over her shoulders up to her ears. At a glance, anyone who came into the room, any maid or cleaner, would think she was in a deep sleep and not disturb her.

As Lukacs fumbled with the oiled leather laces of his boots, he thought back over the last hour. Irina had awakened him, wanting him again, rousing him from his sleep, pressing her body over his, her long hard animal breasts squeezed against his chest. He had let her have her way with him and then, as they approached the moment of climax, he had reached up and, bunching his muscles, deliberately sunk his fingers into her windpipe.

He had often thought about doing this before, but at the last moment, resolution had always failed him. But this time strength came out of the past, the accumulation of years of hatred pumping through his veins with every pounding beat of his heart. She struggled at first, writhing, threshing in a fury to survive, but her strength was nothing against his. Gradually, the struggles had grown weaker and more spasmodic, and then she was not struggling at all but limp in his arms.

Her face had turned to purple and then the lips went blue.

One moment she was an officer in the Chatsny Otdyel, the division concerned with espionage and political murder in the Russian secret police, and the next she was just another corpse, one of the democracy of the dead; another cadaver to add to the thousands who had died in prisons, camps, in the abortive uprisings, in the struggle for or against Communism. But such had been her influence on him that he had lain beside her body scarcely able to believe she was dead. Finally, he roused himself. Once he was out of bed the spell broke. He was his own man again.

Lukacs looked at his watch: the time was five forty-five. He knew where the Mountie Station was, up towards the Fort. He had seen it often enough, with its flag and radio antennae, on his trips to the Hudson Bay Company store. He would take his passport to prove who he was, and then he would tell them his story.

What if they didn't believe him? In that case, he'd use the five single 100-dollar bills he kept hidden in the instep of his right shoe, his getaway money, to buy an air ticket to Winnipeg. And once there, he would try the Mounties again. But whatever happened, he would never go back to Russia and captivity; better to be dead like Irina than to return to the living dead at Vorkuta.

Lukacs stuffed his passport and the black-bound New Testament that contained his codes and recognition signals into a pocket of his duffle coat, pulled on his gloves, took the key from under the pillow where Irina had kept it near her automatic, and let himself out of the door. Then he stood for a moment, holding his breath, listening. The corridor was empty.

Across it, a water tap in one of the bathrooms dripped noisily and regularly like a metronome. Through the thin wall of the room next door he could hear someone snore and then cry out in sleep. But what dream could contain the horror of the nightmare from which he was escaping?

No one else seemed to be awake, at least on that floor, but even so he'd take precautions. He could not risk being questioned by some waiter or cleaner and then brought back to the room. It was imperative that he saw someone in authority before they found the body, otherwise they would never believe what he had to say. He tiptoed to the end of the corridor, past a huge oil-painting of two cats, and then he paused, looking at it without really seeing it, listening. But he heard nothing to alarm him. After all, why should he? He had simply to go down the stairs, slip the two bolts behind the front door, and he would be away. Free.

The word had a wonderful roll to it, a freshness like surf bursting in a flurry of foam on an empty beach.

Irina had been the one who had been set to watch him, so why should there be anyone else? But even though he tried to convince himself that he was being too cautious, the thought persisted that perhaps someone had also watched Irina. His masters took very few chances. They had learned by experience to leave as few loose ends as possible, to offer the minimum hostage to failure. Lukacs turned, and put his foot on the top step.

As he did so, two hands gripped him from behind above his elbows. They had him as tight as pliers. He had to bite his lower lip to stop himself crying out in surprise and pain.

'Who are you?' he gasped in English.

'You know who we are,' replied a voice behind him, also in English, but equally not in an English or a Canadian accent. It was as false as Lukacs's own passport, as false as his name.

'We're Irina's friends. Your friends. Where are you going so early, and alone?'

Ah, alone. That was the giveaway; these bastards went everywhere in pairs, like nuns, in case one defected.

The grip slackened on his arms sufficiently for him to turn round. Two men in snow coats were on either side of him, with stocky, peasants' bodies and pale, sallow faces. Brown eyes Like chips of granite peered suspiciously at him. Their chins were dark with stubble.

'You're no friends of mine,' said Lukacs, looking from one to the other. 'I've never seen you before.'

'Where are you going?'

'To get something for Irina.'

'Come back to your room. She can tell us about it.'

'No,' said Lukacs. 'I'm going out. She asked me to.'

Their grip tightened on his arms. This time he found his voice; once he was back in the room and they found why he had left he would have no chance to speak.

'Help! Help!' he yelled.

The man on his left clapped a hard leathery hand across his mouth. His companion released his hold and gave Lukacs a glancing blow across his Adam's apple with the edge of his hand. Lukacs sagged, sobbing for air, the blood roaring in his ears like the thunder of the sea. They began to hustle him along the corridor, like a sack of beet. All the time, he kept gasping for breath, trying to force another scream for help through his tortured throat before it was too late. But he could make no sound; he could hardly breathe.

They propped him up against the wall outside his door, and one of them went through his pockets for his key, as he lay hunched up like a straw man, weak, feeble, all but beaten. The other tapped on the door in a sequence of knocks. His companion found the key, turned it in the lock and they both drew Lukacs through the door, slamming it behind him. Then they let him drop. He lay where he fell, trying to control the trembling in his limbs, to steady the race of his heart.

One of them looked for a moment at the sleeping girl and then ripped off the bedclothes. She lay in her nakedness; a little mucus and saliva had seeped from her swollen bluish lips to stain the pillow.

'She's dead,' he said flatly, without surprise. 'No wonder you were trying to escape. What happened?'

The two men looked at each other for a moment, unable to comprehend the scope of the disaster, and then they looked at Lukacs. How could they explain this away to their superiors? Would any of the blame brush on to them? Would her death affect their chances of promotion, maybe of survival? Surely, it could hardly improve them? This would have to be handled delicately and with care.

Lukacs said nothing; he could think of nothing to say, and even had words formed in his mind he could not have pronounced them.

'Are you mad?' asked the man who had hit him,

seriously as though he expected an answer: yes or no.

'Don't talk so much,' said the other man. 'Let's see what he's up to.'

He went through Lukacs's pockets, pulling out his passport first, then the Testament that contained his seven recognition phrases, one for each day of the week, and his codes.

'So,' he said softly. 'You were just going out, were you? Going to get something for Irina? What was it - a coffin?'

He lifted Lukacs and hit him across the face with the back of his hand. Lukacs made no attempt to duck the blow. He fell clumsily, still trying to piece together the scattered splintered mosaic of his thoughts, fighting to find a way of escape from this maze of disaster.

'Take it easy,' said the second man. 'We can do no good beating him up. He's as dumb as an ox, anyhow. Let's kill him and dump him in bed with the girl. Say they had a love pact, a suicide pact. We can leave a note. It's the sort of thing that would get no questions asked.'

He took a small green and white capsule from his coat pocket and pressed it between Lukacs's lips. Lukacs clenched his teeth, feeling it cold against his gums, wondering how long it would take for the container to dissolve. The second man kicked him in the groin to make him open his mouth but Lukacs, writhing in agony, still kept his teeth clamped to-gether. They bent down to hold him and prise apart his jaws. Then he found his voice.

'Help!' he bellowed. 'Help!'

At that moment, someone started to beat on the door. 'What you doin' in there - killin' a squaw? Can't

143

a guy sleep in this goddam hotel, for Chrissake?'

The two men said nothing. One pulled a Lüger from his pocket and pointed it at Lukacs's face, holding the forefinger of his other hand to his mouth.

'Open up, you crazy bum!' shouted the man outside the door, inflamed at the silence, the lack of any response. 'Someone was hollerin' for help just now. I heard him come in here. Open up this friggin' door, or I'll break it down!'

Inside the bedroom, the two men looked at each other, fear flecking their brown eyes. They had to make a swift decision, on their own initiative, outside the book of rules, and this was beyond their experience and their capability.

Whoever was outside began to bang on the door until it trembled in its frame. In a second the lock would break and all would be discovered. One of the men shouted: 'Stay where you are or I'll shoot.' In his bewilderment, his accent sounded thick and alien.

'Who the hell d'you think you are, you horse-shaggin' bastard?' roared the man in justifiable Canadian anger. 'You'll shoot *me*. Wait till I get at you.'

At that moment the lock snapped and the door burst open.

The silenced Luger cracked like a whip. The bullet buried itself harmlessly in the lintel, as through the gaping doorway rushed two construction engineers in vests and trousers, tousle-headed and angry.

One felled the gunman with a blow on the jaw before he could squeeze the trigger a second time. The other jabbed his companion's stomach with a fist the size of a ham. As the man's face folded forward, the Canadian brought up his knee. He crumpled like a paperbag.

'What goes on around here?' the first Canadian asked rhetorically. 'A crowd of bum krauts. Christ, look at that dame. Strip fanny naked! Jeeze - she's dead! And who's this guy on the floor?'

Lukacs spat out the death pill from his dried lips.

'Get the Mounties,' he gasped hoarsely. 'For God's sake, get them quickly. It's a matter of life and death!'

Then he collapsed.

***

The original message that Love had sent to Scalpel, Darwin, Australia, regarding folding invalid chairs, had gone on from there to Cape Town in the form of a request for supplies of a specially tempered steel for surgical instruments.

From Cape Town it became an inquiry to a travel agency in Montego Bay, Jamaica, seeking confirmation of holiday reservations. From Jamaica, a cable went to Sensoby & Ransom regarding the export of sunflower seeds and Iraqi dried dates, stoneless and in bulk, for catering purposes. And finally, in an underground office beneath Whitehall, fifty yards from the Cenotaph, decoders turned this innocuous message first into numbers, and then into cipher groups, and finally discovered its hidden meaning. Now, transcribed, decoded and typed, it lay in a blue folder which MacGillivray's duty officer put on his desk in his office in Covent Garden. The folder had a red star on the cover to mark the secrecy of its contents.

MacGillivray put aside that month's issue of *The Country Gentleman's Magazine*, leaned forward in his swivel-chair, untied the pink tape that bound the file and began to read. Then he pushed his magazine into a drawer and pressed a switch on the black inter-com box. His secretary's voice answered.

'Get me Mason at the Yard,' he said.

Within seconds, the green telephone was purring. He picked it up. Superintendent Mason of the Special Branch was on the line.

'What's up, Mac?' he asked. 'Early for you to call.'

'It's always too early to call you. I only do so when I have to. Like now. Can your people do a little job for me, as quickly as possible?'

'Depends on the little job'.'

'It's routine stuff. We've had a word about a Mrs Welcombe, Station Road Newsagency, Ashton-under-Lyne, Lancashire. Mrs I. Welcombe. "I" for India. And Welcombe with a "be".

'There's probably nothing in this at all, for our source is raw and amateur, but he's keen. So he might just have something here. Anyway, I want all you can get about Mrs Welcombe. Who she is. Where she comes from. When she started. The lot. Also I'd like all you can dig out on one Miss Maria Franklin, who writes to Mrs Welcombe from Italy. She gives her address as care of the American Express in Rome.'

'Italy's surely more your neck of the woods than ours, Mac?'

'Surely. But right now it's a bit difficult for us to do a lot there. It shouldn't be too hard for you to find the connexion between the two. They might be sisters. You never know.'

'What do you think, Mac?'

'I'm not paid to think,' MacGillivray replied bluntly.

'Just to find out facts. Like you. When's the soonest I can have some news?'

'Soon as we have it ourselves. Right?'

'Right.'

MacGillivray replaced the receiver and closed the file. Then he selected a cheroot, lit it, and sat back in his chair, letting his mind run over the whole confused, interrupted canvas of events so far. He wondered what his opposite number in Moscow was doing, what his next moves would be. And when. Then he rang down for his car.

He had an appointment to keep with the Prime Minister.

***

In Teheran it was nearly one o'clock. The March sunshine threw yellow bars of light between a gap in the heavy curtains drawn across the lecture room windows in the University. The room was hot and stuffy, the speaker a bore. He was a Dutch professor who had spent so long in New Guinea that his skin was as yellow and dry as old parchment. For three-quarters of an hour he had been discussing the therapeutic uses of malaria in psychiatry, illustrating his long, slow, convoluted discourse with colour slides.

These jerked and jumped and moved on, their crude colours harsh and bright on the screen. The professor's voice, thick with accent, hoarse with the strain of speaking before so representative an assembly, droned away, at times almost unintelligible.

Love, in the second row from the back, his feet stretched out under the chair in front of him, leaned back, eyes closed, willing himself to keep awake.

Important as the therapeutic uses of malaria might be in psychiatry, he could not think they would have much practical application in his practice at Bishop's Combe. Dust motes danced in the beams of sunshine and, finally, overcome by warmth and weariness, he slept.

The lecture ended, and the doctors straggled out, blinking in the strong sunlight, their faces creased and puffy as their suits. A delegate from Goole, one Dr Erasmus Plugge, a slight man with a bald patch in the middle of his sandy hair, like a polished pink island in a ring of pale grass, attached himself to Love. His blunt North Country voice boomed out incongruously amid the elegance of marble pillars and cypress trees.

'He does go on and on a bit, eh?' he said.

'An understatement,' agreed Love, offering him a Gitane.

'No, thanks. Only smoke my own. Guaranteed no nicotine. Made for me specially by my tobacconist. Little fellow in Bradford. Glad to have the chance of a word with you. You're the odd man out, aren't you? Only one in the Park while the rest of us are in the Ambassador?'

'That's right.'

It had been an error not to be with the rest, but there was nothing he could do about that now. The Ambassador had been full and, anyway, MacGillivray thought it a good idea to book him in at the Park, because K had stayed there. Now, Love was not so sure. If this lunatic had noticed he was the only one on his own, might not other people also discover this -

and decide to investigate the reason?

'Yes,' he said easily, as though the matter was only trivial. 'That's me. There was some balls-up in the booking. I had to take what I could get.'

'Oh, well, not to worry. I wondered whether you're coming on the trip to Persepolis? We've got some seats in a special plane if you are, and there are still one or two vacancies. But I must know by tonight at the latest - I'm the honorary organizing dogsbody for the trip.

'Sounds a wonderful place, you know. They tell me that when Alexander the Great captured it more than three hundred years before Christ was crucified, he found twenty-four million quids' worth of gold in the treasuries. Think what *that'd* be worth now!'

The magnitude of the calculation made Dr Plugge shake his head in such baffled amazement that some herbal ash detached itself from his cigarette. He brushed it automatically into his lapel.

'Keeps the moths away,' he explained.

'You going out there, then?" he went on.

Love shrugged.

'I'm not really sure yet,' he said.

'Well, if you want to go, I'm at the Ambassador with all the rest. We've got taxis laid on to the airport and that. We could sit together. Anyway, do let me know.'

'Let's leave it this way,' suggested Love. 'If you don't hear by six tonight, take it I'm not coming. OK?"

'Roger and out,' said Dr Plugge.

He shuffled away in his suede shoes with the plastic soles, puffing acrid smoke over his narrow shoulders. Love watched him climb into a bus with his companions to go back to the Ambassador Hotel. Then he hailed a taxi and drove to the Park. Love let himself into his room.

149

Parkington was sitting in an easy chair, a bottle of whisky on a table beside him. His face looked pale, and his eyes wore dark rings round them.

'Thought you were never coming,' he said irritably.

Love locked the door behind him.

'I think I've arrived in time,' Love remarked professionally. 'You don't look too good, my friend.'

He felt Parkington's pulse. It was erratic; his skin felt hot and dry. He was obviously running a temperature.

Parkington shrugged and poured out some more whisky; his hand trembled so that the neck of the bottle tinkled on the rim of the glass.

'I'm all right.'

'You might be if you'd lay off that hard stuff,' Love went on. 'It's the worst possible medicine after jaundice.'

As he spoke, he remembered the rum and lime-juice he and Parkington had drunk while waiting for the taxi-driver to bring them news on the night he had arrived. What kind of a doctor was he, to let him do this? And yet Parkington, despite the pallor of his face, had seemed so fit that he had thought nothing of it. Now, he thought a lot.

'Come on,' he said kindly. 'I'll take you back to your hotel. I'll get something from the chemist for you on the way and, after a few hours' sleep, you'll feel better. Otherwise, you'll be back in square one again: in bed for weeks.'

'I must say that sounds more agreeable than rushing about round Teheran,' admitted Parkington thankfully. 'But I feel a heel leaving you to cope on your own. After all, I'm the pro here. And I've got a bit of news that might lead somewhere.

'Remember the taxi-driver who told us his cousin had seen K? Well, he turned up here an hour ago. He'd passed word around among his mates that there could be some rials up their shirts if they'd think back to Friday. One of them remembered that on Friday he'd found a screwed-up ball of paper in the yard. It was a note to Mr Offord from someone in the telegraph office. The man remembers the crest at the top.'

'What was it about?'

'Nothing interesting. Just to say that a telegram he'd handed in had been delayed.'

'I see.'

This was the first positive reference to the message K should have sent; did it take them, anywhere or did it just lead to a cul-de-sac?

'I'll run you back to the Ferdowsi, and then on to the telegraph office people who wrote that note,' Love said.

During the drive, they sat in silence, each in a corner of the old Pontiac cab with its split leather-cloth seats. A cheap plastic doll danced from a black rubber sucker on the windscreen. Love felt that he was making little more progress than the doll. He saw Parkington safely to his room, told the manager to call in the hotel doctor to treat him and then drove to the telegraph office.

It was packed with vociferous, rough-chinned men in shirtsleeves milling at holes in wire grilles to buy stamps, which they seemed to need by the sheet. They were sweating a lot and looked as though they would sweat a lot more before the sun went down.

Love caught the eye of a slim young clerk in an

Aertex shirt and white duck trousers who sat in a far corner of the room behind the grille, and beckoned to him. The clerk approached at no great speed. Love smiled, and, extending his right hand through the aperture in the wire, shook hands with him. The clerk took his hand with rather more speed than he had crossed the room, for between the second and third fingers Love had thoughtfully folded a 100-rial note to the size of a postage stamp.

Immediately, and without a downward glance, the Persian's fingers closed around it.

'You speak English?' Love asked him.

He nodded.

'I have matriculated,' he explained simply.

'Good. Well, I'd like to see you for a moment on your own. It's about a private matter.'

'Please come in,' said the clerk. 'I have an office.'

He lifted a flap at the end of the counter and Love walked through, past telegraph operators who sat at bare wooden tables, tapping Morse messages on old-fashioned keys, past ticker-tapes that started and stopped and started again spasmodically and convulsively, into a room where the walls were festooned with long sheets of ticker-tape messages in spring clips.

Above the empty fireplace hung a highly tinted photo-graph of the Shah and his second wife Queen Farah, framed in Persia's national colours. Next to it was pinned a calendar from Iranian Airways; white skyscrapers lined a beach, edged by a sea of unlikely blue.

On the young man's desk was a shabby Royal typewriter and a mass of papers and files held down by lead weights. The young man motioned his visitor to a chair and rang for tea in glasses, without milk. 'Now what can I do for you, sir?' he asked.

Since he appeared willing to help a stranger who put a 100-rial note into his hand, Love took out another note of the same value and laid it on the table under his sunglasses. The young man got the message. Love felt that he would go far in the service of the Iranian Posts and Telegraphs.

Until the tea arrived, they sat in silence; above their head an old fan creaked and whirred. Business of this kind could not be hurried. There was an ancient and rigid protocol to remember, rules by which to proceed. The cries of the stamp buyers seemed faint and distant, muted by the thick whitewashed walls of the building.

An orderly brought in a tray and put it down on the desk, breathing heavily as though he had been climbing a hill. Tea-leaves swam on the brown tide in their glasses; a fly made a slow inspection of a cube of sugar.

Love offered the young man a cigarette and then explained the object of his visit.

'It's about a telegram,' he began.

'A telegram?'

The man appeared puzzled; his brow creased faintly; he might never have heard the word before. Perhaps it hadn't been in his matriculation syllabus.

'Yes. A friend of mine, a Mr Offord, who's staying at the Park Hotel, promised to send a telegram to a mutual friend in Khartoum. But it hasn't arrived and he can't understand why not. I wondered if you would have a copy, by any chance? If you could help, I'd be extremely grateful.'

He glanced casually in the direction of the 100-rial note under the sunglasses.

'Why does Mr Offord not come, sir?' asked the clerk innocently.

Love shrugged, he hoped as innocently.

'He's been called away on business suddenly. I told him I'd look into it for him.'

'And when was this telegram sent, sir?'

'I don't know even that it *was* sent. But I do know that someone here gave him a message saying it had been delayed.'

'Ah, yes. Then that would be last Friday afternoon. Atmospherics were too bad for our radio link to Istanbul. We had to use the land line from here to Basra. And it failed. Tribesmen in the desert cut it now and then when they want some copper wire to make a bracelet or something.

'We had to close down for nearly four hours until the break was found and mended. I'll check that message, sir. In the meantime, please have another glass of tea.'

He walked out of the office, while Love waited on his hard wooden chair, drumming his fingers on the desk impatiently under the creaking fan. The tea grew cold in the glasses; even the fly flew elsewhere.

Now and then dark-skinned messengers and postmen in khaki-drill uniforms with brass buttons put their heads round the doorway and then went away. Telephone bells rang, buzzers hummed and static squealed from an unseen loudspeaker.

After about fifteen minutes, the young man returned; he seemed surprised, perhaps even a little

154

worried.

'We keep records of every telegram sent,' he explained. 'But it seems that your friend's was never sent.'

'Why wasn't it sent?' asked Love, coldness suddenly gripping his heart. 'Why wouldn't it be sent?'

'The clerk concerned is off duty, sir, but a colleague tells me that about an hour after that note was delivered to Mr Offord, two men came in, just as you have done now, sir.

'They said there was no need for the telegram to go, after all. It was addressed to one of them and they'd arrived in Teheran unexpectedly. Could we cancel it? So we did. We tore up the message form.'

'Is that usual? I mean, would you cancel any telegram if someone - not the sender - asked you?'

The clerk swivelled his eyes to the ceiling as though appealing to Allah for aid. Then he lowered them to take in the 100-rial note.

'It's not strictly according to the conduct of the Posts and Telegraph procedure, as laid down in the Manual,' he allowed cautiously. 'But sometimes things like that do happen. If you understand me?'

'Only too well,' Love assured him. 'But can you find that colleague of yours? I want to know - Mr Offord wants to know - what was in that cable.'

'Oh, I can tell you now roughly what it was about.'
'How?'

Well, my colleague is very interested in horse-racing. He's a betting man, as you say in England. This telegram mentioned a number of horses. It said that in the Middle East Stakes - they were run at the racecourse here last week, sir - Kubla Khan was

155

expected to win. The betting was on Oil Baron in second place, with Highway Patrol third.

'The odd thing was, sir' - his voice lowered and he became confidential - 'we couldn't trace any of these horses running in the race, although of course they are racehorses. Perhaps Mr Offord had some inside knowledge?'

'Very likely,' agreed Love.

He pushed the note across the table.

'You're not a gambler?'

'No, sir. It's against my religious principles.'

'And mine,' replied Love. 'If you lose.'

He drove back to the Ferdowsi. Parkington seemed more cheerful but was still far from fit; the hotel doctor thought he should have two or three days in bed.

'What do you make of these three horses?' Love asked him. 'Is it a code that you know?'

'No, siree. But I've got my old code books with me, I expect K had the same ones with him.'

He reached for a pad, paper and pencil and a book with the dust-jacket of *The Oxford Dictionary of Quotations;* pasted inside were several thin sheets of rice paper covered with sets of numbers. He began to write.

Within half an hour he had the rough message: 'Kuwait and Persian oil treaties in danger imminent take over, following assassination of Shah March 23.'

Love looked at his diary. So much had happened so quickly that he had lost count of days and time. What he saw did not reassure him.

The next day was March the twenty-third.

The servant approached Andre Simmias as he lay stretched on the wicker chaise-longue. Silently, he set down the tray of whisky, the bowl of ice, the tall glasses and the gold mesh syphon on the marble table by his side. Simmias nodded his dismissal. Extended, at his ease, his strong brown body warm in the afternoon sun, life seemed very sweet. He poured himself a long drink, dropped in two cubes of ice, and lay back again on the chaise-longue, scanning the morning-edition of the *Teheran Journal*. The constant bickering at the United Nations among representatives of bankrupt countries unable to control their own affairs, yet confident they could control the world; the carefully organized chaos in Africa; the feeble ineptitude of Britain: such items held little interest for him.

The report that the 02.45 flight on March 21 from Rome to Teheran had crashed in the desert was the news that absorbed his attention. His thoughts dwelt on it for a moment, savouring the fearful scene: the scorched, roasting flesh crawling with heat blisters, eyes bursting within calcinated skulls, the reek of burning bones.

The thought of pain always quickened his pulse and tightened his muscles; for Simmias only one thing was more satisfying, and that was to inflict it. He had received a cable from Budapest which had explained how a British agent, almost unbelievably an amateur, would be travelling on this plane. Obviously, the man was coming to see if he could find the other British spy who had been killed in Teheran. Simmias could not afford to risk him doing so when so much else was at risk. Through a contact in Rome he had organized the planting of a crude bomb on the plane.

All that morning he had hoped for a news flash about the crash on the radio, but he had not heard one. Perhaps the bomb had failed to explode? Perhaps one of a dozen things. Now he knew what had happened. He had succeeded.

He poured himself another whisky, stiffer than the first: he deserved it. He felt very happy out there in the sunshine; his brown skin shone with a patina of sweat that accentuated the muscles and strength within. This British agent, this amateur, whoever he was, had been intercepted, eradicated, eliminated, done away with. It was all he could expect, an ending that would teach those lunatics in London to treat the whole business of spying with the seriousness it deserved. Really, events were playing into his hands. His people were so well organized, and they commanded so much sympathy that nothing and no one could beat them.

And in any contest victory must go to those who were best prepared to claim it: all history taught this lesson. Who but professionals would deliberately destroy an entire aeroplane with all its passengers and crew just to make sure that one man died? Certainly, no amateur in the field of espionage would contemplate it - after all, such an operation needed planning and resources.

Simmias looked at his watch. Within fifteen minutes he would have visitors. He decided he just had time for a quick cold shower before they arrived.

Thus, when his manservant announced them,

Simmias was bathed, shaved, clothed, his face smooth as the marble top of the table at which he sat. He smoked his customary black Russian cigarette, in complete command, both of die situation and his visitors: four men of middle height and indefinite nationality.

Now that this absurd British intruder had been dealt with, nothing could go wrong. This would be his triumph, the coup that would make him a legend and, possibly more important, would prove an insurance policy for his own survival. For sometimes even his natural ebullience gave way to concern. How long would - could - his own good luck hold? Yagoda, who had been Head of the Soviet Secret Police when Simmias and his parents were at Kem, had also been successful. But he fell from grace and power and died in one of his own prison camps. Even Lavrenti Beria, Stalin's choice to head the secret police, did not long survive his master.

The uneasy and undeniable fact was that every Chief of Cheka, from the October Revolution on, had died a violent death, usually at the hands of the torturers he had once employed. And the same was true of so many of the lesser officers: few lived to draw retirement pay. Someone drew a knife or a gun against them first.

He forced such ludicrous and unworthy thoughts from his mind so successfully that when he spoke his voice was thick with the thought of his approaching triumph; he addressed them as inferiors and listened with unconcealed impatience to their replies. They accepted this situation; they had, of course, never known any other.

'Are you quite sure you've rehearsed this enough?' he asked the man who sat on his right. They might be discussing some amateur dramatic production; in a sense, he thought bleakly, they were. But for one performance only. And it had to be perfect on the night.

The man nodded. He was in his early thirties, with a pale oily skin and eyes as cold as black beads. His dark hair, brushed closely to his head, was sleek as the skin of a seal. He kept tapping the marble top of the table nervously with the end of a silver propelling pencil. Even in repose, his face appeared tense; a muscle flexed itself continually to the left of his mouth. He was a killer and this was his first important assignment - the previous deaths he had arranged were nothing compared with this. The thought of failure was too terrible to contemplate.

'Yes, sir,' he said briskly. 'We take off from Teheran as soon as the helicopter returns from Persepolis. Our first stop is Leipzig to refuel.

'There we issue a proclamation for world peace, and are interviewed. We explain that we are carrying scrolls dug up from the palace of the ancient kings of Persia. An archaeological find at least as valuable as the Dead Sea Scrolls the Americans made so much fuss about.

'Then we take off for Havana. We refuel again and head north and north-west over Canada to Alaska.

'We have, of course, already received permission to overfly these countries. There is no question of meeting any snag there whatever. I have all the clearances from our embassies in Washington and Ottawa with the ship's papers in the plane. Then we synchronize watches.'

He looked down at the Omega on his left wrist, and by reflex action or imitation everyone else looked at theirs.

'At the agreed hour we go through our pre-arranged drill. If we have engine trouble or anything like that, we signal you to hold up the second phase of the operation. until we're airborne again. Then nothing can prevent the greatest victory for world Communism since October 1917. We will have won the battle for peace - the fight to end war, to isolate the Fascist Imperialist Britain from America, to bring her to her knees - without a shot being fired against her or even a threat being made!'

He stopped speaking and looked round at each man triumphantly. Between ormolu angels, the clock on the mantelpiece ticked away the seconds; the rest was silence.

Simmias did not meet the young man's eyes. Oratory and dialectics bored him: how much was meant for the listeners and how much to reassure the speaker? His mind flitted across the years to a lost, vanished time, to the unreturning, unreturnable peace of anonymity he had once known and not valued. Also, he had taken the chair at too many of these meetings. The exhortations sounded hollow, like actors' speeches in a bad play. But the hired men still seemed to believe them. After all, what else was there for them to believe?

'So,' he said, forcing these thoughts from his mind as he looked from one to the other of the flat Slav faces, all expressionless as bladders of lard.

'There's little more to be said. You all know the

routine. You' - he nodded to the man who had recited the order of events - 'you will receive your final instructions in a sealed envelope tomorrow. A man you don't know and will never meet again will hand a letter to you on your way to air control at Mehrabad Airport.

'He will approach you outside the Middle East Airways ticket desk, and will say: "Here is the letter your wife Magda was expecting." You will reply: "My wife Magda will be very pleased to receive it" and take it. You will not open the letter until you are in flight. No questions? Right. You will now leave here at intervals of not less than ten minutes. But not at regular intervals. Now I must leave you. We will meet again on the plane. Good day to you.'

Simmias stood up, the back legs of his chair scraping on the marble floor. He bowed briefly to the four men, who had stood up with him out of respect, and they clicked their heels and bowed more deeply to him; and then he was gone. It was only afterwards that they remembered he had not addressed any of them by name, or even wished them success.

Simmias crossed the priceless Bokhara carpet in the hall, passing beneath the statues of gilded runners holding torches aloft to candelabra as clear and cold as a waterfall of frozen glass: He entered his study and locked the door behind him. Almost immediately, the two green-shaded desk lamps flashed on and off three times. He was wanted on the secret telephone.

He moved to the bookcase, pressed the concealed button in the spine of the book and picked up the instrument.

'Going over now,' said a metallic voice at the other

end of the line. It belonged to the man he knew as Stanilaus. He heard a click on the wire, as they pressed the buttons that operated the scrambler equipment.

'We have just heard on good authority,' began Stanilaus in his cold voice, 'that the other side have placed a new agent in your area. An Englishman. What do you know about it?'

For a moment Simmias's heart contracted and his breathing stopped. He felt as though he had swallowed a stone that had begun to swell and swell in his throat. Was this how Beria had felt when the Red Army colonels had seized him at the Kremlin door to charge him with, of all things, 'treason to the Motherland'?

How could there be an English spy in Teheran? What had given Stanilaus this crazy idea? Simmias's mind, quick as a snake's tongue, flitted over possible leakages. Perhaps Stanilaus had someone watching him and he was trying to stop him? True, a British spy had been on his way to Teheran, but no one could have survived the air crash. The newspaper report made that absolutely clear. Even so, he would have to be careful.

Simmias spoke slowly into the telephone, choosing his words carefully, holding the fear out of his voice.

'I think there is a misunderstanding, sir,' he said quietly. 'I happen to know that the British agent who was sent from London has been killed in a plane crash between Rome and here. I arranged for the plane to crash with a time bomb. There are no survivors.'

'Then what you happen to know is quite wrong,' said Stanilaus, his voice roughening with anger. 'What you mean is that you made some plane come down. But was this man *on* the plane? Have you confirmed that?'

Simmias swallowed; the stone in his throat had grown to the size of an egg. If it swelled any more, he would choke.

'No, sir, I have no confirmation.'

'Exactly. You make deductions and draw conclusions. I deal with fact. I'm not ringing up to make a social call or have a philosophical discussion. I'm ringing to tell you that there's a new British spy in Teheran, and you've got to find him. Quickly. Before tomorrow.'

Simmias swallowed again. The pressure was easing; he had a few hours in which to escape from the trap. He was not beaten yet; he would never be beaten.

'Very good, sir,' he said meekly.

'And when you do get him, I want him brought to Lubyanka alive. I want to find out why he came to Teheran so quickly. And how - after you tell me you definitely killed him on the way. Report your progress to me at twenty hundred hours tonight.'

The line went dead. Simmias replaced the instrument and stood staring at his reflection in one of the wall mirrors. His forehead shone with beads of sweat; he almost-looked his age. Then his tremendous confidence began to drive out his fear. After all, he had bluffed his way out of traps before; he had always managed to survive. But might there not come a time when his luck ran out? He pushed the thought to the back of his mind.

Stanilaus had said an English spy. Not a Scot, a Welshman, or an Irishman. He'd read that a whole group of British doctors had arrived. He'd try them first. If that drew blank, he'd fall back on his contacts in the airline booking offices and the hotels. It should be a simple routine matter to prove he was right and Stanilaus was wrong.

Even so, his hands were still trembling slightly as he folded the dummy-book spines on the telephone and crossed to his desk.

He picked up the telephone there and dialled a number. The bell rang in a little office above a motor-accessory shop behind the Khiaban Roosevelt. The door carried a small brass plate: The Friends of Iran.

Inside one room a number of filing cabinets with double locks stood against a wall. In the next, two telephones were on a desk next to glasses that long ago had held mint tea. Several ashtrays and saucers overflowed with grey ash and tipped cigarette stubs.

For an organization with an apparently friendly purpose, it seemed to have an unusual amount of Chubb locks on the outer door, and the windows in each room were barred. Thin wires also ran across the glass to alarm bells high up behind the door.

But then, as with much else in this world, The Friends of Iran were not entirely all they seemed. The job of those who used this office was, in fact, to collect and collate material on visiting foreigners who might be of use to Russia, regardless of whether this was friendly to Persia or not. Their interests, hobbies, weaknesses - especially the weaknesses - were all of interest to the men in Moscow who controlled the Communist Central Register, an elaborate and frighteningly efficient card index of all known sympathizers with Communism and, more important, of people who, knowingly, or unknowingly, willingly or not, could be persuaded to help its advancement.

The man who picked up the telephone was slim and slight, with a fuzz of black hair and a bad scar on his left cheekbone. He reached automatically for another cigarette and then lit it, holding the telephone wedged between his jaw and his shoulder, before he spoke.

'I'd like to speak to Hakim,' said Simmias.

'Hakim speaking,' said the young man who looked like a student, but who wasn't one, although he had organized many student demonstrations throughout the Middle East. 'May I know who is calling, please?'

'You know who's calling, Hakim,' said Simmias softly. 'I want you to find out how many English doctors are over here at this conference and where they're staying. And anything that sticks out about any of them. I've a feeling that one may be hostile to us. I want to know this within an hour.'

'Where shall I ring you?'

'At the Ferdowsi. Ask for Mr. Sinejad. I'll be in the bar.'

He replaced the receiver, feeling a little more cheerful. Hakim was a professional, and professionals had no excuses, no complaints that time was too short, the night too dark, or the task too difficult. With professionals, you had results. That was how they stayed in business.

For a moment, Hakim stood looking out of the window at the busy street beneath him, and then he went to one of the filing cabinets. He wore the keys for their double locks on a chain around his waist. He unlocked the metal drawer and selected a buff folder. It was headed 'International Malaria Conference,

March 22 to 30'. Inside were some notes on each of the delegates. He took them out and began to read them carefully.

In the case of the British doctors, the facts he read had been gathered simply enough. Paragraphs had appeared in most of their local papers to the effect that Dr so-and-so was coming as a delegate to this conference. In each locality, the nearest branch of the Communist Party had selected a suitable man to pay a call on the doctor concerned.

He either claimed to be representing a newspaper just out of the district, taking the slight chance that the doctor would be too busy to bother to check his credentials, or else he appeared as the representative of a Famine Relief committee. This was one of the many 'front' organizations formed to further Communist interests; like the others - campaigns for peace, for racial tolerance, for the protection of tenants, and so forth - it would speedily be dissolved as soon as it had served its real purpose.

These callers discovered what they could about the doctors' past, their sympathies towards the so-called underdeveloped countries, their political views, and anything else of value.

This material was sent to a street in Gospel Oak that did not exist. The local post office was instructed to forward all mail for this address on to a man in a rooming house in the Caledonian Road, near King's Cross. There it was copied and posted to many strange and unexpected addresses, including the little office off the Khiaban Roosevelt. From time to time, both London addresses would be changed. There was thus very little chance of the authorities learning about this traffic in letters. And if they did, why should they suspect it? What harm could they prove?

Hakim wanted a man who could help him without realizing the significance of the information he would pass. He wanted a doctor with a chip on his shoulder, preferably from an industrial area; an unsophisticated man who had not been abroad much, naive about foreign matters.

He skimmed through the list of delegates. Only three seemed possible: a Dr Arbuthnot from Pontypridd, a Dr Mackenzie from Newcastle, and a Dr Plugge from Goole. As they were all at the Ambassador Hotel, he would try them in that alphabetical order.

He replaced the file, stubbed out his cigarette, lit another, and locked the cabinet. He left the office, turning each key carefully and then putting his weight against the door to make sure that the locks had caught. Then he went downstairs, past the shop window bright with Cibie lamps and Marchal horns, and hailed a taxi.

The clerk at the reception desk of the Ambassador Hotel rang the rooms of Dr Arbuthnot and Dr Mackenzie for him, but both were out. That afternoon they had discovered that they shared an interest in beaten brass ornaments, and were scouring the bazaar for bargains to take home. Neither knew that the brass had first been beaten in Birmingham and then shipped to Teheran, and as they didn't ask, the shopkeepers didn't bother to tell them. Also, neither ever knew how near they had been to playing an entirely unknowing - and unknown - part in world events.

'Then would you try Dr Plugge, please?' Hakim asked the clerk. Dr Plugge answered his telephone.

'There is a gentleman here to see you, sir,' said the clerk. 'Perhaps you could come down?'

Plugge arrived, wondering who the visitor could be. He didn't altogether take to this rather hard-looking young man with his shock of black hair, his cold brown eyes, his scarred face. But then you never could tell with these foreigners. They all looked so diabolical.

'Dr Plugge,' he said stiffly, introducing himself. 'You wish to see me?'

Hakim switched on a professional smile of welcome, and extended his hand.

'You don't know me, sir,' he said with the unction of an insurance man making a new contact, 'but I represent a charitable society here - The Friends of Iran. I believe a representative from our associated organization in London, Save the Hungry Thousands, called to see you before you left home, sir?'

'He may have done,' said Plugge stonily. 'I don't remember.'

Really, he had met so many different people in the last few weeks that he was bewildered by them all. Yet this fellow seemed quite friendly and harmless. Just showed you could never judge by first impressions or appearances. Nevertheless, he had not thawed completely; you had to keep strangers in their place.

'My time is limited,' he went on importantly. 'What can I do for you?'

'Nothing at all, Doctor,' replied Hakim. 'On the contrary, we'd like to do anything we can to make your stay here pleasant and memorable. We are much honoured by having such a distinguished

169

delegation here, and so I thought I'd check with all the doctors to make sure everything is to their satisfaction. You have no complaints about the hotel, or about transport, or anything? Or if we can help you in any way, arrange any tour or a visit to some historic place - anything at all - we will be most happy to be at your service.'

He paused.

Really, this fellow is damned friendly, thought Plugge, touched and impressed by this approach: What a very different reception would a foreigner receive in Goole! It made you think; first impressions weren't always the right ones.

'I think everything's all right,' he allowed cautiously, not knowing quite what else to say.

'Your colleagues feel the same, I hope, sir?' asked Hakim. 'You are all in this hotel?'

'Oh, yes, we have a block booking. All except for one man who came too late. He's at the Park.'

'Well, I'd better see him too, sir,' said Hakim. 'I thought you were all here. What is his name, please?'

'Dr Jason Love. He comes from a village in the West of England called Bishop's Combe. He's a country practitioner.'

'That's very kind of you indeed, sir,' said Hakim. 'Well, I'll go over and see him. In the meantime, do let me know if I can help you - or your friends - in any way.'

They shook hands again and Hakim was gone. It was only as Dr Plugge was returning to his room that he realized he could not possibly get in touch with Mr Hakim again. Why, the foolish fellow had gone off without even leaving his address. These foreigners!

170

At a quarter past four, Simmias parked his grey Hillman Minx outside the Ferdowsi Hotel. His car was purposely chosen because the make was one of the most common in Teheran and so difficult to identify. The fact that he had six different sets of number-plates and used them all from time to time did nothing to make its identification easier.

The bar was empty at that hour; orange and red lights, which would give such a welcome after dark, seemed sickly and synthetic compared with the bright sunshine outside. He ordered a Scotch, and lit one of his black cigarettes, sitting in a red plastic leather chair in a corner waiting for the call. It came exactly on the stroke of 4.30 pm. Hakim was punctual; professionals always were.

The barman looked around the room inquiringly. It was empty save for Simmias.

'Are you by any chance Mr Sinejad?' he asked him.

Simmias nodded and took the receiver from his hand.

'About the doctors,' said Hakim, coming to the point at once. 'There are fifteen British doctors here. Fourteen are in the Ambassador. Then there's one in the Park.'

'Why aren't they all together?'

'The man at the Park came out after the others were booked in. They hadn't room for him.'

'What's his name?'

'Dr Jason Love. From a country village called Bishop's Combe in the West of England.'

Simmias scribbled down the name, and address on the back of a cigarette packet.

'There's been a reception for all of them at the

171

French Embassy - there are also about ten French doctors here. The British Embassy later gave a coffee party for them, too. But Dr Love attended neither function. No reason given.

'That's all I can find about them being together. I've rung Love, but he's not in his room. I left no message. The English contingent are going on a trip to Persepolis tomorrow. They're staying the night at the Hotel Persepolis, then they come back here.'

'Are they all going?'

'Yes. Except for Dr Love. He doesn't seem to have shown up much at the lectures either, from what I hear. All the others seem to stick together.'

'Thank you,' said Simmias. 'That's all, Hakim. Goodbye.'

He rang off, and the barman bore away the telephone in one hand and Simmias's tip in the other. Dr Love at the Park. The man who had booked late, who didn't go to parties, who wasn't going to Persepolis, who preferred to stay apart from the rest. He might bear investigation.

Simmias drove to the Park, through the wooden archway, around the pond to the reception office, and parked his car near the taxis in the shade of the trees.

'I would like to see Dr Love,' he told the Armenian behind the counter.

The man picked up the house telephone, checked Love's room number, and began to dial it.

'I don't know if he's in, sir,' he said. Who shall I say is calling?'

'A friend. From his home village. Bishop's Combe, in the West of England.'

CHAPTER SEVEN

London, March 23rd, 09.10 hours (GMT)
Teheran, March 22nd, 22.15-22.10 hours (local time)
Persepolis, March 23rd, 11.15 hours (local time)

THE GREEN TELEPHONE buzzed quietly on MacGillivray's desk. He picked it up and pressed the scrambler button. Superintendent Mason of the Special Branch was on the line.

'Some news for you about that Welcombe woman in Ashton-under-Lyne,' said Mason. 'She's a British subject, born in Malta. Said to be a keen stamp collector. Has lots of letters from abroad.

'She was out last night so one of our people got in through an open window and had a quick look-see. In a wall safe behind a picture he found a list of names and addresses, mostly in Canada and America. He took copies. And £2,000 in £1 notes. He left those.

'In her kitchen he steamed the stamps off a letter he found between the pages of a book. They'd got microdots under them. We're working on these dots now.

'He cleared out and went back when Mrs Welcombe had come in. He said he'd got her address from Miss Maria Franklin, in Rome. At once she became very cagey and nervous. For my money, I don't think there is a Miss Franklin in Rome or anywhere else. I've got Interpol on to her but there's no joy so far. Don't fancy there will be, either. I'd say she's just a cover name for someone else.

'We kept an eye on Mrs Welcombe's shop, of course. She locked it up at seven this morning, left a note for the milkman telling him to leave no milk until further

173

notice, and caught the 8.10 fast to Euston.'

'So?'

'So I think she's come to see someone she's afraid to write to, or telephone. Of maybe she just thinks it wiser to move house for a bit.'

'You're keeping an eye on her?'

'But of course.'

'Good. If you can see she stays around for about forty-eight hours, I think we may be able to offer Mrs Welcombe hospitality as a guest of the State.'

'That's the message I get, too. Will do. Over and out.'

As MacGillivray replaced the receiver, his duty officer came into the room with a blue file stamped with the familiar red star.

'A message has just come in from Ottawa,' sir,' he explained. 'I'm not sure whether it's connected with the Teheran business, but I think it may be.'

As MacGillivray took the single sheet of stiff paper, he had a sudden swift image of the teleprinters chattering out the cipher groups in the headquarters of the Royal Canadian Mounted Police in Ottawa, that familiar building rather like a left-over Victorian public library. He thought of the decoding officers working behind the thick green-baize doors in the stuffy fluorescent-lit basement of security headquarters near the Admiralty, where the air-conditioning vents blew their metallic-tasting draughts through the long cold corridors. Thank God he'd never become involved with codes. Reading the messages in clear was bad enough.

He put on his reading-glasses and began to read the decoded message.

'087541 Secret from Security Canada to Security London stop message begins:

1.   Man aged 35 with passport in name Axel Lukacs claiming born Budapest Hungary although he insists born Tirana Albania sought political asylum 0635 hours today Hudson Hotel Churchill Manitoba stop

2.   He admitted murder of Irina Bajder with whom he had been living stop He claims her real name was Irina Solokovsky officer in Russian MVD Otydel stop She entered Canada with Lukacs on March 7 as displaced person stop

3.   With Lukacs in hotel room were two Russians Diemels Studnikov and Pavel Kruglov stop Both were, armed with 9-mm. Lügers and apparently on point of killing Lukacs stop The commotion disturbed two building workers in next room who broke down door and so stopped Lukacs's murder stop He had already been forcibly given lethal pill which he managed unswallow stop Both Russians claimed diplomatic immunity as drivers from Russian Embassy Ottawa stop

4.   Have taken Lukacs into protective custody Churchill flying him Winnipeg and Ottawa under guard soonest stop Also holding armed drivers as long as possible while background check made their activities but owing diplomatic circumstances will have eventually return them to their Embassy stop

5.   Appreciate any details principals involved stop Description Lukacs 5 ft 8 ins 150 lbs brown eyes broad shoulders scar on left cheek two left upper molars missing stop Formerly political prisoner Vorkuta speaks English heavy accent admits being pillar box for messages received unsigned ex Ashton under Lyne Lancashire

175

England which he reposted with identification signal from Your loving son Alex to Madame Eugenia Lukacs 117B Brod-ski Allee Budapest Hungary stop Has no knowledge name or address English sender stop

6.   Irina Bajder about 27 well nourished dark hair figure 38 26 36 5 ft 7 ins brown eyes full set teeth no other identification stop Two drivers refuse answer questions stop Approximate weight Diemels Studnikov 220 lbs height 5 ft 11 ins brown eyes black hair Pavel Kruglov approximate weight 190 lbs 5 ft 10 ins brown eyes black hair no identification marks stop Speak English well believe trained spies stop End message'

MacGillivray took off his glasses and sat looking across the top of his desk at the pigeons on the glass roof of Covent Garden Market. The cries of porters, the dull hooting of lorry horns came up faintly through the double windows. Some of the pieces of the mosaic already fitted in his mind. He thought they might need to look no farther than Mrs Welcombe for the course of the message from Ashton-under-Lyne. But could it be that these events in a remote Canadian hotel had some connexion with K's disappearance in Teheran, on the other side of the world? And, if so - how? What thread could possibly join them?

He crossed the room to the wall map. At one side hung a thin black cord. He picked this up and pinned one end on Teheran, and then drew it west across the map so that it passed through Churchill, Manitoba. Now, what possible connexion could there be between the two places?

MacGillivray opened the file he had examined before he went to, see Love in Bishop's Combe. What the hell was happening in Teheran? There was that Russian archaeological expedition in Persepolis. That Russian plane was still at Mehrabad Airport on some world peace flight. It had already come from Indonesia; so presumably it would go on west, to Europe and then America and Canada.

Was that the clue, was that the tenuous connexion? He pulled the cord from the map, thinking. Then he lit a cheroot and pressed the buzzer on his desk. The duty officer entered.

'I want to send a message, Absolute Priority, to Ottawa,' he said. It was only a hunch, a possibility, but he had no other idea, no other lead; at least, it wasn't worse than nothing.

The officer produced a notebook and sat down, watching MacGillivray pace up and down the carpet, hands behind his back, cheroot between his teeth. Then MacGillivray began to dictate.

'035712 Secret from Security London to Security Ottawa Canada stop message begins:

1.   Received yours 087541 stop Making investigation all points you raise stop Believe already have identity Ashton under Lyne. sender stop British police will hold her on suspicion pending proof stop

2.   Consider positioning Lukacs north Canada could conceivably have bearing on forthcoming peace flight Russian Ilyushin ex Teheran due cross Canada within 36 hours stop

3.   Would appreciate co-operation following matter stop If said plane seen to act in any repeat any way oddly or suspiciously over Canadian territory please

177

endeavour to bring it down to land using peaceable undramatic means only under any plausible pretext stop Make search of plane and passengers but unthreateningly and without force as proof theory held here unobtainable stop Please advise stop
Message ends'

'Send this and then pass over to Mason the names of these Russian characters.: Interpol may know something about them.'

'Very good, sir.'

The duty officer shut his notebook and left the room. MacGillivray crossed the carpet and stood looking down into Covent Garden, wondering what Love was doing, how he was making out. He'd been away for forty-eight hours and. they were still no nearer to finding K. Perhaps, as Sir Robert was reminding him, he'd been a BF to send him. But who the devil else was there?

He recognized the signs of alarm in Sir Robert easily enough. After Vassall and Blake and Ivanov and the rest, the Press were after someone's scalp. MacGillivray hoped they wouldn't get his. Ah, well, if they did, and he was retired prematurely, he might get a large enough pay-out to buy some land in one of the less fashionable parts of the Highlands. He sat down at his desk and took out the copy of *The Country Gentleman's Magazine.* It contained a most interesting article about drainage problems in a peaty soil; maybe he could use the information if the worst happened.

***

Love sat beside Parkington's bed in the Ferdowsi Hotel in Teheran. Parkington, his face yellow as straw, his dull, listless eyes ringed with green, lay back against the pillows under the slowly turning fan.

'I'm sorry,' he said weakly. 'I just can't beat this bloody jaundice. I had a relapse only two weeks ago, and this follows the pattern.'

'You don't exactly help yourself,' said Love. 'Drink's the worst thing in the world for you.'

Parkington shrugged.

'A bit late to remind me. But then if you'd been in this business as long as I have - always on edge, always wondering if the man you're due to meet is really on your side or not, never sure of anything or anyone - you'd find some sort of escape route, too.'

'I hadn't thought of it like that.'

'Of course you hadn't. You're like all quacks - you look on people as chemical equations.'

'Well, at least I think I know the answer to this equation. Parkington plus Booze equals Jaundice again. And you'll have to stay here for four or five days, on a strict diet, as the hotel doctor advises.'

'I surrender, dear. But I feel so bloody useless, just lying here.'

'Well, don't. Give MacGillivray a thrill. Code the names of those horses. Send them to him. Say you're ill and drunk and I'm well and sober, for the whole thing seems too incredible to me to be true. But he's paid to take decisions, so let him decide.

'I'll go to Persepolis under my own steam just in case I can do anything, but you might tell MacGillivray, too, that my job's done, so I'm signing off. After all,

179

I've discovered what happened to K, and that was all I had to do to earn my holiday. Tell him I'm booked on the BOAC Comet that arrives on Saturday afternoon. If he wants to be a friend, he can get one of his minions to ferry my car to London Airport to meet me. And then down the N7, dodging the maniacs, to Antibes and a bowl of bouillabaisse.'

'The way I feel, do me a favour and don't mention words like bouillabaisse. They shorten my life span. By the way, on the matter of life spans, do you know who K was?'

'He was called Offord in his passport.'

'He could just as well be called Pontius Pilate in his passport.'

'What are you getting at?'

'There's no point in telling you his real name, I suppose. It wouldn't mean anything to you. But it would to Simone. Did you know that she's his daughter?'

The news struck Love like a blow: how many more complications were there in what had begun as a simple piece of detection? Or was any detection simple?

'Does she know?'

'Of course not. I only found out by accident once in MacGillivray's office. He was called away to see someone for a moment. He'd left some papers on his desk and I had a gander at them. Simone knew him simply as K, or as Offord whenever she had to pass on a message. They never met or corresponded. After all, she isn't working under her real name, either.'

'Has anyone told her?'

'I should doubt it. Why should they? Why bother the

girl? But enough of that. How are you going to Persepolis?'

'I've got a seat on a plane that leaves about four-thirty tomorrow morning. That's a couple of hours before the one all the other doctors are on.'

'Well, it'll be a change, if nothing more,' Parkington assured him. 'And I'll take money that it will be nothing more.'

But next morning, as Love watched the Shah's, black Cadillac slide slowly past the Apadana Palace in Persepolis, the green, white and red stripes of the Iranian tricolour flapping slowly on its bonnet, he wondered whether they had both been too optimistic.

On came the car, between truncated pillars, past the myths of gods and men frozen in stone two and a half thousand years ago, past staircases that led only closer to the wide and empty sky.

The Shah, in uniform, stood up in the back of the car, its hood folded down behind him, holding a rail behind the driver with his left hand. With his right hand, he saluted the crowds gravely, first to one side and then to the other. Now and then the dark lenses of his glasses caught the sun like polished shields. Had he any clue, any inkling of what was supposed to happen, Love wondered, what reception was planned for him?

Certainly, he seemed well enough guarded. In front of the Cadillac rode six police outriders on Triumph motor cycles. They wore dark-blue brecchcs with polished leather leggings, khaki shirts, black Sam Brownes. But although they all carried Service revolvers - Colts or Webleys - on their right thighs, Love noticed that their holsters were buttoned, and the pipe-clayed lanyards were looped under their arms.

In an emergency, would they be of much more use than the Guardsmen with their ceremonial rifles at Buckingham Palace?

A few feet behind the Shah's car came a grey Pontiac of the Persian Army, containing three officers in gold-braided caps and light-coloured summer uniforms. Even if they carried loaded revolvers they were not primarily guards. By the time they could be out of their car, any. assassin could have done his work, and be away.

Behind the Pontiac again were two open Land Rovers packed with soldiers with fixed bayonets. They sat back to back, the butts of their rifles on the floor, looking out into the crowds. They offered the greatest risk to an assassin, but if he were serious in his intentions he had no doubt made plans to discount them.

And all the while the crowd roared: *'Zindabad! Zindabad!* Their shouts beat back from ancient walls knotted with friezes of foreign kings bringing tribute presents of giraffes, camels, chariots.

To Love, shutting his eyes momentarily against the brilliance of the sun and the glitter of the cavalcade, it seemed that he might be two hundred and fifty centuries in the past. Darius the Great was accepting the adulation of his subjects as he arrived in the huge audience hall - sixty-five yards across - of his palace. Love leaned against a column, feeling the warmth of its rough, crumbling stone through the thin stuff of his light alpaca jacket. He wore a tropical hat with a wide brim; his sunglasses served the dual purpose of protecting his eyes from the brightness of the sun, and also afforded him some disguise should any of the doctors from - the conference think they recognized him.

In his right hand he carried a sword-stick that MacGillivray's gadgeteers had persuaded him to bring. It gave him a comforting feeling to tap it lightly against his leg as he peered over the heads of the crowds towards the Shah's entourage. It had much the same weight and feel as the swagger-cane he'd bought on being commissioned from the OTS in Belgaum - how many years ago? Odd, the psychological uplift a stick gave the holder; it would be interesting to write a paper on it some time, if ever he had the time.

Time. The thought made Love look at his watch and then beyond the long, slow procession to the Royal Mausoleum and the grey mountains, barren of vegetation, rough and bleak as rock. Here, the flapping wings of eagles, the trembling bleats of-sheep and the occasional cheers from crowds on such holidays as this had been virtually the only sounds to break the silence for twenty-five centuries. Would these hills soon echo to a new sound - the crack of an assassin's rifle?

Love looked from the Shah across the miles of ruins shimmering in the morning heat, wondering whether Darius really felt any safer when he arrived at his Spring Palace in Persepolis. Surely insecurity was an integral part of the equation of monarchy, an cntry in the debit account of kingship? If you accepted the acclamation, you also had to take the risk of a violent end.

The faint noise of engines cut into his thoughts. A

helicopter rose like a strange dark bird from behind Apadana, near the Hall of a Hundred Columns. Love glanced up at it with little interest; it probably belonged to the Shah. Then he looked again more closely. If it were the Shah's machine, why should it be airborne again so soon? Others also seemed surprised at its approach. Two of the motor cyclists were looking up towards it, eyes narrowed against the sun.

To the right, above thirty yards away, Love saw half a dozen men standing on the gigantic base of a ruined column. They towered possibly ten or twelve feet above the rest of the crowd. All held walking-sticks and they waved them in the air at the approach of the Shah. So vigorous was their demonstration of enthusiasm that their shirts were already dark with sweat. Now they started to point their sticks at the helicopter, shouting something he could not hear above the cheers of the crowd, but obviously trying to draw people's attention to it.

Love lit a Gitane, watching them, his mind free-wheeling. Now why the hell should they *all* have walking-sticks? He glanced around at the crowds who had come to see the Shah; at the children, the family groups gathered on the bases of other columns. Some held up umbrellas or parasols against the sun's heat, but no one else, so far as he could see, carried a walking-stick. After all, why should they? A walking-stick was surely an English affectation; in this alien place, it looked absurdly incongruous.

Love edged around the side of his column, and pushed his way towards this group, through a mass of loosely packed spectators who chewed nuts and spat out the kernels to tread them into the red dust. He clawed his way up on the far side of the plinth, and stood waiting until the few upturned heads of those who had watched his progress from below were engaged elsewhere.

Then, inch by inch, he sidled around the side of the column in the shade until he was only feet away from the men, with a good view of the machine in the sky beyond them.

The helicopter moved out of the sun, and Love saw this was not the Shah's machine. He had arrived in a grey Air Force helicopter, and this was black. Through its open door Love saw a man sitting behind the pilot, his face in shadow. Could they be photographers? Possibly, but he could see no sign of a camera. Maybe it was a police or security machine; perhaps it had been specially sent because the authorities knew of the attempt that was to be made on the Shah's life. This explanation seemed very comforting, and certainly it was feasible, for the pilot kept hovering above the ruined palace as though it was important for him to be there.

Then the machine moved slowly to the right, over the arches and columns and the pillars, the rotor whacking the air with its harsh, characteristic sound.

At that moment, policemen who lined the Shah's route, standing about twenty or thirty yards apart, began to push back the crowds in front of his car, and the outriders turned to the right, towards the northern court of the palace, where the Russian excavations had been made. Soon the Shah would be out of his car and walking the last few paces towards the trenches that were roped off. There, in a special enclosure draped with the flags of Russia and Persia, the archaeologists, scientists and a diplomatic party waited to receive him.

Suddenly, the earth shook with a rumble like thunder, but yet not thunder. To the right, beyond the old treasury, a column of smoke and dust was already spiralling up towards the burnished sky. The wind carried cries of terror, thinned by distance, across the heads of the crowd.

At the noise, the six men on the other side of the plinth began to wave their sticks towards the cloud of dust. At once, people who only seconds before had been watching the Shah began to crane their necks towards the scene of the explosion; hundreds began to run towards it.

For a moment, Love glanced back towards the Shah. An aide was running alongside his car to open the door for him as soon as it stopped. Behind him, the Army Pontiac was already stationary and the officers were climbing out, adjusting their binoculars in the direction of the explosion.

A sudden movement made Love turn to the right. One of the group on the far side of the pillar, about two yards away, had raised his walking-stick to his shoulder. His companions were still shouting and gesticulating in the direction of the Treasury, but he took no notice of them. Instead, he twisted the handle of his stick with a curious motion and put the crook to his shoulder. Then he looked along the stick as though it was a rifle.

It *was* a rifle. A stick rifle, a gadget to gladden MacGillivray's heart. And he was aiming at the Shah. Love gave his own stick a quick left-and-right shake to free the blade from its leather case. He was not very expert, and he wished he could bend down to recover the case; he hated unnecessary waste, but there was no time.

As the man took aim, following the Cadillac with his stick, turning easily from the waist, obviously a first-class shot, Love edged forward. What the devil should he do? Hit him? Spear him? What if it wasn't a rifle after all? It seemed hardly fair to attack him until he was absolutely certain.

He cleared his throat noisily and, for a second, the man wavered. Love knew from the sudden hunching of his shoulders that his cough had registered in his mind as alien, possibly dangerous. He half turned back towards Love, lowering his stick rifle for a second. In that second, Love saw the tiny sights, the ejector slot; so he was right after all.

But what the hell could he do about it? It was one thing using judo on an attacker, or even putting an antagonist out of the way with a needle, but how to prevent murder in such an open place?

He was just too far away from the man to reach him physically with his sword-stick, so he shouted instead.

'Drop that gun!' It sounded terribly stilted, like a parade-ground command; shades of his time as a private on the square at Chaucer Barracks, Canterbury.

The rifle cracked like a whip. Someone screamed hoarsely in the crowd and fell writhing in the red dust that had already soaked up so many centuries of bloodshed.

For a moment, no one else seemed to move: it was as though a crowd scene on a technicolour wide-screen film had suddenly stopped on the screen, a piece of trick photography. Then everyone moved at once. The two men nearest leaped at him. Love jumped away, knocking one of them back with his stick.

'Arrest that man!' he shouted again, pointing to the gunman who had lowered his rifle, and was now holding it as though it was simply a walking-stick. But no one did a thing: he'd hardly expected that they would, but complete inertia was unexpected.

Down below, the crowd milled around the wounded figure in the dust. Love jumped into their midst. 'Make way,' he shouted. 'I'm a doctor.'

They parted to let him past, and then he felt their hands on his jacket, seizing it, holding his arms from behind. Someone tore at his sunglasses. Another spat in his face. A third hit him across the side of his head. And all the while the men on the plinth kept shouting in Persian, pointing at Love with their sticks.

He struggled free of those who held him; suddenly conscious of his own fantastic danger. Where were the police? Where were the Shah's guards?

He felt the hands on him again, tearing at his sleeves. This was no time to ask academic questions. Unless he escaped, the guards would arrive too late, if they ever arrived at all.

Lifting the sword blade high, and kicking backwards in a judo movement on the shins of those who held him, he started to run. To the left, across the heads of the crowds, he saw that the Shah's Cadillac had stopped. The motor cyclists were already off their machines, had flicked them up on to their stands, and were thrusting their way towards him through the crowds, drawing revolvers as they came.

An officer from the Pontiac was blowing a whistle and the soldiers were jumping down from the Land Rovers. And everywhere fists waved at him like angry branches, and a sea of upturned faces, contorted with hatred, rage and revenge, shouted abuse at him in Persian and English, Love stood for a moment, back pressed against the pillar, trying to assess his best chance of escape. No one in the crowd knew the facts of the matter, and no one cared. They only knew that someone had been wounded; that there had been an explosion and here was a hated Englishman, in his dark glasses, his expensive suit and with a sword in his hand, apparently caught in the act of murder.

At the vortex of this hatred, Love's mind reacted with trained calmness. He had seen death face to face often before in different disguises, in operating theatres, at stricken bedsides. But being close to other people's deaths was one thing; being close to his own, quite another.

Could he hold the mob at bay until some officer reached him, to whom he could explain the rights and wrongs of the matter?

He slipped his left hand into his pocket, and took out one of the marble-sized capsules the gadgeteers had given to him. He flung it into the crowd. It struck the base of a pillar and exploded into a thousand blue and crimson stars that danced over their heads. The people cleared a space for it as it began to burn with an orange, smoky flame.

The capsule was a virtually harmless development of the wartime thunderflash but the sight and sound were frightening and unexpected and thus it was sufficient to draw the crowd's attention for a moment.

In that moment Love ran round the pillar and jumped from its plinth into the only clear patch of earth that he could see.

Those nearest to him drew back, and he was clear. He had no idea where he was, for he had lost his sense of direction. All the ruins around him seemed hideously alike, each wall, each porch a replica of the next; all bearing friezes of goats and bulls and giraffes, presents from subject peoples in a forgotten empire to a forgotten king.

But about one thing he was in no doubt at all. It was imperative to put as much distance between him and everyone else in the shortest possible time. He ran easily, in long loping strides, conserving his energy, but aiming in what he hoped was the direction of the Persepolis Hotel. Perhaps he could find sanctuary there, or even a taxi to take him to Shiraz?

As he ran he saw a little group of Europeans in creased linen suits and floppy hats and sunglasses looking at him in amazement. With shame, he recognized his colleagues from the malaria conference. And there, inevitably, stood Dr Plugge, face blank with surprise.

'But I thought you weren't coming?' he shouted: he had no idea what had happened on the base of the pillar.

'I'm not? shouted Love. 'I'm going!'

And then he was past them. Ahead he saw that some men were running diagonally in front to head him off. They had no idea why he was running, either, only that someone who ran with a naked sword in his hand must be running from fear. And from their point of view, what did it matter what he had done? A pursuit made an interesting interlude in a boring existence. But, like an inexpert and cautious line of threes in an indifferent rugger team, they appeared fiercer and keener than they were. In fact, they were careful not to come too close in case they might be forced to tackle him; the glittering blade he carried had its own uncompromising message.

One bent down and picked up a fallen piece of masonry, about the size of a loaf of bread, and threw it at Love. It missed but, bouncing off a castellated pillar, hit him on the right hand. He stumbled for a moment and almost fell, and his sword dropped on to the red, rough earth.

He swooped down, picked it up and went on more slowly, his hand throbbing with pain. His suit was ripped and torn by hands that had been laid on him as he jumped from the pillar. His sunglasses were smashed and lost, his ankles and knees barked and bleeding.

He paused for a moment to see how near were his pursuers, and realized he was running in a circle, heading towards the Grand Staircase of Persepolis. This led to a majestic throne-room where, centuries before, Darius the King had accepted the presents and tributes from the ambassadors of the twenty-seven nations within his Persian Empire.

If he could reach this staircase and climb a dozen steps, they would not be able to rush him, and surely by then someone in authority could come to his aid? It was not more than an even chance that he could reach the staircase, but it was the only chance he had.

He dodged into a doorway flanked by winged human figures and the towering statue of a bull's body with a man's head, and leaned, against the warm stone to regain breath for the last run to the Grand Staircase. He could feel the rough porous texture of the wall crumble like red sand under his fingers. He flattened himself against the stone post of the door and looked out in the direction from which he had come.

He wiped the sweat from his forehead with his sleeve, and then moved from the protection of the doorway, hoping to dodge from pillar to pillar without being seen. He reached the first one and started to run to the second. In his right bruised and bloody hand he still held the sword-stick; in his left, a stone he had picked up in the gateway. He was more weary than he had realized, and his mouth felt like blotting paper. Blood pounded in his forehead, and the salt sweat, running down his face, stung his eyes.

Suddenly he saw the man with the blue eyes and the tanned face who had shouted to him in English.

'Aim for the Grand Staircase!' he yelled, pointing to the right. 'You can just make it!'

Love nodded; he was already half way there. But who was this fellow? Whose side was he on? Whose side was anyone on?

By now all hope of reaching the staircase unobserved had vanished; roars of anger directed the mob towards him. As he started to run, a man leapt from the top of one of the truncated pillars, and pinned his arms to his sides. They went down together under the impetus of his leap and struggled up again. The smell of sweat and perfumed hair oil was thick in Love's nostrils. He could feel the blood draining from his own hands, his arms, almost from his brain with the pressure of the other man's grip.

Red and orange lights blazed in front of his eyes. He choked for breath, straining to go free, but he might as well struggle against a steel wire. This was the end of the run: buffer-stop, all change, terminus.

Then, dredged up through the layers of experience filed in his subconscious mind, he remembered the judo training. Deliberately, he let his body go limp, and as his opponent grabbed him more tightly, Love hacked out at a knee-cap with the toe of his shoe. The man momentarily loosened his hold; his face came forward. Love brought up the edge of his left hand under his nose. The man rolled away, /writhing in agony.

Love gathered his strength together and stood upright, heart thundering, muscles slowly coming back to life as the blood began to pulse through his arteries. Wearily, every muscle of his body aching as though it had been stretched on the rack, he began to run unsteadily towards the Grand Staircase.

He could see it towering above the ruins, each step cut from a slab of reddish rock, seven yards across, leading to a vast platform at the top, nearly 500 yards long, more than half this in width. Between the pillars and the bottom step the ground was littered with rough, reddish pieces of rock, and behind this rubbish, twenty-five centuries old, the stairway extended to the sky in an infinity of steps.

He paused on the bottom step and turned to face his pursuers, gauging his distance from their leaders. The blue-eyed man had disappeared; or perhaps he had simply merged, chameleon-like, into the background of hundreds dressed in similar white shirts and trousers.

193

Love had no more capsules to throw, but he slipped his right hand into his jacket pocket, withdrew it, fist clenched, and threw a handful of air at the crowd. The ploy succeeded, and, as they ducked, he ran up three steps before the mob realized his trick. Then they charged on up the steps after him. Behind Love, and a hundred steps above him, the columns that once had supported a palace ceiling of enormous size and complexity raised their stone arms stiffly to the sky.

A man charged at him from the crowd, a tall, well-built fellow in green cotton drill trousers, sandals and white shirt open to the waist. The hair on his chest looked as thick as coconut matting.

He leapt towards Love, and the others hung back, watching him, waiting for their chance to come in with stones and fists and feet at no risk of pain to themselves.

Love parried his first blow with the flat of his sword on his wrist, and the man cried out in sudden pain, the knife tinkling on to the red stone steps. Then he closed with Love, his body hunched like a question-mark, fingers extended, his head drawn down beneath his shoulders, waiting for the opportunity of a ju-jitsu hold.

Love took a step back and his right heel came up against the next stair. For a moment he faltered and the man was on him. His left hand seized Love's right wrist, holding it away from him so that he could not use his blade. They stood locked together like two stone figures on the ancient friezes on either side of the stairway, each struggling desperately for mastery. The sight and sound of the crowd melted away. The blood roared in Love's ears, the sky grew dark and the years rolled up like a scroll.

He was at the Officers' Training School in Belgaum, in Southern India, and the old staff-sergeant, his face wrinkled and brown as a walnut from too long in the East, was explaining some of the finer points of infighting and unarmed combat.

'Now, gennelmen, hif you'll be so good has to give me your hundivided hattention - you 'orrible man, Mr Love, sir, pay hattention, sir - Hi'll demonstrate the killing punch.

'Hassuming-the hantagonist his before you face to face, with hay small shoulder movement - thus - you draw the left *hor* right hand - *has* the case may be - hacross the body. *Thus.*

'Hand with han hupward hand houtward movement *thus,* you discharge the hedge of the 'and hunder the hantagonist's nose. *Thus!*

'Not 'aving 'ad the benefit of hay scientific heducation, gennelmen, I cannot say why hit 'appens. But this punch *kills.* Hand so hit his called the *killing punch.'*

The dark mist cleared; the pounding died. The Persian was lying beneath him, head down the steps in the red dust that grew redder with the stream of blood from his smashed face.

Almost subconsciously, the reflexes of Love's mind had delivered the message to his brain: kill or be killed. From out of the past, forgotten long ago, came the automatic reaction of the killer punch, the fearful blow that cracks the skull.

Those in the front of the crowd now drew away; like Horatio's antagonists, those behind cried Forward, but those in front said Back. They recognized a dead man well enough when they saw one; they did not wish to be the next. This strange Englishman in his stained suit deserved respect; they would wait until they could leap on him safely from behind, and then maul him in their own way.

Love stood for a moment, dazed by the nearness of his defeat, his mind swimming against a rushing tide of weariness and nausea. The edge of his left hand, which had struck and destroyed his opponent, was aching; but even the pain seemed to belong to someone else. He felt like a dreamer, on the edge of another man's nightmare, having no part in it himself: he was in the world of horror, but not of it.

But the crowd held back only for seconds. Then three men leapt to the bottom stairs as Love backed up the steps above them. They held staves in their hands, and behind them came one of the Shah's bodyguards, absurdly blowing a whistle, a revolver in his right hand. He did not shoot because he dare not. The crowd, thinking he had come to rescue Love - as possibly he had - held him back, pinning his arms to his side, and all the while the shrill high scream of the whistle, jammed between his teeth, shrieked out its pointless alarum along the columns.

Love backed up the stairs, keeping the men at bay with his flickering blade. They showed no inclination to attack him. They simply wanted to tire him; that way, his end would be easier and quicker for them.

Love glanced behind him for a moment to make sure that no one had in some way reached the platform from behind. He was still secure but, high up against the sun, he saw what appeared to be a tiny dark bird in the sky. He turned to face the mob, but no one had moved any nearer. They were still watching him, waiting for him to show his-hand, to give himself away. He glanced again behind him and the bird in the sky had grown both larger and nearer. And then he saw that it was not a bird at all. It was the helicopter that had been hovering over the crowd before the attempt to murder the Shah.

For a second time he turned to face the mob, and they had taken advantage of his interest in the helicopter to move up two stairs nearer him. He backed away again, remembering from the guidebook he had bought in Teheran that the first staircase had sixty-nine steps, with forty-two more in the second flight that ended on the high platform where once Xerxes had held dominion over his court. He would have to hold them now as Horatio had held the bridge, for every step he retreated brought his own defeat one, stage nearer. Once he reached the platform his main defence - the relative narrowness of the staircase - would be gone.

A hush had fallen over the hundreds who waited beneath him; they also believed that the fight could only have one outcome, and they savoured the thought. Within minutes this Englishman in the torn suit, who had apparently tried to kill the Shah, who had definitely killed another man with his bare hands, would also be dead; and nothing could save him. It would be the will of Allah: a life for a life, a death for a death.

In the distance, Love could still see the Shah's black Cadillac with its flag waving lazily from the bonnet. Officers were standing up on the seats watching the scene through fieldglasses. Nearer to the staircase a handful of soldiers, rifles held high above their heads, were frantically trying to force their way through the mob to reach him. But the crowd had no intention of letting them do so. They stood so close together that the troops could not break through. The edges of the crowd, a thin fringe of women and children, let them past, and then the main body absorbed them, amoeba-like, so that they struggled in a morass of humanity, unable to go either forward or back.

The roar in Love's ears grew louder. He glanced briefly behind him, and saw with surprise that the helicopter was almost overhead, its gigantic four-bladed rotor flagellating the sky. A man crouched in the open oval dimness of the doorway, gripping a handle with one hand, half leaning out. In his other hand he held a dark circle. Then he waved and threw the dark circle towards Love. It uncoiled slowly in the bright clear air - a rope ladder.

The roar of the engine increased, and the wind from the rotor blades blew Love's, damp shirt about his body. The man in the doorway was shouting something, but Love could not make out any words against the bellow of the exhausts and the thunder of the rotor. Yet the message was clear enough. The bouncing ladder spoke it plainly.

Love turned and bounded up the stairs, heart bursting with the effort, until he reached the top platform. He paused, sobbing for breath, leaning against die stone upright of a ruined gateway, at the entrance of a vast roofless room, where petitioners had once gathered to wait the pleasure of their kings.

Doorways opened from crumbling walls eighty feet

apart, decorated with winged human figures and the familiar representation of bulls' bodies bearing the heads of men. To the right Love saw a raised dais and he ran to this; it brought him several feet closer to the dangling ladder. With a roar of almost animal rage and frustration at the thought that their quarry might still somehow escape, the mob surged up the stairs after him, some falling off the edge of the steps to the hard red rocks beneath in their haste to seize him before he could be spirited away.

The helicopter was coming down lower and. lower: already Love could see the joins in the metal body, the rows of tiny rivets, the parallel slots in the screw heads. But still the aluminium bottom-rung of the ladder hung at least ten feet above his head, and the pilot was obviously worried in case he came too close to one of the pillars. Would he come down in time to save him? Could he?

Half a dozen men raced through the entrance archway, stones in their hands, to seize Love. Leading them was the blue-eyed man he had seen on the plinth, who had shouted to him as he ran towards the Staircase.

Down, foot by cautious foot, came the helicopter, and the man in the open doorway, sizing up the danger, threw out a thunderflash at Love's pursuers. It exploded in a white blaze and then fell burning on the red stone floor, throwing off a thick black oily coil of smoke.

The crowd drew back momentarily, not sure whether it would explode again, and the bottom rung of the ladder came within Love's grasp. As his fingers touched the smooth, silvery bar, one man raced at him through the swirling smoke. Others took courage at his example and, shouting to conceal their fear, also ran towards Love.

As Love's left hand gripped the rung, feeling it warm and strong and infinitely comforting against his palm, he threw his sword-stick like a dart at the man. It hit him in the chest. He staggered and sank forward on his knees, clawing at the blade with his hands.

Then Love felt the rung jerk and tighten against his hands as the helicopter began to climb, until he swung like a human pendulum, too exhausted to clamber up hand-over-hand.

As the machine climbed, the rest of the mob rushed in to seize his legs. Love kicked outwards and backwards, losing both shoes, and then, as the rotor blades tilted and bit more deeply into the hot March air, the rate of climb increased. Suddenly, he was looking down at the upturned faces of his pursuers beneath him and at the tops of the pillars, white with twenty-five centuries of bird droppings.

Some of the crowd shook their fists at him and shouted, but he could not hear their voices against the engine. One of the soldiers, now allowed through in the commotion, started to fire his rifle. His aim was wild; the bullets sang away harmlessly through the sunshine.

Love looked up and saw the man in the open, doorway urging him to climb in. He shook his head wearily; he just had not the strength. The helicopter was hovering now about a hundred feet in the air, its rotor clattering above his head. The pilot locked his throttles and left his seat to help his companion pull up the ladder from which Love hung. Slowly, they heaved him in through the doorway and he lay gasping for breath on his stomach, head down on the polished metal floor, legs still sticking out into the air. They pulled him right in, and shut the door behind him.

The man who had thrown the ladder now put his hands under Love's armpits and pulled him upright. He pushed him into one of the two seats behind the pilot, and clipped a grey web safety-belt across his lap. Then he handed Love a drink in an aluminium cup. He took it eagerly and instantly gasped as the neat spirit ran like fire within his tortured body, momentarily robbing him of breath, burning away the tiredness from his tissues.

'Thanks,' he said weakly. 'I needed that.'

The other man sat down in the second seat and looked at him quizzically. He lit a cigarette. Love noticed idly that it was black and that he did not offer him one. Odd, surely?

The man bowed.

'I don't even know who you are,' he said easily, in a voice that held only a trace of accent, probably French. 'But from your appearance and your voice, I'd say you're English. Yes?'

Love nodded. Who the hell was this fellow? And why had he saved his life?

'I was expecting to pick up a colleague who was dressed much as you are - and also with a stick,' the man went on. 'But his loss is my gain. He will have to make his own way home. Tell me, are you by any chance one Dr Jason Love?'

'That's right,' said Love. 'I am. But how did you know my name?'

'What an odd thing life is,' the man went on musingly, ignoring the question. 'I called at the Park Hotel yesterday afternoon at about five to see you. The clerk rang your room but you didn't answer.'

'Five o'clock. I was out, seeing a friend.'

'So I discovered. In the Ferdowsi. Then I come to Persepolis - and so do you. Thus we meet after all.'

'That's right. How did you know that? Who are you, anyway? Some man down there - fellow with blue eyes - told me to make for the platform.'

'Ah, yes. He's one of our people.'

'*Your* people? I don't understand.'

The spirit made Love's head ring; the speaker's voice rose-and fell as though on a long-distance wire; and he was talking rubbish, anyway. *His* people? What the devil did he mean?

'Yes. We're well organized, you know.'

'We?"

'Yes. Or rather, *us.* You must excuse my English. It is not my mother tongue. I mean, *our side.*'

'Your side?'

To Love's fuddled mind it seemed like an old cross-talk act from the halls: 'Who was the woman I saw you with last night?' 'The woman you saw me with last night?' 'The woman I saw you with last night.' 'Oh, that was no woman. That was my Uncle Jock - he walks like that.'

Simmias lit another cigarette.

'I'm sorry about your friend at the Ferdowsi,' he said.

'My friend?'

'Yes. A man named Parkington, I believe.'

'My God. What's happened to him?"

'A tragedy; There was a complete misunderstanding. We heard you had gone there and one of my people - actually the fellow you saw just now, with the blue eyes - confused you both. There was a struggle. Your friend was shot.

'A great pity, although I fancy that Mr Parkington was, as you might say, a professional. Like us. We had a small file on him already. Unfortunately for you, Doctor, I fear you left a lot of fingerprints in the room. And the clerk saw you go up. So I expect the Persian police would like to ask you a few questions - especially when they find the gun in your room at the Park.

'When we do things, we like to do them well.'

'We? You mean - you're with — ?'

He could not finish the sentence; the idea seemed incredible, but Love had been through so much in the last half hour that now nothing was impossible. An intense weariness gripped him, not only physically, but an immeasurable tiredness of the spirit; he had reached the limit of his endurance.

The other man nodded, smiling.

'Exactly. In a sense, I'm almost your opposite number, also a doctor, too, oddly enough. Andre Simmias. Montpelier, class of thirty-three. But not like you, an amateur, Dr Love. I am, as you would say, a pro.'

CHAPTER EIGHT

Persepolis - Teheran, March 23rd, 12.00 hours (local time)

THE NOISE of the helicopter's engine began to thicken. Love looked without hope or interest at the baking, burning desert that lay beneath them, wrinkled as an elephant's scrotum. He saw a ruined tower, an abandoned mosque, a stick with a black flag to mark the grave of a holy man. In the seat beside him sat Simmias, his Lüger cradled in the crook of his arm, pointing at Love's stomach. He was smiling; he seemed to smile a lot. And why shouldn't he? He was enjoying himself.

In front of them, the pilot prepared to land. They came down gently, the wind from the whirling blades flattening the scrubby bushes scattered in the sand.

After the clattering background of the rotor, as the engine spluttered and spat and died, silence rushed in on them. The pilot unclipped his seat belt and stood up. He opened the door, hooked it back and fixed a small aluminium ladder into the doorway.

'Get out,' Simmias told Love, nodding towards the opening.

The brightness of the sun hurt Love's eyes after the semi-gloom of the helicopter's cabin. Instinctively, he put his hand in his top breast pocket for his sunglasses, forgetting for the moment that he had lost them at Persepolis. Simmias jumped out beside him and knocked his hand away.

'Not so fast,' he said. 'You may have a gun in there. Take off your jacket and throw it six feet in front of you on the ground. Then stand with your legs apart and hands in the air until I say.'

Simmias kept him covered with his Lüger while the pilot picked up his jacket, quickly went through the pockets, and shook his passport open to see if anything were stuck between the leaves. He found his fountain pens in his inner pocket, and held them up smilingly to Simmias. He said something in Russian. The pilot handed the jacket back to Love. Simmias nodded for him to put it on, and looked at his watch and then towards the shimmering rim of the desert, where the burnished sky melted into a haze of reddish rocks. A car trailed a long funnel of dust towards them. It slowed, turned and then stopped near the ruined mosque, facing the way it had come. The black flag on the stick flopped listlessly; there was very little wind.

The car turned out to be a red and blue Oldsmobile; Love guessed it was a self-drive hack from Teheran. Its driver was a stocky dark-skinned man, wearing black crocodile shoes already scuffed with dust, a light suit and a panama hat. He looked like every man of his age Love had seen in Teheran, which was why he was so useful to Simmias. No one would ever recognize him a second time. He opened the lid of the hoot and took out a pair of white overalls. He threw them on the ground at Love's feet.

'Put them on,' said Simmias. 'And hurry up. We haven't got all day. We've another plane to catch.'

The overalls were freshly laundered and stiff with starch, embroidered on the back in red with the two words: Ilyushin Aeroflot.

'Now get in the back of the car. Don't try anything smart. You'll only make things hard for yourself.'

The pilot climbed back into the helicopter, pulled in

the steps, shut the door, and started the engine. The rotor began to spin round limply, and then more smoothly, with increasing speed. Slowly, the plane moved up the sky. They shut their eyes against the sudden, prickling cloud of dust it created.

The driver slipped into the Oldsmobile's driving seat; Simmias climbed in behind Love. The car shot away, a hot, dry air from the desert blowing in through the driver's open window; it felt like warm sandpaper on Love's face.

From the position of the sun - almost overhead, and slightly to the right - Love calculated they were driving roughly north, presumably back to Teheran.

Simmias leaned back in the corner, against the door, a soft hat pulled down over his eyes, his gun crooked in his right elbow.

This man Love, or whoever he really was, would be his passport to survival, the living answer to any suggestion that he might not be as efficient as he should be, as he used to be. His capture alive would satisfy not only Stanilaus in Baku, but also the unknown heads of the Secret Service in their headquarters in Lubyanka Square in Moscow. Simmias felt entitled to be pleased with himself; once more he was on the winning side.

Not so, Love. He sat back in his corner, eyes closed, wondering where and how and when he could make an attempt to escape, and what would happen if he couldn't and didn't and, not for the first time, why and how he had ever allowed himself to be persuaded to come on such a ridiculous jaunt. And to think that MacGillivray had assured him it would be such a simple, routine task! He'd tell him what he thought of him when he got back. The idea cheered him and then his cheerfulness died: for 'when' read 'if'.

He glanced casually at the doors; as in the old Packard in the garage of the house along the airport road, the handles had been removed from inside them. This minimized any chance of wrenching them open.

Worse, he was in his stockinged feet, for the mob had torn off his shoes as he hung from the helicopter above Persepolis. So, even if he should manage to escape from the car, which in itself seemed unlikely, he could not march for long in the burning, rasping sand. Or could he overpower Simmias and leap out of the car? But the driver would almost certainly be armed. So what the hell was he going to do? It was like a game of snakes and ladders: he couldn't get away from the snakes.

'Where are we going?' he asked Simmias. 'To Russia?'

'Eventually.'

In the distance, through the shimmering haze of heat, he saw a line of palm trees with dusty-green fronds, then a cluster of wind-towers and the strangely shaped *ab-anbars:* big water reservoirs fashioned like buildings. Blue cones and domes marked shrines and holy places. Across the dried-up river bed, he saw golden minarets behind buildings of baked brick, and recognized the scene from a description in his guidebook.

This was the town of Qum, site of a shrine to Fatima, Mohammed's daughter, one of the four perfect women of Islam. The information was only of value to him in confirming his belief that they were going north; Teheran was still ninety miles on, possibly two-and-half-hours' drive away. After half an hour, the heat, the smooth ride on the big soft American springs, the realization that for the moment he could do nothing but endure his captivity, soothed away some reaction and fatigue. *Che sera, sera:* whatever will be, will be. His head fell back against the dusty cushions; soon, he slept.

Simmias watched him. Then he relaxed in his corner; within minutes he was also asleep. In front, the driver slid a Beretta from the hip pocket of his trousers, slipped the safety-catch and laid the automatic on the empty seat by his side. From time to time he glanced in the rear mirror to make sure the prisoner slept. He had his instructions if he tried to make trouble.

Much of the heat had left the sun by the time they drove into Teheran, and headed towards the airport. Simmias shook himself awake. He tugged Love by his left wrist. Love grunted but still did not wake. Simmias reached up behind him to the shelf at the back of the seat. He selected a small syringe from a cardboard box, broke the noose of a tiny glass phial, filled the syringe, depressed the plunger until a bead of colourless liquid wept from the end, and then jabbed the needle through Love's jacket into his left arm. The sudden sharp prickle of pain woke Love, but Simmias was already replacing the syringe in the box.

'Don't worry yourself,' he said. 'As one medical man to another, I'll not kill you yet. That's just to keep you quiet. From now on, you're an Ilyushin technician suffering from heat stroke. Look, no hat. No sunglasses. And you'll have all the symptoms, too, by the time we arrive. So there's nothing for it but to carry you aboard.'

'Aboard where?'

'The Bird of Peace.'

The car turned into the airport enclosure, under the squat flying-control tower, with its curious rounded end, the long colonnade, like a leftover from some architectural folly of the thirties. Love saw that the white ropes still ringed the Aeroflot Ilyushin, as they had on the day he arrived. Now a flight of steps was being wheeled against the plane, and men stood about, in white overalls like his own, arms folded, looking towards their car. It was expected; but was he?

They drove into the fenced-off car park and stopped. Simmias and the driver took hold of Love, one on either side, and pulled him out of the left-hand rear door between them. Love felt weak and dizzy; needles of pain bored behind his eyes, so that he was almost grateful for the guiding arms of his captors. He tried to speak, but his fuddled brain could not select words.

'Don't get the idea that you can shout for help,' said Simmias casually, 'even if you could shout. I've got one of your fountain pen gadgets in my pocket, too.'

Love's feet were so heavy that he could barely drag them across the tarmac; his legs had turned to sponge. Immigration officers in plain clothes approached them, with uniformed police wearing distinctive caps with the peaks bent down over their forehead, like runaway Guardsmen. Love saw their faces grow large and recede, and tremble and disappear. Hell, that drug was strong.

Simmias spoke in Arabic, showing them papers that

209

the driver had handed to him. They nodded sympathetically. One produced a rubber stamp. Love tried to speak, but he could not even croak; his mouth was as dry as a blotter, and his throat belonged to someone else. A helpful orderly brought a pair, of plimsolls for him to put on his feet. At least, they were better than crossing the hot tarmac in his socks.

When they reached the steps by the Ilyushin his legs refused to go any farther, so Simmias and the driver simply carried him inside. He noticed that half the seats had been taken away down one side of the aisle, and crates that looked like tea-chests were lashed with webbing straps on sorbo rubber blocks. Idly, he wondered what they could contain to need treating with such care. But what use would the knowledge be to him now?

A canvas stretcher was clipped to the floor. They lifted Love on to it. The driver tucked a blanket around him and strapped him in, hands to his sides.

'It's for his own safety,' Simmias explained to the immigration officers. 'In these cases of sunstroke, when you come from a northern climate, they can get quite violent. You'd be surprised, the trouble they cause.'

The official nodded understanding, tut-tutting. Love gave up trying to fight the waves of sleep that washed over him, and the tide came in and drowned him.

***

When he awoke, it was night. Shaded blue lights glowed above his head, and from the slight motion of the stretcher, the tiny dip and rise of the aeroplane, he knew they were in flight. But where to? And what awaited him at the end of the journey?

Under his blanket, Love's fingers felt for his watch,

but it was missing. He had no means of telling the time but, worse, the midget transistor transmitter that the gadgeteers had built into its back was gone, too. Not that it would have done much to help him, but as it had been tuned to the No. 3 RAF Distress Wavelength, there was just the faint chance (admittedly so slim as to be little more than a hope) that its tiny bleep-bleep signal could have been received and acted upon. But by whom, and how? Anyway, it didn't matter now. For a moment, he felt a sense of complete desolation, utter isolation; then he remembered why MacGillivray had insisted he had a long session with his dentist in Wimpole Street; the memory cheered him and he slept again.

This time, Simmias shook him awake. He bent forward and undid the straps that held him.

'Sit up,' he said roughly.

Love did so.

'Where's my watch?' he asked, rubbing his wrists to restore the circulation.

Simmias took it out of his pocket.

'From your dear father, in memory of the boy you used to be,' he said sarcastically, and opened the back with its left-hand thread so that the tiny screwhead of the transmitter control was visible. 'Mr Parkington had the same inscription on his wristwatch, too. I thought that if you had fountain pens to shoot needles, your watch might also do more than tell the time. And I was right. But what good would a homing signal be to you out in the Persian desert, or up here over East Germany? You'd better ask Mr Parkington what he thinks of your arrangements, too - when you see him.'

Sitting on the arm of a seat on the other side of the centre aisle, Simmias looked down at Love with contemptuous amusement.

'Where are we going?' asked Love.

'You've asked that already, and I've told you. Russia. Only we're taking the long way round. We've got some relics of the great Iranian past aboard. That's one of the reasons the Shah was in Persepolis early today - to see what the Russian scientists, had been digging up.

'You probably saw all the flowers around, the plane when you arrived? We're on a peace mission, too. We land at Leipzig and then next stop Havana. Then up to Canada, over to Alaska, and then across Siberia to Moscow. A flight of peace in the Bird of Peace.'

Love flexed his muscles under the blanket; the effects of the drug had worn off. He felt rested, physically at ease, ready to exploit any opportunity of turning the situation to his advantage. The news of Parkington seemed incredible. The pain would grow, but now it was only a numbness of the mind. Things like that only happened to other people; you read about them in the papers, for they never happened to you.

'Why take me?' he asked.

'Why not?' We want to discover why a country doctor from Somerset goes to Persepolis with a sword-stick, fountain-pen guns and a radio in his wristwatch. Among other, things. But that's not why I woke you. We're coming in to Leipzig in minutes to refuel. So I'll give you a warning once more. Don't try anything. No matter who comes aboard, you'll be covered all the time. And, anyhow, what could you try? They're

212

our own people who'll be coming in.'

As he spoke, the plane began to dip slightly, preparing for the long climb down through the sky, into the thick clouds, groping towards the darkened land. Love closed his eyes and feigned sleep.

He lay under his blanket as the plane bumped once, twice and taxied down to the end of the runway. Two stewards in white linen jackets came out of the crew compartment to adjust the white covers on the seats, and the lights came on brightly above the aisle.

Three men in dark suits, who had been sitting in the back of the plane, and whom Love had not noticed before, moved up and sat down beside him. The one nearest the aisle held a briefcase across his knees, with one hand inside its open flap. Love guessed that he gripped a pistol aimed at him.

Through the oval windows above his head, amber and blue lights blazed as they passed the airport buildings, and the pilot ran up his engines. In the sudden, ear-singing silence that followed, Love lay listening to the German voices outside; a set of steps was wheeled to the door. Some officials came in, saluted and shook hands with Simmias. They went off together, leaving the door open.

Soon the inside of the plane grew cold and Love was grateful for the blanket. Time passed. He lay in a hinterland between sleep and wakefulness, reality and fantasy - how could all this possibly be true? Then lights dimmed, engines hummed, fired and began to run, and. the aircraft started to move.

The lights came on more brightly once they were airborne and the three men who had moved up beside Love now went back to the rear of the plane. Simmias came out of the crew room, undid the straps that held Love down, pulled away his blanket and threw it over an empty seat. He was at ease, relaxed, in command of events.

'You can get up if you want,' he said. 'The lavatory's in the back. But remember, there's nothing you can do to harm us, so don't get silly ideas.'

Love slipped free of the safety-belt, flexing his stiff muscles. Simmias looked at him sharply, and then turned to the men at the back of the plane.

'Come over here, Josef,' he called.

The man who had held the briefcase put it down on a seat and started to walk up the carpeted gangway. He was a squat man with anthropoid features, and long arms that reached almost to his knees; he walked like a sailor, with a slight roll. He stopped a few paces behind Simmias, standing respectfully at attention.

'Search this man,' said Simmias briefly.

He sat down, felt in his pocket for his gold cigarette case, withdrew a black Russian cigarette, smiling to himself. Nothing could go wrong now, he thought. He was home and dry, as the British would say. He could afford to relax and enjoy himself, and he intended to. His eyes grew bright at the thought of another man's pain.

Josef stood facing Love, about a yard away, and when he moved, his right fist was so quick that even Simmias, who had seen him in action often and was expecting the blow, did not see it. The punch caught Love unawares in the solar plexus. He crumpled on the floor like a discarded suit of clothes, his whole body one living, throbbing focus of pain. Josef bent down and tore off his jacket and then, ripping away

214

the tie, pulled Love's shirt over his head without undoing the buttons. He stripped him naked, and then turned him over with his foot, examining the body orifices, in case they concealed a phial or capsule; but there was nothing.

'You're quite sure?' Simmias asked him.

Josef nodded.

Well, then, dress him again,' said Simmias.

Love, still swimming against waves of pain, was propped up against the arm of the seat. His body felt damp and clammy with the sweat of the fearful blow, but the mist of nausea had receded, although his whole stomach still ached like one gigantic bruise. Nevertheless, he was fairly fit; his judo training had hardened his muscles. A blow like that could have killed a man out of condition; as it was, he only felt like the walking dead. There was a difference.

'I'm not quite satisfied,' said Simmias slowly when Love was dressed. 'There's one place you've overlooked. His mouth.'

He leant forward and pushed the glowing end of his cigarette against Love's lip. Love jerked away his head, but Josef caught him by the hair, wrenched open his jaw, and peered inside.

'Ah!' he cried triumphantly, and pulled out the single false tooth that MacGillivray's dentist had so carefully fitted in the space left by an extraction years before between two lower molars. He held it up in triumph. Simmias unfolded his handkerchief from his breast pocket, and Josef dropped the tooth into the silk square.

Simmias looked at it for a moment without touching

it. 'Break it,' he said briefly.

Josef picked the tooth out of the handkerchief, placed it carefully on the carpeted floor and ground it with his heel. Then he bent down and picked up the little pieces. Among them lay the round blue dot of the transistor, the size of a match-head.

'So,' said Simmias. 'You nearly got away with it, doctor. But nearly is not quite. Although what good another homing device could do you, God only knows. Right, Josef, that is enough.'

A steward appeared with a tray of plastic cups of steaming coffee. Simmias handed one to Love. He sipped it gratefully, but it was too hot to drink. He placed the cup on the seat beside him, a sentence from Sir Thomas Browne's *Hydrio-taphia* floating through his mind: 'The long habit of living indisposeth us for dying.'

True. And whereas, until his experience at Persepolis, Love had regarded his role as a part-time secret agent simply as a fragment of an entertaining charade, with a free holiday as his prize, now he was determined to win the last battle. He had to: he'd lost all the rest.

At that moment, the crew-room door opened and a girl came out. She wore black slacks and a loose fisherman's knit sweater of charcoal grey. At the sight of her, Love's stomach contracted with surprise and amazement so that he thought he was going to be physically sick.

She was Simone, the British agent, the woman in Rome.

'*You*,' she said softly, as though disbelieving the evidence of her eyes. She might have been staring at a ghost.

'You, too,' replied Love with a grin. Even the effort of smiling hurt his stomach. The thought of what he would like to do to Josef flickered its comforting message to his brain. Correction. What he would do.

She sat down across the aisle from him, glancing back rapidly at the three men in the tail of the plane. They were engaged in some earnest discussion together with papers spread out on their laps.

'I joined the plane through the crew door up front. In Leipzig. I didn't know you were here,' she said. 'I thought —' She stopped awkwardly.

'I'll tell you exactly what you thought. You thought I'd died in that air crash, didn't you? Probably something you'd arranged for me. But I don't like people arranging things for me. I try to arrange my own life. It's a habit I've grown to like. That's why I'm still single. Why I'm still alive.'

Her mouth tightened, and she looked at him again, not quite meeting his sardonic gaze.

'Was that the only reason?' she asked.

'No, not the only one. I didn't like your assumption in Rome that I was going to Teheran. It struck a wrong note somewhere. Or maybe a right one, depending what side you are on.'

'Tell me,' she asked softly, changing the subject, womanlike. 'Why wouldn't you make love?'

'What a bloody question,' said Love disgustedly. 'You reminded me of someone else, someone I once loved. And I don't like imitations. I like originals. Any more questions?'

'I don't suppose you've really any idea why I acted as I did?' she said.

217

'None at all. And I don't care a damn, either. I only know you did.'

He shut his eyes and sat back in his seat. The future held about as much promise as a blank wall. All systems stood at stop. But, in fact, why had she gone over to the other side? (Again that spiritualistic phrase.) There must be some deep psychological reason. The doctor in him was inquisitive; Browne's dictum that 'No man can justly censure or condemn another, because indeed no man truly knows another,' ran in his mind.

'Tell me about yourself,' he said, his eyes closed. 'What do your parents think of you? What do you think of them?'

'They're dead. My mother was killed in the war at Plymouth in an air raid. I lost my brother in Italy.'

'Your father? What about him?'

'Well, what about him? I've not seen him for nearly ten years. When I did see him it was only off and on.'

'What did he do for a living?'

'Did? You speak as if he's dead.'

'Yes, I do,' agreed Love. 'What was his line of country?'

'A professor. But he always seemed to be moving about the world. I hardly ever saw him. I hated not seeing him, not being important enough for him to come to prize days and so on at school. He'd promise to be there but always, at the last moment, he'd back out. He'd be off on some business trip. Yet he'd never tell me where, or why. He wasn't like other fathers at all.'

'So you worked off your resentment for what you think the world owes you, or what you thought your father owed you by becoming an undercover Communist? You found that there were lots of others like you, all with chips on their shoulders as big as sacks of coal. If you couldn't be like other people, you'd make them like you. Everyone was out of step but you.'

'More or less. Of course, I'd forgotten. You must know psychology: you're a doctor.'

He looked at her, smiling for the first time on this trip. What would be her reaction if he told her that she had been responsible for the death of her father? Would it be disbelief, amazement, acceptance? He opened his mouth to tell her, and then thought better of it. The knowledge couldn't help him, and might not harm her. It was like knowing a patient had cancer when he only thought he had indigestion. Why spoil the dream? The awakening would probably come soon enough in any case.

'Tell me,' he said gently. 'What happens to me? Where's this plane heading for?'

'Russia, eventually. It's come from Indonesia - the usual peace mission stuff. Speeches against Imperialism, thousands of signatures against the bomb. All that jazz. We were due to call at Havana, but that's off now. We fly over Canada and Alaska and then home.'

'What happens then?'

'God knows. You'll be questioned, of course. They'll be interested to know how many other amateurs are being used. We've got most of the names of the pros from Blake.

'Then I suppose there'll be a trial and a few years in Lubyanka, and eventually a discreet exchange with someone we want who's in a British prison.'

'You mean, like Lonsdale?'

'You've a very high opinion of your value. I wonder if MacGillivray will share it.'

'I'll tell you when I see him. But why the long way round? Why didn't we just go north over the border from Teheran?'

'Because we've to be over America at a certain hour.'

Love looked at her blankly. He guessed that, woman-like, if he asked her directly why, she would refuse to tell him, basking in her own self-importance. But if he expressed no interest whatever the chances were she'd have to tell him, just to make sure he knew and was impressed. He'd used this technique often enough in dealing with women patients; he saw no reason why it should not work again.

'All right,' she said at last. 'I'll tell you part of it.

'We seize power in Teheran, take over the radio station and the newspapers. We've got our people there already, waiting for the word. And don't say it wouldn't work, that it can't happen here, etcetera. It's always happened before - in Czechoslovakia, Syria, Cuba, Iraq. And elsewhere.

'Next, we deal with the Sheikh of Kuwait. A pro-Russian Kuwait government also takes over. Another bloodless coup, as the papers say. *That's* timing for you. Both these new governments - of their own free will, of course - end their oil treaties with Britain. They nationalize the oil companies, send home the British technicians, block the Sterling payments. That oil's lifeblood to Britain. Without it, the country will just bleed to death.'

'But what about British reactions? What about

UNO? What about America?'

'You ask the questions, Doctor. I'll supply the answers. *What* about them? I'll tell you what about them. Right on top of these two coups there's a crisis in America.'

'A crisis? What do you mean?'

'What I say. Their TV screens go blurred. They can't see a proper picture. Worse, their radios can't pick up stations. So they can't hear any news bulletins. Even the radio-telephone links don't work.

'And suddenly every set picks up the Stars and Stripes followed by an official announcement from the White House, Everyone is to stand firm. No panic. America expects. All the sort of patriotic crap that'll make them worried as hell.

'Then the news - America is being invaded from Cuba. Red Chinese subs are off San Francisco. Russian nuclear subs are sighted near Miami. Rockets, heading for Washington, have been seen approaching Bermuda. And so on.'

'They'll never fall for that,' said Love.

'No? Do you remember what happened in thirty-eight when Orson Welles produced a radio play in New York claiming the Martians were invading America? That play brought out so many cars with people fleeing that the roads were blocked. Telephone exchanges were swamped with calls, police stations mobbed. People ran out into the streets screaming with terror.

'We'll get the same reaction there now. Only more so. For that was only one programme - all the other stations were still OK. Now, ours will be the only news *anyone* can pick up. Sure, we'll be rumbled in an hour or two, maybe less. But by the time the hysteria dies down, we'll be solidly in power in Persia and Kuwait. And there we'll stay, for as history shows, possession isn't just nine points of the law. It's the whole damn lot.

'You mentioned UNO. What'll they do? What did they do over Hungary? Nothing. Tibet? Nothing. India and China? The same again. And they'll do nothing now, except talk. A motion of censure will be passed, of course: ten for it, three against, two abstaining. That's all they, will do - all those old women can do.

'And where would Britain get the troops to turn out the new Persian and Kuwait governments? If you couldn't keep the Suez Canal from a crowd of Gyppoes, you certainly couldn't do this.'

'How do you blackout America?' asked Love, ignoring the torrent of her argument, but recognizing the underlying causes of personal inadequacy, of some inner, perhaps even childhood resentment, that caused it.

'Easily,' she said. 'At the moment the Sheikh of Kuwait is killed we'll be over Alaska, ten or twelve miles up. We've a device in one of those crates that acts on several sputniks that are already orbiting a hundred or two hundred miles up. They contain H-bombs to blow dirty great holes in the Heaviside Layer. *Now* do you understand?'

Now Love understood. He had not heard of the Heaviside Layer since his student days, but he remembered its importance quickly enough. Its seam of ionized air bounced back radio waves to the earth. Without this trampoline, these waves would suddenly disappear into space. An explosion of the right size - say fifty megatons - and at the right height could destroy the Layer over a large area. A series of such explosions could rip a vast tear in it across North America Radio messages would then simply disappear through this hole.

And if the explosions were large enough, they might damage the Van Allen Layer, which is above and beyond the Heaviside, and which would affect radar. They could even disturb the earth's magnetic field. The size and extent of possible damage seemed almost endless.

'Who makes the broadcast about invasion?' Love asked, pushing these thoughts from his mind.

'We do. From this plane. The gear's in those boxes. The message has been taped in Moscow. We've enough Americans there who've seen the light. We do things thoroughly, you know.'

'So it appears.'

Love sat back in his seat, eyes closed. So this was the plot that K had discovered, either completely or in part. It had the simplicity of genius. Love could easily imagine the entire subsequence of events unfolding in Britain, stage by stage.

First, there would be the newspaper calls for action - carefully unspecified, but at least preferable to inertia and acceptance. Then would come the government assurances, the ponderous TV appearances of politicians, the frequent references to 'the Atlantic Alliance', 'our allies across the ocean', and other such empty phrases long ago wrung dry of meaning. Third stage would be the cries for caution, for second thoughts, for UNO mediation by those who abhorred all action, all declension of will.

It was most unlikely that the extraordinary blackout of radio and TV in America would be associated with two assassinations in the Middle East. And, in the end, what would happen? At the most, a half-hearted, ill-equipped British attempt to land troops in Kuwait and possibly Persia. As at Suez, this would bring a resounding warning from Khrushchev about massive rocket retaliation - the cue for the nuclear disarmament rabble to turn out, manipulated by Communists behind their covers of peace groups and peace committees. Pale, bearded, unwashed, they would appear in Trafalgar Square and Whitehall, expertly marshalled and dragooned, almost overwhelming the patient weary police by their numbers. Finally, a worried, enfeebled government would gratefully accept any terms that they could extract from those who had seized the initiative.

'There,' said Simone triumphantly. 'I thought that would surprise you.'

'You thought correctly. Full marks,' replied Love. 'Tell me, what time does all this begin?'

Simone looked at her watch.

'We've lost so many hours flying that I'm not sure,' she said evasively. 'But I'd say it'll be around noon tomorrow, local time, wherever we'll be then.'

The plane droned on above the clouds, above the rain already pitting the heaving, grey Atlantic far beneath them. Love felt very cold, as though the foreknowledge of disaster was already chilling his bones. One of the stewards turned up the heating and then the hot, dry, artificial blast of air grew almost as uncomfortable as the cold had been. He clipped a plastic tray to the arms of Love's chair, and produced one of the pre-cooked, pre-digested meals that taste the same on every airline.

How long since he had last eaten on the flight to Teheran? Only a few days, as one counted time; but all the immeasurable distance between naivety and knowledge as one counted experience. Love ate, not because he was hungry, but because he did not know what lay ahead. His training and common sense told him that it was better to face the unknown on a full stomach.

After the meal the main cabin lights went out, and blue bulbs came on in their place. In the back of the plane, the three men still sat together. A reading lamp threw a warm yellow halo around them. Two were playing cards; the third was reading a magazine. Beyond them, Love noted, was the passengers' washroom.

Simone went into the crew-room, and Simmias came out and sat down across the aisle from Love.

'Can I still go to the lavatory in the back?' Love asked him with deceptive meekness.

Simmias nodded.

'Surely. But don't be too long. We like to have you where we can see you.'

Love pushed the tray to one side, and walked down the aisle into the little cloakroom with its quilted pink and plastic walls, its socket for an electric razor, the tiny white and gold taps in the plastic basin, the pink-tinted mirror. He washed his face and hands thoroughly, bathed his eyes in cold water and opening his shirt, massaged into the bruised muscles of his trunk some of the yellow after-shave lotion from a bottle above the basin. The sharp spiritous liquid stung his flesh; afterwards, he felt better, more toned up.

He looked at his face in the mirror: his eyes were still reasonably clear. He flexed his muscles tentatively. Despite deep pain from his solar plexus if he moved quickly, he felt fitter than he had any right to be after so long driving to patients through Somerset lanes. But his judo had not been wasted: he was basically in good trim. If he ever returned to Bishop's Combe he'd take more care to keep himself in top physical shape. Again the 'if' struck him like a blow. To hell with it. For 'if' read 'when'.

He towelled himself dry, and returned to his seat. He had no means of telling the time, and behind the plastic curtains the night stretched endlessly, bright with stars like pinpricks in the floor of heaven. There was nothing he could do to influence his destiny until the plane came down, and probably not much then. He tilted back his seat, loosened his plimsolls and slept.

It was early morning when he awoke; Simone was shaking his shoulder. She looked tired, as though she had not slept, and her eyes were puffy. Perhaps she wasn't as confident as she had seemed; perhaps a whole lot of unknown things.

'We're coming in to Winnipeg,' she explained. 'We've got permission to land and remain on board, so stay in your seat.'

The three men moved up from the back of the cabin again and sat down opposite Love. The business of the hand in the briefcase was repeated. The plane stopped a little way from the airport building. A health official climbed aboard, glanced around the cabin, nodded pleasantly to them all, and left. He came and went so quickly that even if Love could have overcome the sudden dryness in his mouth at the nearness of possible rescue, he had not time to do so. He sat on in silence, ears strained for the sound of anyone else approaching, but apart from the growl of a diesel engine as a fuel tanker was backed alongside, and some man shouting directions to the driver, above the rattle of hose nozzles, he heard nothing; and no one else entered the plane.

Within an hour they were airborne again, and in the strengthening sunshine Love looked down out of the window at the endless desert of snow beneath them. Land and lakes, merged together, both covered by waves of snow, blown by. the wind, frozen like the enigmatic smile on a dead man's face. The clouds were giant rolls of cotton wool, huge puff-balls pulled between the plane and the earth. Beyond them, millions of acres of fir trees stretched out of sight without a road, a house or any sign of human occupation. They crossed the tree-line - the most northerly point, beyond which it is too cold for any trees to grow - and then the white wastes beneath them raced on to infinity.

To Love, looking through the cabin window, it was impossible to tell where snow ended and sky began. All was a white emptiness that matched the desolation of his mind. The plane climbed speedily and effortlessly, its great jet engines pouring out their long, thin vapour trails, as they soared above the clouds where the sun was bright and the sky blue. Love gathered his energies and thoughts to concentrate on his last hope. Simone sat down beside him and offered him a cigarette. He took the packet clumsily and, his mind apparently elsewhere, dropped it on the floor. As he bent to pick it up he nicked a small piece of the silver foil inside the carton between his thumb and finger.

He kept this concealed while he lit his cigarette from Simone's, apologizing for his carelessness. Then he carefully transferred the tiny triangle of paper to his trousers pocket. In his mind, like a layer of pearl forming around a speck of grit, the tiny glimmering of a plan began to grow.

CHAPTER NINE

Covent Garden; London, March 25th, 12.45 hours (GMT)
Baker Lake, North West Territories, Canada, March 25th, 08.10 hours (local time)

MACGILLIVRAY SAT in his office in Covent Garden marking advertisements for Scottish estates in *Country Life.*

There was a fine one of 2,000 acres outside Coupar Angus, but it wasn't priced. Nine-bedroomed house, usual offices, stabling, garage for four cars - how could he ever afford *four* cars? - lodge and farm buildings. Another, near Callander, with only fifty acres, was advertised at £14,000. So what would the Coupar place fetch?

Ah, what was the good? He was ten years too late for anything worth while. The syndicates, the property men, the used-car millionaires had ruined the market for people like him. But how wonderful to be there, a good 500 miles away from the trouble that now engulfed him.

He lit a cheroot and wished something would happen. Something pleasant, for a change. He'd received an appalling report from the Foreign Office about some ghastly business at Persepolis during the Shah's state visit. Apparently, an Englishman had gone berserk. A shot had been fired - whether by him or not no one seemed quite sure - then he had. drawn a sword arid behaved in a most abominable manner. He'd actually killed one man and then had been spirited away by a helicopter. A delegate to the malaria conference, one Dr Erasmus Plugge, of Goole, had positively identified the Englishman as a

229

Dr Jason Love of Bishop's Combe, Somerset.

Then the DNI had been through to him with news that his operative, Richard Mass Parkington, had been found shot in an hotel bedroom in Teheran. Moreover, a clerk had identified this same Dr Love as visiting him. Fortunately, a cleaner must have opened Parkington's door within minutes of this affray; he was still alive and had been rushed to hospital. There was a faint chance that he might survive, but he was unconscious and could not help them with any details.

Luckily - or unluckily, MacGillivray wasn't quite sure Parkington had sent the message about the racehorses just before he'd been shot, but no one in the Service could make much of it. The Shah was popular, his Government seemed fairly secure. Why should he be assassinated - and by whom? And how would that necessarily endanger the oil treaties?

He'd told the FO, of course, and no doubt they'd passed on the news in a tactful way to the Persian ambassador, or maybe they hadn't, for the Shah had obviously still gone to Persepolis, otherwise this fiasco would never have arisen.

Just how reliable was this fellow Love? Had he gone mad in the heat - or was this his idea of humour?

What about all this? the DNI wanted to know. What about compensation for the Persian who'd been killed at Persepolis? That was the question asked by the ambassador.

Was there any background that the Foreign Minister needed to know in case questions were asked in the House? Was this yet another fatuity, a further boob by British Intelligence? Was Love just a nutcase, a country doctor who couldn't stand a hot climate? Or was he a British agent? Pray let them have answers in writing at the very earliest moment.

Well, what about all this, then? What answers could he give? Sir Robert had been quite right: no good came of using amateurs for this type of work. But how could anyone have imagined, let alone foreseen, what a shambles would erupt from what had seemed, at first sight, a very reasonable scheme? And where was Love now?

MacGillivray had even taken the unprecedented step of telephoning to him direct at the Park Hotel, giving his name as Smith, and saying he was Love's brother-in-law. But the hotel receptionist repeated that he wasn't in his room; he hadn't been seen for some time.

This was not surprising to MacGillivray; but what did he do now? And whose could that helicopter have been? It wasn't a Persian machine, and it wasn't British.

The green telephone buzzed into his reverie. He picked it up. If this was more bad news, he might as well know quickly.

'Interdominion Exports of New York on the line, sir,' said his adjutant. 'Shall I put them through?'

MacGillivray groaned. This was the code-name of the British Intelligence operations headquarters in America. It could only mean that Sir Robert was now involved. At the rate this was going, he'd better give up all thought of a Scottish estate: he'd be looking for a job as a lodge-keeper or gardener: Without references.

'Put them on,' he said in a resigned voice. 'And don't monitor.'

The scrambler buttons clicked; Sir Robert's voice came over the thousands of miles of wire, aggrieved, a little puzzled.

'Doesn't look like that doctor fellow has done us a lot of good, Mac,' he said. 'I told you at the time I didn't like using amateurs.'

'I know, sir. But there didn't seem to be much choice just then.'

'Well, I wish to God you'd made a different choice. I've just seen some of the cables. They've come down on the 'printer from Washington. So far, no Americans are involved, and as far as I can gather, the CIA's got no reason for thinking this character is one of our men - and of course he isn't. But what if he's captured and talks? What then? The poor sod may be in Siberia now. What'd you say to that?'

MacGillivray said nothing to that.

'Well, you got this fellow in, so you'd better get him out. Think up a cover for this man - if he does talk. That he's a drunk or off his head or some damn thing, so that I can disclaim him convincingly, if I have to. I'll be here for another two hours, so ring me direct if need be. Otherwise put your story on the wire. Goodbye to you.'

The telephone went dead; MacGillivray replaced it thoughtfully and pulled *Country Life* to him again. Here was just the place for him: Shepherd's bothy on the Grampian foothills. Very isolated. No electricity, running water or main drainage. Suit thinker or recluse.

Suit me, thought MacGillivray wistfully, and lit another cheroot.

***

The tip of Love's tongue explored his mouth and settled on the back, upper molar from which MacGillivray's dentist had carefully removed a filling and substituted one of his own. The dark grey amalgam in the cavity concealed a minute transistor, smaller than the head of a spent match, smaller than the one Josef had discovered in his false tooth. This could be a key to freedom, or it could simply be another filling, unnecessarily more complicated than the rest. Love did not know which: he would try to discover.

At least, he still had the darn thing. He'd jibbed at what seemed an absurdly childish idea, but MacGillivray had insisted: it was part of his survival kit, as important as the L-pill concealed in his top shirt button, for use if the going became unbearable. They'd be bound to find the first transmitter in his watch, and almost certain to find the-second in his false, tooth. But it was less likely that they'd think of scraping the fillings in his teeth. But what use would the bloody thing be? Love had asked irritably, and MacGillivray had only shrugged.

'Maybe of only psychological value, dear boy,' he'd said vaguely. 'You know, a bit of one-upmanship. Or maybe it could lead us to you - maybe it could even throw some of their electronic gadgets. Ask me another.'

Love looked out of the window at the endless white wool of the clouds billowing below the plane, and asked himself a question. Surely there was just a chance that someone in this white frozen desert of loneliness might

233

see the plane and radio an emergency request for it to land? The chance was slight, but it was the only one he had.

Somewhere beneath the clouds would be tiny, scattered settlements of. Eskimoes and Indians; missions, trading stations, perhaps a small first-aid post where a trained nurse coped with the health of families scattered over an area of ten or twenty thousand square miles.

For generations, the only means of communication between these outlying groups living off the land, fishing and hunting, had been sled and teams of Husky dogs. But now they had their own radios with call-signs in case of distress or emergency. And at night, men would talk on the air to friends, although separated by hundreds of miles of snow. Sometimes, if a patient in one of the nursing stations needed urgent treatment, the sister in charge would ask the radio operator to put out a request for any plane nearby to land and take the patient to hospital.

These little settlements were usually on the banks of some great lake and, during the cold weather, the ice was swept clear of snow each day so that a plane could land and take off again in such an emergency. Love reckoned that a pilot would have to have a fairly strong reason for not landing in response to such a request.

Above the clouds, of course, the Ilyushin would not need to answer such signals simply because it could not be seen from the ground.

But if it came down lower to fly visually - what then? His only hope of bringing the plane down to fly visually lay in his transistorized tooth-filling. If its signals were strong enough to interfere with the Ilyushin's automatic direction-finding equipment, then the pilot might - repeat might - be forced to lose height in order to fly by landmarks and the map, which was how many smaller planes in the area flew all the time.

Love knew that a radio set of, any power could speedily induce such a reaction in the electronics of the plane, which is why no airline allows passengers to use portable radios when in flight - but was his tiny set strong enough?

There was only one solution: to try it and somehow to bring it as close as possible to the electronic gear to give its feeble signals every chance.

He left his seat, walked as casually as possible down the aisle again, and locked himself in the lavatory. Then he pulled from his pocket the tiny triangle of silver paper he had torn from Simone's cigarette packet. He opened his mouth before the mirror, rolled the paper into a pellet and held it over the transistorized filling. He bit hard on it, rubbing the silvery fragment on the dark amalgam a dozen, two dozen times, until it shredded, and he was left with a tiny piece of tissue paper and flecks of silver on his tongue.

He spat them out, and rinsed his mouth into the basin. The friction had produced the tiny electrical impulse needed to activate the transmitter. With a toothpick from a glass jar on the shelf above the basin he scratched away the shallow filling and loosened the transistor. It felt like a hard grain of rice against his gum.

His tongue tingled as though it had touched two terminals of a torch battery, as he used to do at school

235

to see whether the battery still contained any 'juice'. This meant that the transistor was working. But he was certain that its signals would not be strong enough to penetrate the metal bulkhead between the cabin and the pilot's compartment. So now for the difficult part. He had somehow to smuggle it up front.

He returned to his seat and picked up his half-finished beaker of coffee. He sipped it, made a face at its coldness and spat out some of the skin from the coffee into the beaker; and with the skin went the tiny transistor.

'Foul,' he said. 'Ugh. Excuse my manners. A legacy of the Army and a scientific education. But I do hate skin on coffee.'

He handed the beaker to Simone. Dear God, he prayed, let her carry it into the crew-room with her and not leave it here. She put out her hand and took it.

'I'll go and see,' she said. ·

'Can I come?' He wanted to make sure that the beaker was not dumped somewhere on the way.

'No. You stay here.'

'Well, let me at least open the door for you.'

She looked at him for a moment, surprised at his sudden politeness, but his face was a mask of charm; she could read nothing in his eyes but a willingness to help, simple and almost naive. The three men in the rear of the plane watched him follow her to the door. For a moment, Josef stood up, a frown on his face, wondering what Love was doing; but Simone shook her head in answer to the question on his face. The Englishman was harmless. Josef sat down again. He expected no trouble; also, the man had no weapons.

Josef relaxed.

Love opened the door for Simone, bent down, wincing at the pain in his bruised muscles, and slipped the catch at the base to hold it open.

'Perhaps I could have a new cup? Save you washing that one.'

Simone nodded, despising his attentions as a sign of weakness.

'I'll see,' she said. Obviously, he hoped that such courtesy would make things easier for him. Christ, how feeble and sycophantic and cringing could a man become and still stay a man? But after the pathetic way he'd behaved in Rome, he wasn't a man at all; not even a mouse, but a neuter.

Five minutes went by. What the devil was she doing? Grinding the beans herself? Had she rinsed out the beaker and found the transistor? Then Simone came back and handed him a new beaker of coffee. Through the open doorway he could see the backs of the pilot and co-pilot. The transistor must be in there, for the good reason that in a pressurized aircraft she could not have thrown it away.

There was nothing he could do now but hope and pray; and if the BBC could transmit 'Panorama' by way of a transistor pill in Richard Dimbleby's stomach - as they had then surely his set would work in half an inch of cold coffee? Another minute passed. Two. Three. Love sipped his coffee with apparent gratitude, wondering what had happened to the other beaker and the transistor it contained. Suddenly, without warning, he had his answer. The floor of the Ilyushin tilted almost imperceptibly away from him, and then the angle increased sharply. They were going down.

Simmias came through the door, an unlit cigarette between his lips.

He didn't feel happy about all this. It was bad enough that the Shah was still alive; this meant that they would have to pin everything on killing the Sheikh of Kuwait. The plan would still, work, of course, for they had discounted misadventures in their timetable; but this left them with only one chance. And how many more changes could their plan stand? Worse, how many changes could he afford?

To have failed once was regrettable, although he could talk his way out of that. After all, his seniority and his record were excellent advocates. But what would his superiors say - or worse, what would they do - when they learned the plane was coming down over alien soil without their knowledge or permission? This was something no one had anticipated or imagined. Yet what else could he do?

He needed a shave and his suit looked unpressed. For the first time, Love thought, he seemed a bit ragged round the edges, not quite so assured, so urbane.

'What's wrong?' Love asked.

Simmias shrugged. Tiny pinpricks of anxiety flickered in his eyes and were just as swiftly masked.

'Nothing,' he said shortly.

'Then why are we going down? Are we landing?'

'Don't be a bloody fool. We're going to fly lower for a while.'

'Why? If nothing's wrong?'

'Shut up with your questions or I'll get Josef to deal with you again.'

So. The tiny transistor must be working. Love could imagine the turmoil in the delicate instruments before the captain's surprised eyes. The trembling needles, the white pointers spinning on their hidden hairsprings, the confusion behind the ebonite control panels as the incomprehensible signals poured in, feeding- the direction-finding equipment until its complex electronic brain suddenly became fuddled, bemused, unable to cope, and threw them all back. Messages received but not understood.

***

The telephone purred in the little wooden Mountie Station that stood up to its eaves in snow on the edge of the frozen Baker Lake. In Baker Lake, all the telephones are interconnected. Each organization: the Anglican and Roman Catholic Missions, the Department of Northern Affairs, the Royal Canadian Mounted Police, and so on, have their own codes of short and long rings. Thus, whenever a telephone bell tinkles, everyone listens automatically in case the call is for them. This has one great advantage; as long as the person wanted is in a building with a telephone, he can be reached.

The Mountie took the receiver from its-hook on the wall, 'Hello, yes,' he said, lighting a cigarette. 'Corporal Douglas here.'

'Aeradio here, Phil,' said the voice in his ear. 'Bill Dodds speaking. You asked about that Russian plane. Well, we've just had word that it's starting to lose height. One of the long-range radars over at Goose Bay is tracking it. If it comes down through the clouds, d'you want me to put out that emergency call?'

'Yeh, Bill. Do just that. I'll get down there on the lake with Jack and Tony all wrapped up and the nurse to give it a bit of colour. Let's know when you've made the call. And what their reply is.'

'Roger,' said the radio operator.

He replaced the telephone, threw two switches, and when the blue light began to wink on his desk, he began to speak into the microphone, reading from the note the Mountie had given him half an hour earlier.

Back in his hut, Phil Douglas, the Mountie Corporal, picked up for the twentieth time the sheet of paper on which he had transcribed the laconic code message from the headquarters of the RCMP in Ottawa.

> 'RUSSIAN ILYUSHIN JET LINER ZKB 77521 OVERFLYING NORTH WEST TERRITORIES EAST WEST DURING DAY STOP SHOULD PLANE BEHAVE IN ANY REPEAT ANY WAY UNUSUAL EXAMPLE LOW FLYING CIRCLING OR OFFCOURSE FLYING ENDEAVOUR BRING DOWN PLANE PEACEABLY STOP SUGGEST RADIO THEM CLAIMING MEDICAL EMERGENCY STOP BOARD PLANE FRIENDLY WAY EXAMINE INTERIOR AND PASSENGERS CLOSEST STOP IF ANYTHING REPEAT ANYTHING SUSPICIOUS ADVISE URGENTEST MEANWHILE HOLDING PLANE ON ANY CONVINCING PRETEXT STOP UNDER NO REPEAT NO CIRCUMSTANCES BECOME INVOLVED

VIOLENCE STOP REPORT NEGATIVE
OR POSITIVE FINDINGS URGENTEST
HEADQUARTERS OTTAWA ENDIT'

Well, that was clear enough. He smoothed out the sheet of paper, and placed it under an Eskimo soapstone carving on his desk. It might be needed as evidence for his actions if anything went wrong, although he'd done his best to make them go right.

He'd written out a message for the radio operator to send. He'd even persuaded two other Mounties who were spending a few days with him from Churchill to be ready to lie on stretchers, wrapped up in rugs, as casualties. The plane could turn back and drop them off back at Churchill before flying on again. It wouldn't take long at the speed that thing could make.

If they did so, he'd radio Churchill airport and tell them to expect the plane on an unscheduled stop. The trip should give them a chance to see if anything odd was going on aboard the plane, so long as they kept their traps shut. But he hoped they wouldn't be kept away for too long. He was getting married on Monday, and Jack was going to be his best man.'

Douglas went into the kitchen; his two friends, tough, broad-shouldered, clear-eyed, with fair hair cropped close to their heads, were sitting at the scrubbed table brewing coffee, listening to the radio.

'The Russkie plane's comin' in,' said Douglas. 'Come'n get wrapped up on the stretchers. You've gotta act sick.'

'With the head I've got, I don't have to act sick - I

241

am sick,' retorted Tony.

'Come on, you old Eskimo bastard. You're the unlikeliest sick Eskimo since Christ was a carpenter.'

'You don't look so good yourself.'

'You'll be all right,' Douglas told them. 'The nurse is in on this, and we're putting bandages all round your faces. You'll just have room to see out, but they won't be able to tell who you are. Hell, its only for an hour. The plane'll be back in Churchill again in less'n that time. You can be back here this afternoon on the next Transair.'

'So I should hope. We're meant to be on leave.'

'Oh, quit all this bitching. The plane'll be down at this rate before you're even out there.'

***

Through the wedged-open door, Love watched the captain and his co-pilot at their controls, earphones on their heads, the green and red and blue warning lights glittering on the black dashboards. The radio operator had switched the radio over to the loudspeakers, and through the crackle of static and Morse, the rise and fall of call signs and coded messages, he heard a Canadian voice in clear: 'Calling all airplanes radius five zero miles Baker Lake. Please reply on this wavelength. Are you receiving? Are you receiving? Over to you. Over.'

And then, silence. Love listened, gripping the arms of his seat until his knuckles went white. The voice spoke again in a rush of atmospherics.

'This is Baker Lake Aeradio Department of Transport. Department of Transport Baker Lake

Aeradio calling. We have two urgent stretcher cases. Two urgent stretcher cases here for Churchill hospital. Two Eskimoes with facial and spinal injuries. Two serious cases here.

'Will any airplane receiving this message please land on the lake? I will repeat. Will any airplane receiving this message please land on the lake?

'Wind fresh, north, north-east. North, north-east, freshening. Runway marked with red and yellow drums. Red and yellow drums mark runway. This is urgent. I will repeat. This is urgent. Come in now on this wavelength. Over to you. Over.'

Love imagined the Eskimoes in their caribou parkas, upper lips slimy with catarrh - because to blow their noses in the ferocious cold only aggravated the flow of mucus - lying patiently, while the radio operator from Baker Lake, wherever that might be, flung his optimistic appeal for help to the empty, unreplying sky.

He cleared his throat.

'What's all that mean?' he asked Simmias, as if he didn't already know.

'Damn all,' retorted Simmias irritably. 'Don't ask so many questions.'

Simone went up front to see the pilot.

'The pilot says we've got to go down,' she explained to Simmias on her return, and again the spark of fear showed in his eyes, reflecting a flicker of anxiety in hers.

'Why?'

'It's the custom, so he says. Any plane who picks up an emergency call of this sort up here has to put down. If we don't, they'll think it odd. And the last thing we want is to draw attention to ourselves.'

'How the hell can they see us? I thought we were still above the clouds? It's so white down below you can't tell what's cloud and what's snow.'

'Something's gone wrong with the instruments. Only a little temporary thing, the pilot says, but he can't get a proper bearing. He dropped down to fly visually for a spell while the others checked the instruments. Then this call came in.'

Simmias looked out of the window at the white emptiness beneath him. He liked neither the sight nor the sound of all this; on every side, far farther than he could see, the white smoothness of the snow extended in an eternity of silence.

A warning bell began to ring in his brain: there was something odd, off-key, false about all this. He couldn't say exactly why it was, yet he felt he had been through it all before, years ago. Then he remembered: he had felt like this when, as a boy in his teens, he had arrived with his parents in Kem, and the camp commandant had lectured the new arrivals on the wonderful chance they would have to-redeem themselves through their labours. He hadn't liked it then, and he liked his present situation less.

'Not to worry. We've plenty of time,' Simone assured him. 'We've hours yet before we're to do anything. Far better to come down for twenty minutes or so on the ice, pick up these characters and take off again, and that's the end of the matter. *Finite*. If we don't, we've still got to hang about in the sky till zero hour. We'd only call attention to ourselves - for we've no possible excuse for not landing.'

'I suppose you're right,' said Simmias without

conviction. 'But I don't like it, all the same.'

He turned to Love.

'We're coming down on the ice to pick up two Eskimoes, as you probably heard. Some locals may come aboard with the stretchers. As I'm a doctor, I suppose I'll have to have a word with them. We'll put you in the back of the plane. Josef will sit behind you, so don't get any ideas about escaping.'

Love allowed himself a wintry smile to conceal his inner feelings of hope. He was half way home now; pray God he could make the full distance.

The smile annoyed Simmias. It seemed a comment on his own sudden feeling of unease and insecurity. He brought the back of his hand across Love's face; a thin trickle of blood began to ooze from his nose.

'Take it easy,' said Simone irritably. 'Why make a scene? We don't want these people to think anything's wrong. Now he'll have to stop the bleeding. Relax.'

This was the moment, the unconscious cue, for which Love had waited. Without a glance at Simmias, he walked slowly up the gangway to the lavatory, his handkerchief held to his nose. Inside, he bolted the door, dipped his face into a bowl of cold water, wiped away the blood, disregarding the urgently flashing sign in English and Russian above the basin: 'Return to your seat at once,' as the plane banked for its final circle above the frozen lake, beforc landing. He stayed where he was until Simmias began to beat on the door outside, shouting: 'Come out, or I'll smash the lock!'

'You really don't give me much option, do you?'

asked Love mildly, slipping the bolt. Through the windows across the aisle he could see two parallel rows of oil drums painted with red and yellow stripes, marking the runway in the snow. Behind them, on a slight slope, a cluster of hutments stood up to their roofs in drifts. Half a dozen radio pylons were grouped around the radio station; a red windsock fluttered at a masthead. Two vehicles with half-tracks at the rear and skis in front, one yellow, one dark green, and a crowd of about fifty Eskimoes and Indians, wearing fur parkas and boots, waited on the edge of the runway.

Bump. The plane came down and up again. A spray of soft snow fluttered from their double wheels.

'Now, listen,' said Simmias, urgently, gripping Love by the arm. 'As I said, Josef is behind you. He's got a pistol at your neck. It's silenced, and if you shout, he shoots, and to hell with what happens. We'll say you went mad and had to be restrained or something. So for the last time - don't get ideas. Now sit here.'

He pushed Love down roughly into a seat. Love glanced behind him at Josef's impassive Slavonic face. He didn't like what he saw. Josef stabbed the muzzle of the Lüger into the base of Love's skull as the Ilyushin bumped again on the ice, a flurry of snow fled past the windows, and they were down.

The pilot ran up his engines as he turned the plane and then cut them one by one. A steward opened the door and lowered an aluminium ladder over the white ice. The sudden, unexpected cold made Love gasp for breath in his thin tropical suit. The almost unbelievable chill of minus seventy degrees Fahrenheit made him feel his joints were being taken apart and hammered together. His bruises ached like fresh, raw wounds; the moisture in his nostrils turned to ice, and his eyes pricked as though polished with sand.

He had a sudden sight through the oval doorway of smooth impassive Eskimo faces framed in fur, like a scene from a children's calendar put out by the Society for the Propagation of the Gospel in Foreign Parts. Then Simmias and Simone appeared from the pilot's compartment. They also were feeling the cold, and their breath hung like fog in the freezing air.

'I'm a doctor,' Simmias announced in English to the crowd at large. 'Who's in charge? Where are the casualties?'

'They're right here, Doc,' called a man in a fur-lined parka with the flaps of his fur hat pulled over his ears. 'Let me come aboard and I'll explain.'

'Come up, then.'

As the man began to climb the aluminium ladder into the plane, Love saw he was a Mountie; he recognized the dark blue trousers with the familiar thin red stripe down the seam. With him came a girl in fur boots and a red parka trimmed in white fox fur. She carried a khaki webbing bag, with a red cross on a white circle on one side; obviously she was the local nurse. They came through the oval doorway, bowing their heads to miss the roof. I'll count ten, Love told himself, and then I'll act.

The Mountie and the nurse walked up the aisle towards the open crew-room door. He was a big, broad-shouldered man with a revolver in a leather holster at his belt. Love saw that the holster was unbuttoned. *One. Two.*

'Reckon we can strap 'em on this side, Anna.

There's one stretcher here already,' the Mountie said, pointing to the stretcher where Love had been tied. 'Mebbe we can use it - unless it's being used?'

Three,

Simmias shook his head.

Four.

'One of our fellows got a touch of the sun in Persia and he slept there for a while. He's fine now, though.

'I'll take a look at the two casualties you've got outside,' he went on. 'You've got their case histories, I take it, sister? And where we're to drop them off? We haven't a scheduled stop on our flight, so I hope you've fixed all this?'

'Surely,' said the nurse, following him down the aisle towards the door. 'I've put all the details of their accident, blood groups, their names and so on in envelopes I've tied to their wrists. They were playing football on the ice and they collided and fell. It often happens here, and the ice is so hard. Their noses are smashed, too. That's why we've bandaged them so heavily.'

Five. Six.

Simmias and Simone climbed down the ladder into the ' snow.

Seven. 'Big fellows for Eskimoes,' said Simmias thoughtfully, looking at the two men on the stretchers, wrapped in caribou skins, red Army blankets and rugs. The Mountie walked down the aisle towards Love and Josef in the rear seats. He patted one of the wooden crates easily with his hands as he passed it.

Eight.

'Hi,' he said, nodding towards Love pleasantly.

Nine.

Love nodded slightly. Josef held the gun pressed hard into his neck.

Ten.

'Hi!' shouted Love - and dropped forward into his seat, head on his knees.

For a second, Josef's Lüger pointed uselessly down the aisle towards the Mountie. Josef dared not fire with him so close, and in the split second of Love's unexpected movement, he could not hide the gun.

'Hey, what the hell?' Corporal Douglas began, as he saw its blue-black barrel resting on the back of the seat, and Josef's impassive Slavonic face. His hand dropped for his 45.

Love whipped back his left arm in a scything blow that caught Josef down the side of his face, between the ear and the jawbone. Josef tried to roll the punch, but Love brought down the edge of his hand on his right wrist. The Lüger clattered uselessly to the floor.

'Have you guys gone mad?' shouted the Mountie. His Colt was now in his hand.

'Hold him!' shouted Love. 'He's a spy!'

The Mountie lumbered down the aisle, not sure whether to believe Love or not. But at least he spoke English. That was something. And how right headquarters had been to ask for this plane to be brought down! But how the hell could he help this English guy without using violence?

Love and Josef wrestled furiously, first to one side and then to the other. Josef's muscles were like coiled steel. He was in perfect physical condition and not even out of breath, although a slight trickle of dark blood stained the left corner of his mouth, where Love's blow had smashed a tooth. His hands grew up

like the knotted roots of trees to grip Love's throat.
Love was tired, in pain, but he was fighting for his life.
If this chance failed, he would not have another. If
Josef beat him, Simmias would simply explain away
the incident by telling the Mountie that he was off his
head, a violent lunatic; the effect of the Persian sun;
no doubt.

Josef's fingers tightened round his neck. The
deepening red mist of defeat began to fill his eyes, his
mind, as blood hammered in his ears, and his lungs
sobbed for air. He was dimly aware of the Mountie
shouting something behind him, but he could not hear
anything above the roar of blood in his ears, as he
arched his body and, clasping his hands together,
brought up his wrists between Josef's forearms. Then,
with both arms, he struck outwards and upwards.

The old judo move took Josef for a second by
surprise; he had not thought his opponent had the
strength for such a blow. In that second, Love could
breathe; and with breath came action.

A quick left-scythe with the edge of his hand to
Josef's throat and, as he doubled up, two hard hooks:
a left and a right to his solar plexus. He fell forward
and Love brought up his knee. Josef dropped like a
sack of shale.

'Put the clips on him,' Love gasped to the Mountie.

'Christ,' said Douglas with feeling, although he was
not a notably religious man.

As he spoke, the pilot, who had seen all this with
mounting horror through the open door of the crew-
room, started his engines. Gouts of black smoke and
orange flame poured from the jet nacelles. The
Eskimoes and Indians near the open door scattered

with cries of alarm. Some of them dragged the stretchers to one side as the thick oily flames seared the snow.

Then the plane turned and Love could see nothing but an expanse of snow broken by small hillocks: the Eskimo igloos. The Ilyushin began to amble slowly across the lake, still with its door open and the ladder sticking out over the snow like a pointing silver finger.

'Jump!' Love roared to the Mountie. He picked up the dead weight of Josef and threw him out into the snow. The man collapsed on his shoulders and rolled over and did not move. Douglas jumped after him, gun still in his hand, and Love followed, landing on all fours in the hard, trodden snow.

The plane began to gather speed, the door flapping to and fro like a bird's broken wing. A steward threw the aluminium ladder out after them and banged shut the door. As the jets turned, snow blew in their faces, stealing their breath.

'Listen,' Love shouted to the Mountie against the spiralling scream of the engines. 'It may sound bloody crazy to you, but get me to a radio, where I can put out a call to stop that plane. Don't ask why. Just help me.'

'What's going on?' asked Douglas, his homely brown face creased with perplexity. This was entirely outside his daily routine of following an Eskimo family 'on the land', when they set off to hunt caribou, and carelessly left one of their children behind in their igloo; or settling a dispute over the ownership of a husky or a cache of caribou skins. But it was also a whole lot more exciting. This sort of experience made the routine bearable. The shriek of the Ilyushin's jets grew to a frenzy. Clouds of snow streamed out behind the plane as the pilot turned her farther into the wind.

'All right,' Douglas shouted. 'Follow me.'

He ran to the yellow half-tracked Muskeg that stood waiting, its engine puttering, and jumped inside. Love climbed up beside him and slammed the door. The Mountie swung to the right up through the snow towards the radio pylons.

'My name's Douglas,' he shouted above the roar of the engine. 'Corporal Phil Douglas.'

'Pleased to know you, Corporal,' replied Love. 'I'm a doctor - Dr Jason Love. The story's too complicated to tell you here. Just get me to some radio where I can send out a message. I'll tell you all about it afterwards.'

'We had orders to intercept that plane if we could without a great commotion,' shouted Douglas. 'I didn't know why, and I still don't; but we certainly had some commotion!'

He stopped the Muskeg near a gaping hole in the snow.

'Follow me,' he commanded.

They jumped out together and Douglas led him down steps cut into the packed drift, through a burrow in the snowdrift thirty feet high, to a round aluminium tunnel dug still deeper beneath the snow. At the end, near a wooden barrel containing a brush of twigs to wipe snow from visitor's boots, a door opened into a mess hall with long tables and chairs. Behind a stainless-steel counter two Indian women stirred huge cauldrons of porridge and cocoa on a long electric stove.

Douglas and Love ran through this hall, past a

storehouse packed with shelves of shiny, polished apples, cans of food the size of oil drums, through a swing door and into another corridor. This was in a building buried to its chimneys in snow, and so cold that the nuts and bolts holding the aluminium framework together had grown long beards of ice inside the walls. Ice also glittered like black glass where doors had been opened. The cold was a physical pain in their marrow, in their blood; even to breathe was an effort.

They ran lip a wooden ramp, through two more swing doors and into the Aeradio room. This was a warm contrast, with a plastic-topped counter where people brought their telegrams. On the far wall hung a huge map with coloured pins marking other radio stations. Standing against the other three walls were grey metal cabinets six feet high, full of radio equipment. At a table with a Morse key, surrounded by dials and switches and lights, sat the man in charge, Bill Dodds, the duty operator, who had sent out the emergency call that had brought down the Ilyushin.

'Hi, Phil,' he said easily. 'See we got the plane down OK. Now what's the rush?'

'Feller here has an urgent message to send,' replied Douglas breathlessly. 'That Russkie plane has tooken off again in a hell of a hurry. Didn't even take the patients. Guy in there holding a gun.'

'So we're in business,' said the operator, looking at Love. 'What can we do for you?'

'Two things,' said Love. 'First, I want a general call put out to stop that plane by any means short of war. Next, I want to send a cable. I've no money and no passport but you can take my word that it's official. And it's absolutely vital.'

'That OK by you, Phil?'

'Sure. He seems genuine enough. Says he's a doctor.'

'What you wanna say, Doc?'

'You do shorthand?'

'Surely. Hundred a minute.'

'Right. Here are the messages. First. A general alarm call to all Royal Canadian Air Force Stations. Bring down and detain Russian Aeroflot Ilyushin airliner flying west from Baker Lake towards Alaska. Number ZKB 77521. This aircraft has permission to overfly Canada and America, but imperative to hold it on any pretext with all aboard pending further instructions.'

Love paused.

'That all?' asked Dodds laconically. 'Don't want no general mobilization or call-up yet?'

'Not right now.'

'Well, that's sump'n, for sure. How should I sign it?'

What could he sign it? Love held no rank, no authority, nothing to back up a message that could conceivably result in the rupture of diplomatic relations between Russia and Canada. He said: 'Sign it: Jason Love, care MacGillivray, Sensoby & Ransom, Covent Garden, London, England.'

Perhaps someone would know what that meant; he wasn't sure whether he did himself any more. All he wanted was sleep and a bath, and time to forget this nightmare come to life.

'Well, I hope you know what you're about,' said the Mountie with some awe. 'I'll reckon you'll be singing alto in the choir if this isn't genuine.'

'Yeah,' said Dodds soberly. 'Padre tells me Anglican Mission could use three altos in our choir now. Hope they won't be us. Well, what's the second message, Doc? Wanna make it to Khrushchev this time?'

Love felt in his pocket for the Diners' Club card, forgetting for the moment that it was left locked in his luggage in the Park Hotel. Hell, he'd have to send the message to MacGillivray in clear. What did it matter who read it now? Maybe MacGillivray would have to move his office more speedily than he had anticipated, but that was not his concern.

'Send it to MacGillivray, Sensoby & Ransom - you've got the address - from Dr Love.

'One, Simone acting both sides. Two, attempt outrub Shah already reported to you but foiled to be followed similar attempt Kuwait Sheikh within hours, then denunciation of oil treaties. Suggest extract digit; forewarned, forearmed, etc. Three, am currently care Aeradio Baker Lake, North West Territory, Canada, having jumped ex-captivity Moscow bound Aeroflot Ilyushin, number ZKB 77521, thanks your transistors. Four, have sent out radio call to RCAF to detain this plane pending further orders. Five, please explain soonest how I can contact Canadian representatives. Six, without passport, money, authority. Would be grateful early remedy these lacks. Otherwise fit, well. Very cold here. Balls now in your court.'

'Is there an apostrophe in ball's? or shall I put it "Ball is"?' asked Dodds, seriously.

'Put it as I say it. Balls,' Love told him: that was how he felt about the whole affair; no doubt MacGillivray would get the message.

'What shall I sign it?' asked Dodds.

'Love. He can take it any way he likes.'

The man's hand flew to the red plastic handle of the Morse key. Love crossed the room and looked out of the window, its edges thickly encrusted with frozen snow, past the radio masts and the wide web of wires from which his messages were now flying, across the frozen lake to the scattered oil drums that marked the landing place.

The Eskimoes and Indians still stood waiting hopefully in a rather abject but colourful crowd behind the stretchers. They had nothing more pressing to do, nowhere else to go; the excitement of a plane landing and taking off again so soon brought a spark of novelty and colour to an existence as monotonous as the landscape, and they were reluctant to disperse in case it should return.

Josef had been put on a stretcher and a group of men were carrying him slowly in the direction of the nursing station. Behind them, on the lake shore, a motor launch, usable only in the summer, lay on its side, half covered with snow and ice. To the right, he could see the nursing station, a small oblong shack, and the meteorological station, a big round building like an oil tank, painted with red and white squares. A tractor was pulling a huge roller over the churned snow after the Ilyushin's arrival and departure to prepare the surface in case it should return or another plane should call. Life went on; life had to go on.

At that moment the telephone rang, in a series of long and short tinkles.

'For you,' the operator said, looking at Douglas.

Douglas picked up the telephone and listened, his face darkening with worry; then he replaced it on the stand.

'What's wrong?'

'That feller who said he was a Russkie doctor and the girl have escaped in the Bombardier.'

"What's the Bombardier?' asked Love.

'I forgot. You don't know. It's a half-track. Bigger than the Muskeg. Green job. It was out there on the lake near the plane. We'd carried the casualties out in it.'

'Where could they go from here?' asked Love.

'Nearest place of any size is Churchill, five hundred miles off. But they'd never make it without a guide. Anyway, they'd never make it, period. They've only gas for about one hundred miles, for one thing and, for another, the exhaust gasket's blown. You can only run the motor for a few minutes without almost gassing yourself. It was going into Workshops today.'

'That doctor,' said Love grimly. 'I've got to find him. Could your Muskeg catch the Bombardier?'

'Nope,' said Douglas. 'But I've got a pretty good Eskimo hunter, name of Tamutnik, with his team of dogs. He'd follow their trail easily enough once they leave the Bombardier and take to the snow. As they'll have to, when the gas runs out or when the smell gets too strong.'

'Can you lend me some warm clothes, Douglas? I'd like to go out with your man.'

The two Canadians looked at him, and then at each other.

'You seem to be taking a lot on yourself, Doc,' said Douglas slowly. 'But, well, I don't see why you shouldn't go. After all, you're the most closely involved. I'll have to go, as that Bombardier's

Canadian Government property. You could tag on with me, easy enough. I'll fix you up with a parka and some boots and glasses.'

He grinned at the prospect of a trek, a fight, a capture. Hell, they'd almost surely make him sergeant after this.

***

The telephone rang as MacGillivray came into his office from a quick lunch in 'The Nag's Head'. He debated whether to answer it or pretend he was still out: it could only mean bad news. Then he told himself not to be such a bloody pessimist and picked up the receiver.

His adjutant spoke with excitement in his voice.

'Top priority just come in from Canada, sir,' he said. 'In clear.' He began to read Love's message.

MacGillivray sat down, still in his overcoat, his hat pushed to the back of his head, and scribbled out the message.

'Right,' he said when the adjutant had finished reading. 'Advise the Foreign Office and the DNI. Then get me an Absolute Priority call to Sir Robert at Interdominion Exports. He'll still be at their New York number.'

'Very good, sir. What do you think Sir Robert will say?'

'I'll tell you exactly what he'll say. He'll say it just shows how right we were to take his advice and use an amateur.'

'Oh, *no*, sir. Not after all he's said about that already.'

'Oh, *yes*, sir. That's how he became Sir Robert. Now take this message for Dr Love.'

***

Love stood outside the Mountie's hut in the borrowed Eskimo boots, wearing a caribou skin vest with the hair towards his flesh, and on top of this a caribou skin parka with the hair outside. Thick mittens encased his hands, and his belt was plugged with thirty rounds for the Colt 45 which had been specially treated to prevent the action freezing. He felt warm, but a bit light-headed with the cold air, the reaction, the unbelievability of it all.

Phil Douglas and Tamutnik adjusted the leather lead reins and harnesses on the team of huskies; then they set off, walking slowly, heads bent forward against the wind that blew out of the emptiness, robbing them of their breath, burning their eyes, prickling the inside of their nostrils like wire.

The twin 'tracks of the Bombardier were easy to follow, and soon Love grew accustomed to the blinding whiteness of snow and sky, grateful for Douglas's pair of dark glasses. Although, at first, the caribou skin tickled him and made him want to sneeze, he even grew used to this, and soon its warmth made sweat trickle down his back between his shoulder blades.

From the air the snow had appeared flat, like a desert, but on the ground it rolled on endlessly in hills and dunes and valleys. And, although the parallel tracks were clear, without Tamutnik Love would have slipped on a dozen occasions into drifts as deep as a house, as soft as spun silk, from which he could not have extracted himself on his own.

They toiled to the top of one of the dunes, and there beneath them in the hollow, half dug into the snow, stood the green Bombardier. One of its tracks had snapped and lay spread out uselessly, like a shining metal serpent. Douglas unslung his Lee-Enfield from his shoulder and cocked it. The driver's door swung open, banging in the wind against the body with a lonely, echoing metallic sound. The three men walked on towards the vehicle, the dogs growling and snapping suspiciously.

'Woman driver,' said Douglas laconically, nodding towards die severed track. 'Takes time to learn how to handle these things in snow.'

'How far d'you think they'll have gone?' asked Love.

'No distance at all. Look inside.'

Love crunched his way through the crisp crush of snow and peered inside the metal cab. Simmias lay back in his seat as though asleep. The skin on his face was blue. A little saliva had frozen on his chin; it glittered like glass. Simone had fallen across the steering wheel. Love touched her arm, but her body was as stiff as a board. They were both dead.

'Gassed, I reckon,' said Douglas laconically. 'I told you there was a bum gasket on the motor. They must've had a struggle to get as far as this. I suppose they kept opening the door to let some fresh air in. But they didn't have much of a chance really, did they? It was three to one against survival, let alone escape. The shortage of gas, the cold, the leaking exhaust. Well, that's life, Doc'

'And death.'

'Surely. And death. Reckon we'd better get these

stiffs back to Baker. Then we can send out some fitters to fix up this track and bring it back too.'

'Must we take them now?'

'Best to. Otherwise the wolves may pay a call.'

'I see.'

Love suddenly felt immeasurably old, immeasurably weary. A chain reaction against intense heat and cold, against violence and death and danger swept over him. He sat down shakily on the edge of the wooden sled, ignoring the snapping, slavering jaws of the huskies. Douglas uncorked a hip flask.

'Have a shot,' he said sympathetically. 'You'll feel better then.'

Love gulped down the rye gratefully and it ran like fire in his veins. But although it warmed him, the spirit could not remove his deathly feeling of distaste and horror, as though his soul was in cold storage, beyond all warmth of human contact. He stood up, shaking his head to try and drive away the nausea that engulfed him, as Tamutnik and Douglas pulled the bodies out of the cab and tied them firmly, with ropes on the sled, under a red blanket. Then they set off in silence towards Baker Lake. As they approached, they saw the little crowd of people still down on the frozen surface, now playing football. Against the vastness of the sky that loomed with white immensity, they looked like toy puppets pulled by hidden strings. And that is just what they are, thought Love wearily; just what we all are. Most of us don't even know who pulls the strings. But all of us dance.

The words of Henry V's speech before Agincourt came back like an echo in his mind: 'He which hath no stomach to this fight, let him depart; his passport

261

shall be made.' But who made out the passport for an unsuccessful spy? And to what undiscovered country was it valid? They measured out their strange lives in make-believe and falsehood. And finally, as with K and Simmias and Simone, as with the fat man behind the old Packard in Teheran, they left the stage abruptly to voyage out, unsorrowed and unknown, on passports to oblivion.

'Lucky you radioed for that emergency,' he said to Douglas, making conversation to break his train of thought.

'Lucky my arse,' retorted Douglas inelegantly. 'I'd got orders from headquarters in Ottawa to bring the plane down if it seemed to be behaving oddly. So when it came down under the clouds we sent off that message. They even suggested what I should say.'

'Oh. I didn't know that.'

But why should he have known? There was so much he hadn't known, hadn't imagined. He'd gone out to Teheran convinced of his superiority over these ludicrous professionals, confident that he could solve the mystery of K's disappearance within days, if not hours. But, in fact, instead of leading, he had been led; he had not taken the initiative but had followed it; even the transistors had been MacGillivray's idea.

Events had carried him on their tide; he had not influenced them at all. His only value had been as a kind of human catalyst, necessary to start the chain reaction that would make his opponents take one course or another, but at least show their hand.

All MacGillivray had needed was someone to go to Teheran - anyone new, inexperienced and unknown to the other side, to make them take some action. And when they had risen to this bait, Love's work had already been done. The humiliating thing was that it seemed to him that anyone else could have produced the same results - perhaps far more quickly and cheaply and less lethally. There was so much he didn't know and would never know; perhaps it was better that way.

They walked on in silence, heads down against the wind that blew across the aching emptiness of cold.

Back in the little RCMP hut, Douglas showed him a message that had just arrived. Two RCAF fighters, on a routine patrol over Eskimo Point, had buzzed the Ilyushin and forced it to land. No shots had been fired, no papers burned.

The crew were being detained in the local Mountie Station, on a technical charge of flying too low, while the contents of the plane were being discreetly examined.

A message also awaited Love from MacGillivray.

'THANKS YOURS WHICH HAVE ACTED UPON STOP SORRY TO HEAR LOVE IN COLD CLIMATE BUT WILL ARRANGE WARMER WORKING CONDITIONS NEXT TIME STOP CORD AWAITS YOU AT LONDON AIRPORT STOP ALL OTHER NEWS WILL KEEP ON ICE TILL THEN STOP THANKS MACGRLLIVRAY'

There were also instructions, addressed to Corporal Douglas, for his return. Tomorrow, if the weather held, a Transair DC4 was due in on a routine trip. The Aeradio operator reported that there were a couple of vacant seats in it; Love could have one of them.

He would spend that night in the Mounties' Station where Douglas had a spare bunk, and he should be in Ottawa on the following day. Then, allowing for time changes, he would be back in England within another twelve hours. He had moved so far, so fast, that he still felt he had not quite caught up with himself. Like the Red Queen in *Through the Looking-Glass*, he had had to run very hard simply to stay where he was - alive. Or, as Hippocrates had put it, more philosophically, 'The life so short, the craft so long to learn.'

And in the last analysis, what did one learn? Simply that the more you learned, the more you realized how little you would ever know.

He walked to the window and looked out. The hour was late, but Baker Lake lies so far north that for much of the year there is no real night; and on this March evening the moon hung like a huge veiled light in the pale sky. In the distance, tireless Eskimoes still played football on the ice. Beyond them, four men with a string of dogs and a sled were off 'on the land' to hunt for caribou, the animal that provided them with food and clothing. From where Love stood, they all looked like tiny toy puppets, as the figures on the lake had looked in the afternoon. But each was his own man, with his own hopes and plans and dreams. It was something that they could still play and hunt; something that he could still watch them. This in itself was part of the victory.

And next time. What was this next rime that MacGillivray mentioned? Would there be a next time? Of course, there always was.

'Damn!'

A cry from Douglas broke into the pattern of his thoughts, scattering them like pieces in a fallen jigsaw. Blood dripped from the Corporal's right hand; in the left he held a tin of beer with froth oozing out of a jagged tear in the top.

'Beer's scarce up here,' he explained. 'In fact you only get a strict ration in case of trouble, but I felt that this called for a can. Only now I've gone and cut my thumb on the bloody edge.'

'Here, let's see,' said Love, examining the gash. '*Hm.* Maybe a stitch would help. They'll have the things I want at the nursing station, I take it?'

'Surely. Of course, I'd forgotten you're a doctor.'

'Thanks for reminding me. I'd almost forgotten myself.'

Together they walked out through the double doors, across the crisp snow, under the wide arched sky, the pale moon and the spangle of unwinking stars beyond. Next time, thought Love, I'll not need reminding.

Stogumber, Somerset; Teheran, Iran; Churchill and Baker Lake, Canada.

265

IF YOU ENJOYED THIS BOOK WHY NOT TRY SOME OTHER BOOKS BY JAMES LEASOR AND NOW AVAILABLE AGAIN:

PASSPORT TO PERIL

Passport to Peril is Dr Jason Love's second brilliant case history in suspense. An adventure that sweeps from the gentle snows of Switzerland to the freezing peaks of the Himalayas, and ends in a blizzard of violence, hate, and lust on the roof of the world. Guns, girls and gadgets all play there part as the Somerset doctor, old car expert and amateur secret agent uncovers a mystery involving the Chinese intelligence service and a global blackmail ring.

"Second instalment in the exploits of Dr Jason Love… Technicolour backgrounds, considerable expertise about weapons… action, driven along with terrific vigour" *The Sunday Times*
"It whips along at a furious pace" *The Sun*
"A great success" *The Daily Express*

PASSPORT IN SUSPENSE

'A superb example of thriller writing at its best' *Sunday Express*
'Third of Dr Love's supercharged adventures... It starts in the sunshine of the Bahamas, swings rapidly by way of a brunette corpse into Mexico, and winds up in the yacht of a megalomaniac ex-Nazi... Action: non-stop: Tension: nail-biting' *Daily Express*
'His ingenuity and daring are as marked as ever' *Birmingham Post*

When a German submarine mysteriously disappears on a NATO exercise in the North Sea, and a beautiful girl was brutally murdered in the Bahamas, there at first seemed little connection between the two events. But the missing sub was a vital link in a deadly plan to conquer the West, master-minded by a megalomaniac ex-Nazi. And the dead girl was an Israeli agent intent on bringing to trial the ex-Nazis hiding in South America.

Dr Jason Love, the Somerset GP–turned part-time British secret agent, was enjoying a quiet holiday in Nassau, on his way to an old car rally in Mexico, when he witnessed the girl's murder. Before he knew it, he found himself dragged into the affair. He duly travels to Mexico, thinking he has left this behind, but becomes plunged into a violent situation, with his life in danger – and a desperate mission to foil a terrifying plot to destroy Western civilisation as we know it…

THEY DON'T MAKE THEM LIKE THAT ANY MORE

It introduces the randy, earthy and likeable proprietor of Aristo Autos who deals in vintage cars - not forgetting Sara, supercharged with sexual promise, who whets his curiosity and rouses his interest.

In the process of becoming a reluctant hero, he spins across France, Spain and Switzerland, on the track of a rare Mercedes too badly wanted by too many dangerous men. . .

'Devoured at a sitting. . . racy, pungent and swift' *The Sunday Times*

'Number one thriller on my list ...sexy and racy'

'A racy tale . . . the hero spends most of his time trying to get into beds and out of trouble . . . plenty of action, anecdotes, and inside dope on exotic old cars'
Sunday Express

NEVER HAD A SPANNER ON HER
In the sequel to "They Don't Make Them Like That Any More" our vintage car dealer gets involved in a scheme to import some vintage cars from Nasser's Egypt. From the run of the mill trades of London our hero finds himself in Cairo and trying to export a Bugatti Royale, probably the rarest car on the planet. The story has suspense, guns, a beautiful girl and of course masses of old cars. It races from Belgravia, to Belsize Park to the Pyramids and Alexandria. Leasor combines his proven thriller writing skills with an encyclopaedic knowledge of vintage cars to deliver a real page turner.

`Mr. Leasor has a delightful sense of the ridiculous; he also has an educated style which stems from more than 20 very good books.'   *Manchester Evening News*
`All good reading, with accurate detail of the cars involved.' *Autocar*
`Vintage adventure for auto-lovers and others alike.' *The Evening News*

HOST OF EXTRAS
The bawdy, wise-cracking owner of Aristo Autos is offered two immaculate vintage Rolls straight out of a collector's dream: one is a tourer, the other an Alpine.

The cars, and Aristo, get in on a shady film deal which leads to a trip to Corsica with the imperturbable Dr Jason Love - Somerset GP and part-time secret agent - his supercharged Cord and the infinitely desirable Victoria – and to the cut and thrust of violent international skulduggery.

"An entertaining and fast moving adventure" *Daily Express*

'It's all great fun and games, with plenty of revs.' *Evening Standard*

'. . . a clutch of thrills and sparks of wit.' *The Yorkshire Post*

FOLLOW THE DRUM

James Leasor's fictional tale, based on the events surrounding the Indian Mutiny.

India, in the mid-nineteenth century, was virtually run by a British commercial concern, the Honourable East India Company, whose directors would pay tribute to one Indian ruler and then depose another in their efforts to maintain their balance sheet of power and profit. But great changes were already casting shadows across the land, and when a stupid order was given to Indian troops to use cartridges greased with cow fat and pig lard (one animal sacred to the Hindus and the other abhorrent to Moslems) there was mutiny. The lives of millions were changed for ever including Arabella MacDonald, daughter of an English regular officer, and Richard Lang, an idealistic nineteen-year-old who began 1857 as a boy and ended it a man.

Pulling no punches, it shows up the good and the bad on both sides - the appalling stupidity and complacency of the British which caused the mutiny to happen, the chaos and venality of the insurgents, the ruthlessness of the retribution. It has everything, with a story based on the actual events.

MANDARIN-GOLD
The first of James Leasor's epic trilogy based on a Far Eastern trading company:

'Highly absorbing account of the corruption of an individual during a particularly sordid era of British imperial history,' *The Sunday Times*

'James Leasor switches to the China Sea more than a century ago, and with pace and ingenuity tells, in novel form, how the China coast was forced to open up its riches to Englishmen, in face of the Emperor's justified hostility' *Evening Standard*

'In the nasty story of opium - European and American traders made fortunes taking the forbidden dope into nineteenth century China, and this novel tells the story of their deadly arrangements and of the Emperor's vain attempts to stop them. Mr. Leasor has researched the background carefully and the detail of the Emperor's lavish court but weak administration is fascinating. The white traders are equally interesting characters, especially those two real-life merchants, Jardine and Matheson.'
Manchester Evening News

It was the year of 1833 when Robert Gunn arrived on the China coast. Only the feeblest of defences now protected the vast and proud Chinese Empire from the ravenous greed of Western traders, and their opening wedge for conquest was the sale of forbidden opium to the native masses.

This was the path that Robert Gunn chose to follow... a path that led him through a maze of violence and intrigue, lust and treachery, to a height of power beyond most men's dreams — and to the ultimate depths of personal corruption.

Here is a magnificent novel of an age of plunder— and of a fearless freebooter who raped an empire.

THE CHINESE WIDOW
James Leasor's two preceding books in his chronicle of the Far East a century and half ago - FOLLOW THE DRUM and MANDARIN-GOLD were acclaimed by critics on both sides of the Atlantic. THE CHINESE WIDOW is their equal. It combines the ferocious force of the Dutch mercenaries who seek to destroy Gunn's plan; the pathos of a young woman left alone to rule a fierce and rebellious people; the gawky humour of Gunn's partner, the rough, raw Scot MacPherson; the mysterious yet efficacious practice of Chinese medicine, handed on through thousands of years...

When doctors in England pronounced his death sentence, Robert Gunn-founder of Mandarin-Gold, one of the most prosperous Far Eastern trading companies of the nineteenth century-vowed to spend his final year in creating a lasting memorial to leave behind him... to pay back, somehow, his debt to the lands of the East that had been the making of his vast fortune. He had a plan - a great plan - but to see it through he had to confront a fierce and rebellious people, a force of Dutch mercenaries and the Chinese Widow. Who was the Widow? What was her past-and her power...?

Action, suspense and the mysterious splendour of the Orient are combined in this exciting and moving novel.

BOARDING PARTY

Filmed as The Sea Wolves, this is the story of the undercover exploits of a territorial unit. The Germans had a secret transmitter on one of their ships in the neutral harbour of Goa. Its purpose was to guide the U-boats against Allied shipping in the Indian Ocean. There seemed no way for the British to infringe Goa's Portuguese neutrality by force. But the transmitter had to be silenced. Then it was remembered that 1,400 miles away in Calcutta was a source of possible help. A group of civilian bankers, merchants and solicitors were the remains of an old territorial unit called The Calcutta Light Horse. With a foreword by Earl Mountbatten of Burma.

'One of the most decisive actions in World War II was fought by fourteen out-of-condition middle-aged men sailing in a steam barge...' *Daily Mirror*

'Mr. Leasor's book is truth far more engrossing than fiction... A gem of World War II history' *New York*

Times

'If ever there was a ready-made film script...here it is'
Oxford Mail

GREEN BEACH
In 1942 radar expert Jack Nissenthall volunteered for a suicidal mission to join a combat team who were making a surprise landing at Dieppe in occupied France. His assignment was to penetrate a German radar station on a cliff above 'Green Beach: Because Nissenthall knew the secrets of British and US radar technology, he was awarded a personal bodyguard of sharpshooters. Their orders were to protect him, but in the event of possible capture to kill him. His choice was to succeed or die. The story of what happened to him and his bodyguards in nine hours under fire is one of World War II's most terrifying true stories of personal heroism.

'Green Beach has blown the lid off one of the Second World War's best-kept secrets' *Daily Express*

'If I had been aware of the orders given to the escort to shoot him rather than let him be captured, I would have cancelled them immediately' *Lord Mountbatten*

'Green Beach is a vivid, moving and at times nerve-racking reconstruction of an act of outstanding but horrific heroism' *Sunday Express*

THE RED FORT
James Leasor's gripping historical account of the

Indian Mutiny.

'This is a battle piece of the finest kind, detailed, authentic and largely written from original documents. Mr. Leasor has a formidable gift of narrative. Never has this story of hate, violence, courage and cowardice been better told.'
Cecil Woodham-Smith in the *New York Times*

A year after the Crimean War ended, an uprising broke out in India which was to have equal impact on the balance of world power and the British Empire's role in world affairs. The revolt was against the East India Company which, not entirely against its will, had assumed responsibility for administering large parts of India. The ostensible cause of the mutiny sprang from a rumour that cartridges used by the native Sepoy troops were greased with cow's fat and pig's lard — cows being sacred to the Hindus, and pigs abhorred by the Mohammedans. But the roots of the trouble lay far deeper, and a bloody and ineptly handled war ensued.

The Red Fort is a breath-taking account of the struggle, with all its cruelties, blunderings and heroic courage. When peace was finally restored, the India we know today began to emerge.

THE MARINE FROM MANDALAY

This is the true story of a Royal Marine wounded by shrapnel in Mandalay in WW2 who undergoes a long solitary march to the Japanese through the whole of

Burma and then finds his way back through India and back to Britain to report for duty in Plymouth. On his way he has many encounters and adventures and helps British and Indian refugees. He also has to overcome complete disbelief that a single man could walk out of Burma with nothing but his orders - to report to HQ - and his initiative.

THE MILLIONTH CHANCE
The R101 airship was thought to be the model for the future, an amazing design that was 'as safe as houses ... except for the millionth chance'. On the night of 4 October 1930 that chance in a million came up, however. James Leasor brilliantly reconstructs the conception and crash of this huge ship of the air with compassion for the forty-seven dead - and only six survivors.

'The sense of fatality grows with every page ... Gripping' *Evening Standard*

THE ONE THAT GOT AWAY
Franz von Werra was a Luftwaffe pilot shot down in the Battle of Britain. The One that Got Away tells the full and exciting story of his two daring escapes in England and his third and successful escape: a leap from the window of a prisoners' train in Canada. Enduring snow and frostbite, he crossed into the then neutral United States. Leasor's book is based on von Werra's own dictated account of his adventures and makes for a compelling read.

'A good story, crisply told' *New York Times*

THE PLAGUE AND THE FIRE

This dramatic story chronicles the horror and human suffering of two terrible years in London's history. 1665 brought the plague and cries of 'Bring Out Your Dead' echoed through the city. A year later, the already decimated capital was reduced to ashes in four days by the fire that began in Pudding Lane. James Leasor weaves in the first-hand accounts of Daniel Defoe and Samuel Pepys, among others.

'An engrossing and vivid impression of those terrible days' *Evening Standard*

'Absorbing ... an excellent account of the two most fantastic years in London's history' *Sunday Express*

WHO KILLED SIR HARRY OAKES?

James Leasor cleverly reconstructs events surrounding a brutal and unusual murder. It is 1943 and Sir Harry Oakes lies horrifically murdered at his Bahamian mansion. Although a self-made multi-millionaire, Sir Harry is an unlikely victim - there are no suggestions of jealousy or passion. Leasor makes the daring suggestion that Sir Harry Oakes' murder, the burning of the liner Normandie in New York Harbour in 1942 and the Allied landings in Sicily are all somehow connected.

'The story has all the right ingredients - rich occupants of a West Indian tax haven, corruption,

drugs, the Mafia, and a weak character as governor'
Daily Mail

James Leasor was educated at The City of London School and Oriel College, Oxford. In World War II he was commissioned into the Royal Berkshire Regiment and posted to the 1st Lincolns in Burma and India, where he served for three and a half years. His experiences there stimulated his interest in India, both past and present, and inspired him to write such books as Boarding Party (filmed as The Sea Wolves), The Red Fort, Follow the Drum and NTR. He later became a feature writer and foreign correspondent at the Daily Express. There he wrote The One that Got Away, the story of the sole German POW to escape from Allied hands. As well as non-fiction, Leasor has written novels, including the Dr Jason Love series, which have been published in 19 countries. Passport to Oblivion was filmed as Where the Spies Are with David Niven. He died in September 2007.

James Leasor's books are available again. Please visit www.jamesleasor.com for details on all these books or contact info@jamesleasor.com for more information on availability. Follow on Twitter: @jamesleasor and facebook for details on new releases.

Jason Love novels
Passport to Oblivion (filmed, and republished in paperback, as Where the Spies Are)
Passport to Peril (Published in the U.S. as Spylight)
Passport in Suspense (Published in the U.S. as The Yang Meridian)
Passport for a Pilgrim
A Week of Love
Love-all
Love and the Land Beyond
Frozen Assets
Love Down Under

Jason Love and Aristo Autos novel
Host of Extras

Aristo Autos novels
They Don't Make Them Like That Any More
Never Had A Spanner On Her

Robert Gunn novels
Mandarin-Gold
The Chinese Widow
Jade Gate

Other novels
Not Such a Bad Day
The Strong Delusion
NTR: Nothing to Report
Follow the Drum
Ship of Gold
Tank of Serpents

Non-fiction
The Monday Story
Author by Profession
Wheels to Fortune
The Serjeant-Major; a biography of R.S.M. Ronald Brittain, M.B.E., Coldstream Guards
The Red Fort
The One That Got Away
The Millionth Chance: The Story of The R.101
War at the Top (published in the U.S. as The Clock With Four Hands)
Conspiracy of Silence
The Plague and the Fire
Rudolf Hess: The Uninvited Envoy
Singapore: the Battle that Changed the World
Green Beach
Boarding Party (filmed, and republished in paperback, as The Sea Wolves)
The Unknown Warrior (republished in paperback as X-Troop)
The Marine from Mandalay
Rhodes & Barnato: the Premier and the Prancer

As Andrew MacAllan (novels)
Succession
Generation
Diamond Hard
Fanfare
Speculator
Traders

As Max Halstock
Rats – The Story of a Dog Soldier

www.jamesleasor.com

Follow on Twitter: @jamesleasor

Printed in Great Britain
by Amazon